continued . . .

Berkley Prime Crime titles by Victoria Thompson

MURDER ON ASTOR PLACE
MURDER ON ST. MARK'S PLACE
MURDER ON GRAMERCY PARK
MURDER ON WASHINGTON SQUARE
MURDER ON MULBERRY BEND
MURDER ON MARBLE ROW
MURDER ON LENOX HILL
MURDER IN LITTLE ITALY
MURDER IN CHINATOWN
MURDER ON BANK STREET
MURDER ON WAVERLY PLACE
MURDER ON LEXINGTON AVENUE

MURDER ON
WAVERLY PLACE

A Gaslight Mystery

Victoria Thompson

BERKLEY PRIME CRIME, NEW YORK

THE BERKLEY PUBLISHING GROUP
Published by the Penguin Group
Penguin Group (USA) Inc.
375 Hudson Street, New York, New York 10014, USA
Penguin Group (Canada), 90 Eglinton Avenue East, Suite 700, Toronto, Ontario M4P 2Y3, Canada
(a division of Pearson Penguin Canada Inc.)
Penguin Books Ltd., 80 Strand, London WC2R 0RL, England
Penguin Group Ireland, 25 St. Stephen's Green, Dublin 2, Ireland (a division of Penguin Books Ltd.)
Penguin Group (Australia), 250 Camberwell Road, Camberwell, Victoria 3124, Australia
(a division of Pearson Australia Group Pty. Ltd.)
Penguin Books India Pvt. Ltd., 11 Community Centre, Panchsheel Park, New Delhi—110 017, India
Penguin Group (NZ), 67 Apollo Drive, Rosedale, North Shore 0632, New Zealand
(a division of Pearson New Zealand Ltd.)
Penguin Books (South Africa) (Pty.) Ltd., 24 Sturdee Avenue, Rosebank, Johannesburg 2196,
South Africa

Penguin Books Ltd., Registered Offices: 80 Strand, London WC2R 0RL, England

MURDER ON WAVERLY PLACE

A Berkley Prime Crime Book / published by arrangement with the author

PRINTING HISTORY
Berkley Prime Crime hardcover edition / June 2009
Berkley Prime Crime mass-market edition / June 2010

Copyright © 2009 by Victoria Thompson.
The Edgar® name is a registered service mark of the Mystery Writers of America, Inc.
Cover illustration by Karen Chandler.
Cover design by Rita Frangie.

ISBN: 978-0-425-23520-1

BERKLEY® PRIME CRIME
Berkley Prime Crime Books are published by The Berkley Publishing Group,
a division of Penguin Group (USA) Inc.,
375 Hudson Street, New York, New York 10014.
BERKLEY® PRIME CRIME and the PRIME CRIME logo are trademarks of Penguin Group (USA) Inc.

PRINTED IN THE UNITED STATES OF AMERICA

10 9 8 7 6 5 4 3 2 1

To Ryan,
the very newest Thompson!

I

WITH A WEARY SIGH, SARAH BRANDT PUSHED OPEN THE
front door of her house. She'd been awake for more than thirty-
six hours, and she wanted nothing more than a quick bite to
eat and a long night in the comfort of her own bed. But as
she closed the door behind her, she heard a childish shriek of
joy and all her fatigue fell away.

She looked up to see her daughter, Catherine, clattering
down the stairs to greet her. "Mama!" she cried in a voice that
was almost normal and threw her small arms around Sarah's
legs.

Sarah blinked back tears. When she'd found Catherine at
the Prodigal Son Mission a few months ago, she wouldn't
speak at all. She'd appeared on the doorstep of the Mission
one morning, and no one knew a thing about her life up until
that moment except that something had frightened her into
total silence. For months she'd remained mute, and only after

coming to live with Sarah had she finally begun to speak again.

"What have you and Maeve been doing while I was gone?" Sarah asked, setting her medical bag on the floor so she could hug Catherine back.

The child looked up, her brown eyes wide with excitement. "Mrs. Decker is here!" she reported happily.

Sarah looked up in surprise to see her mother coming down the stairs at a more sedate pace than Catherine had used. Elizabeth Decker wore a simple dress that gave no indication her husband was one of the wealthiest men in New York City.

"Home at last," Mrs. Decker said with a smile that didn't quite reach her eyes. Sarah thought her mother must have been worried about her.

"It was a difficult case," midwife Sarah Brandt explained apologetically, thinking of the breech birth that had taken forever, only to be followed by an unexpected twin sibling. The surprised parents had needed more than a little reassurance. "Have you been here long?"

"All afternoon," Mrs. Decker said. "But Catherine and Maeve kept me entertained."

"We played with my doll house," Catherine reported. "I got new furniture for the nursery."

"Did you?" Sarah asked with a meaningful look at her mother.

"Yes, she did," Mrs. Decker confirmed without apology.

"It's beautiful," Maeve added. The young woman who served as Catherine's nursemaid had come down the steps behind Mrs. Decker.

"I'm sure it is," Sarah said.

"We saved you some ham from supper," Maeve said. "I'll fix you something to eat."

"Thank you," Sarah said with heartfelt appreciation. "I'm starving."

"And you're exhausted, too," Mrs. Decker said with the slightest trace of disapproval. She didn't like the idea of her daughter earning her own living, especially when she had a family who was more than able to support her in grand style.

"Come see my new furniture," Catherine begged, taking Sarah's hand and tugging her toward the stairs.

"Let your mama take off her things first," Mrs. Decker said, and Catherine obediently dropped Sarah's hand and waited with ill-disguised impatience while Sarah removed her hat and jacket.

The next hour passed in a blur as Sarah went upstairs to admire the new doll house furniture, then ate the hearty supper Maeve had reheated for her while listening to a recounting of Catherine's day. While Sarah was eating, her mother's driver returned for her, but to Sarah's surprise, she asked him to wait while she visited with Sarah a bit longer. Finally, Maeve took Catherine up to get her ready for bed, and Sarah had a chance to speak to her mother alone.

"Won't Father be wondering where you are?" Sarah asked as they sat across the kitchen table from each other.

"He's out of town on business," she said, giving her another of those tense smiles. Only now did Sarah realize that the strain she'd sensed earlier in her mother went deeper than simple worry over Sarah's safety.

"What's wrong?" she asked, certain now that something must be. Why else would her mother ask her driver to keep the horses standing in the street? "Are you ill? Is Father ill?"

"No, no, don't be silly," Mrs. Decker said. "What makes you think something's wrong?"

"You came here to visit, but instead of going home at a

decent hour, you've been waiting for me to come home, and . . . Well, I can see that something is bothering you. What is it, Mother?"

Mrs. Decker smiled again, sadly this time. "I'm amazed at your powers of perception, Sarah. But nothing's wrong, nothing at all, I assure you. I just . . . I wanted to ask a favor of you."

"A favor?" Sarah couldn't think of a single favor a poor midwife could do for a society matron like her mother.

"Yes, I . . . It's difficult to explain, so please, Sarah, have an open mind and don't judge me until you've heard me out."

"Don't *judge* you?" Sarah echoed in dismay, wondering what her mother could have done to merit judgment. "When have I ever judged you?"

"You can be quite uncharitable about other people's . . . weaknesses, Sarah," her mother said.

Sarah gaped at her in astonishment. "I'm not uncharitable!" she insisted, stung by the accusation. "And what weaknesses could you possibly . . . ?" Her voice trailed off as she had a most horrifying thought. "Have you taken a *lover*?"

Her mother gaped back at her in equal astonishment, and Sarah watched the emotions race across the familiar face—surprise, amazement, revulsion, and then amusement that finally dissolved into hysterical laughter. Elizabeth Decker, one of New York society's four hundred most elite members, was suddenly howling with laughter at Sarah's kitchen table.

"I suppose this means I was wrong about the lover," Sarah guessed wryly as her mother tried to compose herself.

"Oh, dear me, yes," Mrs. Decker assured her as she wiped the tears from her eyes with a lace-trimmed handkerchief that cost more than Sarah earned in a month. "A lover! What on earth made you think of such a thing?"

"You asked me not to judge you," Sarah reminded her

tartly. "And you said I was uncharitable. I tried to think of what you could have done that I would find unforgivable."

"And moral turpitude was the only thing that came to mind?"

"It also had to be something you were embarrassed to tell me," she said, realizing it for the first time herself. The strain she'd sensed in her mother was embarrassment, not worry.

Mrs. Decker sobered. "Oh, yes, well, perhaps that is part of it. Not embarrassment, exactly, but a bit of . . . discomfort."

"Oh, for heaven's sake, just tell me," Sarah said in exasperation. "It can't be worse than what I was imagining."

Her mother straightened in her chair, as if gathering her courage, and drew a deep breath. "I . . . I would like for you to accompany me to a séance."

This was so far from anything Sarah had imagined that she needed a moment to make sense of it. "A séance?" she repeated stupidly. "You mean where they talk to ghosts and rap on tables?"

"I'm sure I don't know what they do," her mother said, no longer trying to hide her discomfort. "I've never attended one."

"Then why do you want to attend one now?"

"A friend of mine, Mrs. Burke . . . Do you remember her? We were in school together."

"I think so," Sarah said, remembering a gentle lady who had visited her mother from time to time.

"Well, she . . . she lost her sister several years ago. They had been quarreling, and Kathy never had an opportunity to . . . to say good-bye or ask forgiveness. Then she heard about this medium . . ."

"What's a medium?" Sarah asked with a confused frown.

"That's what you call the spiritualist who conducts the séance. Kathy heard about this medium who is able to speak to the dead—"

"Mother!" Sarah cried in dismay. "No one can speak to the dead."

"I knew you'd be judgmental. I asked you specifically—"

"All right, all right," Sarah said, lifting her hands in surrender. "Go on. She heard about this . . . this medium person."

"So she went to see her. Madame Serafina, that's her name. She was able to contact Kathy's sister."

This was all so ridiculous that Sarah didn't even know where to begin. She drew a fortifying breath and tried not to be uncharitable on top of being judgmental. "Are you saying that this . . . this medium person—"

"Madame Serafina," her mother supplied.

"Madame Serafina," Sarah repeated dutifully. "That she was able to speak to Mrs. Burke's dead sister?"

"Well, not directly, you understand. She apparently has a spirit guide who speaks to those who have passed to the other side."

Sarah rubbed her forehead where a knifelike pain was pulsing. How she wished her mother had chosen to have this conversation on a day when Sarah had had a full night's sleep beforehand. "Mother," she tried patiently, "this isn't possible. We can't speak to the dead."

"Of course we can't," her mother readily agreed. "That's why you need a spirit guide to do it for you."

Sarah stared at her mother in disbelief. Had she lost her senses? "Why on earth would you want to talk to the dead in any case?"

"Because," her mother said, and to Sarah's horror, Mrs. Decker's eyes filled with tears. "I want to talk to Maggie."

At the mention of her sister's name, Sarah's own eyes stung as a pain so great she could hardly bear it filled her chest. Of course. Why hadn't she realized it immediately? "Oh, Mother," Sarah said, reaching across the table to take her mother's hand.

"No," Mrs. Decker said, snatching her hand away and blinking fiercely at her tears. "Don't give me sympathy. I don't deserve sympathy. I don't deserve forgiveness either, but I want to ask for it anyway."

"Maggie forgave you long ago," Sarah assured her.

"No, she didn't," her mother insisted. "How could she? She died before she even knew I was sorry for what I did to her."

"Mother, listen to me—"

"Kathy spoke to her sister," Mrs. Decker insisted, the pain like a flame burning in her eyes. "She hadn't been able to eat or sleep for months, and then she spoke to her sister and apologized, and her sister forgave her."

Sarah's heart was breaking over her mother's anguish. "Mother, these people who do this, they're charlatans. They trick gullible people just to get their money."

"I know many of them are," Mrs. Decker agreed too easily. "But not this one. Kathy said she knew things about her and her sister that no one else could have known. She's done this for other people, too. She's amazing, and she's developing quite a following."

Sarah asked the only other question she could think of that might discourage her mother. "What does Father think of all this?"

Mrs. Decker stiffened defensively. "He knows nothing about it, and there's no reason he should."

"He would never allow you to go to a spiritualist," Sarah reminded her.

"He will never find out. Unless you tell him, of course," she added.

Sarah couldn't imagine doing any such thing, and she was sure her mother knew it. She'd have to try a different tack. "Why have you started thinking about all this now?"

"You mean why have I suddenly started thinking about

Maggie?" she asked with a trace of sarcasm that Sarah hadn't expected.

"Well, yes," Sarah admitted.

Her mother's lovely face twisted with the pain of loss that Sarah would have sworn she no longer felt. "I never *stopped* thinking about her, Sarah. She's my daughter. I think about her every morning, when I wake up, in that one blissful moment when I emerge from the sweet oblivion of sleep, and for one second, one single second, I don't remember that she's dead. For that one second, there's the possibility that she's still in the world and I might see her happy for one more day. And then I remember. I remember that she's dead and that I'll never see her again, not in this life at least. And I feel that pain all over again, the pain of losing her and knowing it was my fault that she died."

"It wasn't your fault!" Sarah cried, tears streaming down her cheeks now.

"Whom should we blame then?" her mother asked bitterly. "Your father?"

Sarah had always blamed him the most, but she wasn't going to say that now. "Mother, Maggie made her own choices—"

"The only choices we left her," Mrs. Decker reminded her. "And don't think for one moment your father made any decisions without my approval. We are equally damned for what we did to her."

"Mother, please!" Sarah reached out again, alarmed to see that all the color had drained from her mother's face. She looked as if she might faint.

This time Mrs. Decker let Sarah take her hand, and she clasped it tightly, nearly bruising Sarah's fingers. "I know it's not possible to talk to the dead," she said, shocking Sarah. "At least I've always believed it is, but suppose I'm wrong? Suppose we're both wrong? Suppose someone *can* reach Maggie? Suppose it's possible to make my peace with her here and now instead of waiting for some fragile hope of eternal forgiveness? I have to find out, Sarah. I have to at least try!"

Sarah stared at her mother, reading the desperate hope and the anguished need. She'd suffered this guilt for years and suffered far more than Sarah could have imagined. How could she deny her mother this one chance to end it? "All right," Sarah said, defeated. "If it's so important to you, I won't try to talk you out of it."

"And you'll come with me?" she asked, her eyes lighting with renewed hope.

"I can't do that," Sarah said without apology. "I don't suppose they allow nonbelievers to attend in any case."

"But you have to go, Sarah. You must!"

"Why?"

"Because . . ." Mrs. Decker had to swallow the tears from her voice. "Because Maggie may not want to speak to me at all, but she'd speak to you. If she'll come back for anyone, it will be you."

Sarah stared at her mother in wide-eyed astonishment, having no idea how to respond. Fortunately, Maeve appeared at that moment, saving her from having to decide.

"Catherine is ready for bed and . . . Oh, I'm sorry," she said quickly, sensing the tension in the room. "I didn't mean to interrupt."

"That's all right, Maeve," Sarah said, jumping up in her desperate need to escape. "I suppose she wants me to tuck her in."

"Yes, she always misses you when you've been gone awhile." Maeve's shrewd glance was flicking back and forth between Sarah and her mother, trying to gauge the situation. Were they quarreling? Disagreeing about something? Sarah wasn't about to explain.

"I'll be back shortly," Sarah said, not daring to meet her mother's eye.

Catherine was more demanding than usual, begging Sarah for just one more good-night kiss and asking question after question. She knew Sarah's attention was focused elsewhere and tried every trick she knew to draw it back. Hating herself for giving the child less than her due, Sarah finally managed to break away. She found her mother still sitting at the kitchen table. Maeve had made herself scarce.

"I'm sure this was a shock to you," her mother said before Sarah could open her mouth. "I shouldn't have asked you so soon. I should have given you time to get used to the idea. It's just . . ."

"How long will Father be out of town?" Sarah asked, having figured out the rush.

"Only three more days. It's not really necessary that he be out of town, of course, but I thought—"

"You thought it would be easier if he were," Sarah supplied for her. "I just don't know . . ."

"Sarah," Mrs. Decker said, her blue eyes clear now, and full of determination. "You've finally been able to lay your own ghosts to rest. Please, help me with mine."

Sarah knew she was referring to Sarah's husband, Tom. She hadn't even realized how haunted she had been by his tragic murder almost four years ago until her friend Detective Sergeant Frank Malloy had finally tracked down his killer. While Sarah would still miss Tom until the day she died, at least she understood why he had died and had seen his killer punished. While nothing would ever ease the pain of losing him, she did have some measure of peace now. Could she deny her mother the chance at some peace for herself?

"I'll go with you, Mother," Sarah said.

Mrs. Decker's relief was palpable. "Oh, Sarah, thank you. I can't tell you how much this means to me."

"Don't thank me yet. I'm not promising to support you in this or believe for one second that it's possible. I'm just going to make sure no one takes advantage of you."

"It *is* possible," her mother said, her voice almost breaking from the strength of her emotions. "It *has* to be."

For her mother's sake, Sarah could almost hope it was.

AFTER SEEING HER MOTHER OFF, SARAH CLOSED THE front door to find Maeve standing on the stairs that led upstairs to the girls' bedrooms. "Is everything all right?" the girl asked with genuine concern. "Mrs. Decker seemed upset."

Sarah looked at the young woman who, like Catherine, had also come from the Prodigal Son Mission. Maeve had sought refuge there to escape a life Sarah knew little about. She had recently learned some important facts about that life, though, and about Maeve's special talents.

"Do you know anything about spiritualists?" Sarah asked.

"Spiritualists?" Maeve repeated with a frown. "What kind?"

"Are there different kinds?"

Maeve shrugged, telling Sarah more than she wanted to know.

"My mother wants to go to a séance."

Maeve's eyes widened with surprise. "Mrs. Decker? I wouldn't've thought she's the type."

Sarah's head began to throb again. "Would you come into the kitchen and tell me everything you know about it?"

"Are you sure?" Maeve asked with unfeigned concern. "You're awful tired. Maybe tomorrow . . . ?"

"I won't be able to sleep," Sarah assured her. "At least not until I know more about this."

Maeve nodded and led the way back to the kitchen. When they were seated at the table, Maeve folded her hands expectantly.

"What do you know about people who do séances?" Sarah asked.

Recently, Sarah had learned that in her former life, Maeve had been a grifter, or at least that she'd come from a family of grifters, people who made their living by conning people in elaborate schemes. Although Maeve had never given Sarah any reason to suspect she was dishonest, Sarah's friend Detective Sergeant Frank Malloy had recognized her abilities immediately when Maeve had employed them to help him solve the murder of Sarah's husband, Dr. Tom Brandt.

"I never knew anybody who did that kind of thing," Maeve replied. "You need a house in a respectable neighborhood, and most of all, you need some way to get people with money to come to you. You know, classy people who can vouch for you." She smiled apologetically. "My family never could even have managed the house part of it."

"But you know that it's all fake, don't you?"

"I always figured it was. People talk, so I heard about it. There's a lot of money in it, I guess."

"How do they get money from people?"

"Not by stealing or anything," Maeve hastened to assure her. "The marks . . . I mean, the customers, they come back of their own free will. The trick is to make them want to. You tell them some little thing the first time, just enough to make them believe it's on the up and up. Then they have to come back again to hear more. Next time you tell them a little more and promise that the next time there'll be even more. There's no end to it, and they'll pay more and more each time to hear what they think the spirits are telling them."

Sarah sighed wearily. "That's what I was afraid of."

"Mrs. Decker wouldn't let herself get taken in, though," Maeve said.

"What makes you say that?" Sarah asked in surprise.

"She's smart. She's . . ."

"Rich?" Sarah guessed when Maeve hesitated. "That's no guarantee you won't be gullible. In fact, she's probably much more innocent about these things than you are. She's led a very sheltered life."

Maeve frowned, considering this. "If you don't mind my asking, what's made her want to do this in the first place?"

Sarah sighed again, absently rubbing the ache in her forehead. "She wants to contact my sister, Maggie."

"I didn't know you had a sister," Maeve said in surprise.

"There's no reason you should. She died a long time ago, and we don't talk about her," Sarah admitted. "We're too ashamed."

"Ashamed?" Maeve couldn't believe it. "I'm sure you've got nothing to be ashamed about, Mrs. Brandt."

Sarah only wished that were true. "Guilty then," she said. "We've got more than enough guilt to go around."

"I don't believe it!"

"Then I'll have to convince you, won't I?" Sarah said with another sigh. "Maggie was my older sister. I suppose she was a bit of a rebel. She didn't think it was fair that our family had so much when many other people had nothing. She wanted to do something to help."

"Like the ladies who volunteer at the Mission," Maeve guessed.

Oh, if only Maggie had confined herself to such conventional good works. "No, she wanted more than that. She wanted to convince businessmen like my father to treat their workers more fairly."

"Did she?" Maeve asked doubtfully.

"Not at all. She tried to convince our father first, of course, but he completely dismissed her, which only made her more determined."

"I can understand that."

"I'm sure you can," Sarah said with a small smile. "Telling Maggie no was always the surest way to make her dig in her heels. And then she fell in love."

Maeve's eyes lit up, thrilled to hear about a romance. "With who?"

"A man who worked for my father. He was young, just a clerk, but he probably had a bright future. He would never be good enough for Felix Decker's daughter, though."

Maeve's face fell with disappointment. "So Mr. Decker wouldn't let them get married," she guessed.

"Of course not. Not even when she told them she was with child."

"Oh, no! But wouldn't she *have* to get married? With the baby and everything?"

"No. My father was determined she wouldn't waste herself on a nobody, so my parents arranged for her to take a trip to Europe. She would have the baby there, give it to some orphanage, and return home with no one the wiser."

Maeve made an anguished sound of protest. "That's horrible!"

"Of course it is," Sarah agreed bitterly. "Didn't I tell you we were ashamed?"

"Is that how she died? Having the baby?"

"Not exactly. As you already know, Maggie wasn't one to meekly go along with our father's plans. She escaped before the ship set sail, and she found her lover, and they eloped. But they didn't live happily ever after," Sarah warned quickly when Maeve's face lit up again.

"But they were together!" Maeve protested.

"My father is a very powerful man. He had dismissed Maggie's husband when he found out about the affair, and he'd made sure the man couldn't get work anywhere else. He had to labor on the docks, when he could find work at all, and when he couldn't, they went hungry." Sarah had to close her eyes to shut out the visions that still haunted her.

"That must've been awful hard on your sister," Maeve said. "With her being used to living in that fancy house and all."

"None of us ever imagined how much they suffered. I tell myself that if we had, my parents would have helped them, but . . . Well, we'll never know, will we?"

"They would have," Maeve assured her. "Mrs. Decker is such a nice lady."

Sarah wished she was as certain. "At any rate, we had no idea where they were. I think my parents believed that if they were truly in need, they would ask for help. In fact, I think that was exactly what my father had planned. They'd come crawling back, he'd make them beg forgiveness for defying him, and then he'd help them."

"Except your sister would never give in, so they never asked."

"No, she wouldn't, not until it was too late." Sarah drew a deep breath and let it out in a weary sigh. "I was home alone that night when he finally came," she remembered. "My parents were at some party, and there wasn't time to find them. Maggie was dying."

"Oh, no!"

"He took me to the place where they were living. It was a rear tenement, on the fifth floor." Sarah didn't have to explain to Maeve that this was the cheapest of lodgings. Rear tenements were built in the spaces behind the buildings that fronted onto the streets. They got little air and less sunshine, and the fifth floor would be the least desirable location in a building where no one ever wanted to live in the first place. "The front room was full of lodgers who rented out floor space at night. That was the only way they could afford the rent."

Maeve's eyes were filling with tears. She didn't want to hear the ending to this story, but she held Sarah's gaze, determined not to flinch.

"Maggie had given birth with no one to help her, and she was dying. I know now that the afterbirth hadn't been expelled properly, but I didn't know anything about childbirth then. She was bleeding and no one could make it stop. She wanted me to take care of her baby." Sarah's voice caught on a sob as the horrible memories overcame her.

"You did, didn't you?" Maeve cried. "Please tell me you didn't leave him there!"

"He was already dead," Sarah remembered, wiping the tears from her own face. "Such a tiny little thing and so perfect. I'll never forget how beautiful he was. But I promised her I'd take care of him, and then . . . then she was gone."

"And that's why you became a midwife," Maeve guessed, her voice filled with wonder.

"Yes," Sarah said simply. "There were other reasons, too, but that was probably the most important one."

"And when you married Dr. Brandt, your parents had learned their lesson and didn't stand in your way."

"I suppose you could say that. At least they didn't stop me. I didn't see them much after I was married, and after Dr. Brandt died, we quarreled and didn't speak at all for several years."

"But now you've made up."

"Yes, although none of us can really forget what happened to Maggie."

"But that wasn't *your* fault. You were so young, you couldn't've done anything."

"I knew Maggie wasn't going to Europe. She told me she was planning to elope. I'll always wonder what would have happened if I'd told my parents and they'd been able to stop her."

"You couldn't do that! She wanted to be with the man she loved!" Maeve protested.

"But if I'd spoken up, she'd still be alive and her baby would, too. Even her husband . . . He hanged himself after Maggie died. Three lives lost, because I kept her secret."

"That's foolishness, Mrs. Brandt," Maeve insisted. "You can't know what would've happened. Maybe Maggie wouldn't want to be alive like that. Imagine knowing your baby was out there somewhere and you'd never see him again!"

Sarah smiled at the girl. "Thank you, Maeve, for trying to make me feel better."

"I'm not trying to make you feel better," she protested. "I'm telling the truth!"

"Yes, you are," Sarah said. "And you're right. We don't know what would have happened, but now you know what *did* happen and why my mother is so interested in contacting the dead."

"Does she want to tell your sister she's sorry for what happened?"

"Yes, she does, and since we both know this spiritualist is a fake, she's not going to be able to do that."

"But what if she could?"

Sarah looked at her in surprise. "I thought you didn't believe."

"I don't, but Mrs. Decker does, and that's all that counts.

If she believes this person can talk to your sister, then she can say she's sorry and she'll feel better. Would that be wrong?"

A very good question. Sarah considered it.

"Or maybe," Maeve ventured, "you think she doesn't deserve to be forgiven."

"Oh, no! I know how sorry she is. I've always known that, but tonight I finally realized how much she's suffered. I don't want to see her suffer anymore."

"Then what harm could it do? So long as you're there to make sure nobody takes advantage of her, I mean."

What harm *could* it do? Sarah had no idea. She just hoped she wasn't going to find out.

2

BY THE TIME THE DECKERS' COACH STOPPED IN FRONT OF
Sarah's house the next day, she was certain she'd made a terrible mistake by agreeing to accompany her mother. Her growing apprehension had infected Catherine, who started crying
when Sarah kissed her good-bye and started out the door.

"It's all right, sweetheart," she assured the child. "I'll be
back in a little while, and when I am, Mrs. Decker will be
with me."

"Hush, now," Maeve soothed the child. "Mrs. Ellsworth
will be here in a minute, and we'll bake some cookies," she
said, naming Sarah's next-door neighbor. "You'll like that,
won't you?"

Catherine shook her head in misery, big tears rolling down
her cheeks as Sarah forced herself to turn away and take her
leave.

The Deckers' coachman was holding the door for Sarah,

and she climbed inside to find her mother looking pale and drawn.

"Mother, are you ill?" Sarah asked in alarm. "We don't have to do this if—"

"No, no, I'm not ill. I just couldn't sleep a wink last night for thinking about Maggie. What if she appears? Oh, Sarah, I don't think I could bear seeing her again."

"She's not going to appear!" Sarah exclaimed, horrified. "There's no such thing as ghosts. You taught me that yourself."

"Sometimes there are . . . apparitions at these events," Mrs. Decker said as if she hadn't heard. "My friend Mrs. Burke told me."

From what Maeve had said last night, Sarah felt reasonably certain that any apparitions that appeared would be staged by the spiritualist, and her mother wasn't likely to see an apparition on her very first visit in any case. She'd have to return several times and pay a large amount of money for such a dramatic display. "Has Mrs. Burke actually seen an apparition?"

"No, not herself," Mrs. Decker admitted reluctantly. "But she's heard about it from others. I don't think I could bear it."

"Then perhaps we shouldn't go at all," Sarah suggested gently.

Sarah could see that her mother's gloved hands were clenched tightly in her lap, and she really did look as if she might be ill. "I have to go," she said after a moment. "I've got to try, or I'll never have any peace."

Sarah sank back against the seat cushions, resigned to enduring whatever the next few hours might bring.

The trip didn't take long, or at least not long enough for Sarah. If she'd been called to deliver a baby on Waverly Place,

just off Washington Square, she would have walked from her
house on Bank Street and counted herself lucky she had a delivery so close to home. Women like her mother didn't walk
around the city, however, even though it took longer for the
carriage to navigate the heavy traffic than it would have taken
Sarah on foot.

The streets in this part of the city were quiet and well
kept, inhabited by respectable people who worked hard and
took pride in their accomplishments. Maeve would no doubt
approve of this location for a spiritualist who wanted to at-
tract a clientele with financial resources.

When the coach finally stopped in front of one of the long
row of identical town houses, Sarah looked at her mother one
last time. "Are you sure you want to do this?"

Her mother refused to meet her eye, but she nodded with
just a hint of her normal determination. When the coachman
opened the door, Mrs. Decker drew a deep breath before taking his offered hand and climbing out. Sarah followed her
across the sidewalk, into the tiny, gated yard and up the
small stoop and waited while her mother rang the bell. After
a few moments, a well-dressed gentleman with carefully po-
maded hair answered the door.

"You must be Mrs. Decker," he said in a deep, reassuring
voice. "I am Professor Rogers. Please come in. Your friend
Mrs. Burke is already here." He stepped back to allow Mrs.
Decker to enter, and only then did he notice Sarah. "Is this
lady your guest?" he asked with just the slightest hint of disapproval.

Her mother had heard the disapproval, too. Although
Sarah couldn't see her face, she saw the slight stiffening of her
mother's spine as she squared her shoulders in silent resistance, in case the man intended to deny Sarah entrance. "Yes,

my daughter, Mrs. Brandt." No one could mistake the tiny thread of steel that ran through the words. Every trace of the uncertainty Mrs. Decker had felt mere moments ago was gone.

The gentleman was suddenly uncertain. "Madame Serafina was not expecting *two* new clients today."

"Then perhaps you will ask her if it would be all right for my daughter to join the sitting today as well," Mrs. Decker said in a tone that brooked no argument. "I have included an additional fee for my daughter," she added, starting to hand the Professor an envelope but stopping just short of actually doing so. "But if my daughter is not welcome, I will have to leave with her."

The poor man was caught between following what were obviously his instructions to admit only invited guests and the prospect of losing Mrs. Felix Decker as a client. "I'm sure that won't be necessary, Mrs. Decker," he said, instantly contrite. "I'll speak with Madame Serafina. These matters are very sensitive, you know. Madame Serafina must maintain a delicate balance."

"We will most certainly be guided by her wishes," Mrs. Decker said, although her tone implied that Madame Serafina's wishes would doubtless coincide with Mrs. Decker's. She allowed the Professor to have the envelope.

Professor Rogers—Sarah wondered just what kind of a professor he was—guided them inside, took their wraps, and escorted them into the parlor before disappearing, presumably to ask Madame Serafina's permission for Sarah to attend the séance. A large silver tray had been set on a low table in the middle of the modestly furnished room. On it were a tea service and an assortment of small cakes. Two people had already arrived. A woman sat on the sofa and a man stood on the other side of the room, staring out a window.

"Elizabeth," the woman said, nearly upsetting her teacup

in her haste to put it down and rise from where she was sitting. "I was beginning to think you'd changed your mind."
The woman hurried over and took Mrs. Decker's hands in
her own, as if to reassure her.

"Kathy, you'll remember my daughter, Sarah Brandt,"
Mrs. Decker said. "Sarah, Mrs. Burke."

"So nice to see you again, Mrs. Burke," Sarah said politely.
Mrs. Burke looked vaguely familiar, although Sarah probably
wouldn't have recognized her under other circumstances. Her
clothes marked her as a member of the wealthier members of
society, and she had the well-tended look of a hothouse flower.
Is that how her mother appeared to others? Sarah wondered
fleetingly before Mrs. Burke returned her greeting.

"So nice to see you again," she said. Her tone was too
hearty, and now that Sarah had an opportunity to look into
her eyes, she saw a strange anxiety reflected there. What did
Mrs. Burke have to be anxious about? She'd already made
contact with her dead sister and made up their quarrel.

"I'm glad I was able to come," Sarah replied noncommit-
tally.

Mrs. Burke turned back to Mrs. Decker. "I didn't know
you were bringing someone else." Now the strain in her voice
was unmistakable.

"I only decided last night," Mrs. Decker replied with a
frown. "The gentleman who answered the door seemed to
think it would be all right."

"He did?" she replied uncertainly, with a nervous glance
toward the doorway. "Then perhaps it is. Mr. Sharpe, do you
know how Madame feels about unexpected visitors?" She
turned slightly toward the older gentleman who had been
standing by one of the long windows that overlooked the
street. He must have been listening to their conversation,
because he looked up and came forward as if on cue.

"I'm afraid I can't speak for Madame Serafina," he said to Mrs. Burke. "Perhaps Mrs. Gittings can tell you."

Mrs. Burke glanced uncertainly at the doorway again, as if expecting the answer to her question to appear there, before remembering her manners. "Oh, may I present Mr. John Sharpe?" she asked Mrs. Decker.

He was impeccably dressed, and his clothes fit without the slightest wrinkle, as only a skilled tailor could manage. His hand, when he took Sarah's, was smooth, but his eyes were razor sharp.

"I believe I've met your husband, Mrs. Decker," he said when he'd greeted them both.

Sarah saw a small flicker of alarm pass over her mother's face, and she quickly stepped in. "Are you well acquainted with my father?" she asked.

"Just enough to admire his success, I'm afraid," he said, easing her mind.

Footsteps in the hallway alerted them to another arrival, and a woman entered the room. She wore a hat and gloves, but she had obviously come from somewhere else inside the house, since they would have seen her coming in the front door.

"Mrs. Gittings," Mrs. Burke said with renewed alarm, which she covered with a bright smile. "Mrs. Decker has come, and she's brought her daughter, Mrs. Brandt."

Mrs. Gittings took them in with a swift, measuring glance. "So I see." She was a small woman with an ordinary face. Although her dress was the height of fashion and her hat very stylish, Sarah could see she wasn't quite comfortable in her finery, as if she'd only recently acquired the means to own such expensive things.

"Do you think it will be all right?" Mrs. Burke asked. "With Madame Serafina, I mean?"

"She must tell us that herself," Mrs. Gittings said and turned to Mrs. Decker expectantly.

Mrs. Burke took the hint and quickly introduced her to Sarah and her mother.

"Pleased to meet you, I'm sure," Mrs. Gittings said, although her expression betrayed no pleasure at all.

Sarah was beginning to think her coming was not just an uncomfortable situation for her but a genuine problem. Should she offer to leave? Or simply to wait in another room during the séance?

"We might as well sit down," Mrs. Gittings said before she could decide. "Mr. Cunningham hasn't arrived yet, and we can't start without him."

"He's always late," Mr. Sharpe observed with disapproval. "The young have no manners."

"He's an orphan, Mr. Sharpe," Mrs. Burke reminded him too brightly.

"He's only fatherless and his father died when he was twenty-two, Mrs. Burke," he reminded her right back. "That was plenty of time to learn propriety."

Sarah wondered if the missing Mr. Cunningham wanted to contact his late father, but she didn't ask. She wasn't quite sure what the rules of etiquette were for séances. Was it rude to ask whom one wished to contact? Would Madame Serafina ask them outright or would she just know?

Mr. Sharpe turned back to the window, and the ladies took seats around the center table with the tea things on it.

"Would you like some tea while we're waiting?" Mrs. Gittings asked them, almost as if she were their hostess.

"Nothing for me," Mrs. Decker said. Sarah figured her mother's stomach was tied in knots, just as hers was. Sarah also declined. She didn't think she could swallow a thing.

"In any case, it's nice to see some new faces," Mrs. Gittings remarked in an attempt at small talk.

"Yes, it is," Mrs. Burke said with forced enthusiasm.

Sarah could stand it no longer. "Is there something we should know before . . . before it starts?"

"Oh, my, no," Mrs. Burke assured her. "Madame will explain everything. There's nothing to worry about. The spirits want to help us, don't they, Mrs. Gittings?"

"I'm sure they do," Mrs. Gittings replied with studied neutrality.

"Yellow Feather does, in any case," Mr. Sharpe offered from his station by the window.

"Yellow Feather?" Sarah repeated in surprise. "Who's that?"

"That's Madame Serafina's spirit guide," Mrs. Burke explained eagerly. "He's an Indian warrior who passed away over a hundred years ago. He——"

The sound of the front doorbell ringing surprised them all, and every head turned toward the doorway to see if Mr. Cunningham had arrived at last. They saw the Professor pass by on his way to answer it, and then heard a young man's voice making apologies for being late. In another moment, he appeared in the doorway.

He couldn't have been much older than twenty-two now, so Sarah judged he couldn't have been "orphaned" very long ago. He was tall and gangly and rather plain, although his manners were just fine as he looked around the room, greeting everyone he knew by name and offering his excuses for being late.

"A terrible tangle at Madison Square," he was saying. "A wagon overturned and no one could move an inch down Fifth Avenue for an hour! I finally gave up and walked the rest of the way. Hello, do we have some newcomers today?"

Mrs. Burke hastened to make the necessary introductions.

"Pleased to meet you," he told both Sarah and her mother. "I know Madame can help you. She's helped me more than I can ever tell you," he added earnestly.

Sarah wasn't sure how to reply to that and neither was her mother, so they simply smiled politely.

Cunningham walked over to where Mr. Sharpe stood and began inquiring after the older man's health. Sharpe had only a moment to reply before something caught everyone's attention, and they all fell expectantly silent. Afterward, Sarah could not remember hearing anything, but she must have. Something had warned them all and compelled them to look up just in time to see a figure clad entirely in black step through the open doorway. In an instant, they were all on their feet.

Sarah needed no one to tell her this was Madame Serafina, and she was nothing like Sarah had imagined. First of all, she was very young, hardly more than twenty if Sarah was any judge. She was also strikingly attractive. Not conventionally beautiful or merely pretty, but her large, dark eyes shone with an intensity that was almost magnetic. Her fair, flawless skin seemed to glow, and she wore her glossy dark hair pulled severely back into a chignon, a style that truly flattered few women but which actually accentuated her marvelous eyes.

"Good morning," she said. Her voice was as soft and sweet as Sarah had expected from one so young.

"Madame," Cunningham exclaimed, coming toward her eagerly. "I'm so glad to see you." He looked more than glad, and for an instant, Sarah thought he might take her in his arms, but he stopped just short and took her offered hand instead.

"I'm glad to see you, too, Mr. Cunningham," she said, sounding not even a tiny bit more than politely pleased. Her gaze touched him only for a moment before moving back to Sarah and her mother. "You must be Mrs. Decker," she said.

"Yes," Mrs. Decker said in a feathery voice Sarah hardly recognized. The determined Mrs. Felix Decker had vanished once again in the face of the amazing Madame Serafina.

Madame reached out and took both of Mrs. Decker's hands in hers, then closed her eyes for a few long seconds. "I sense pain," she said without opening her eyes. "Great pain. You have suffered a terrible loss. Someone very close to you. Someone who . . . A child."

Mrs. Decker gasped and snatched her hands away.

Madame Serafina opened her eyes and said, "I'm terribly sorry. I didn't mean to frighten you."

"No, no," Mrs. Decker assured her, clutching her hands to her breast. "It's just . . . I wasn't expecting . . ."

"I know, I know," Madame soothed, then turned her implacable gaze on Sarah. "I am so pleased you brought your daughter with you today." She smiled mysteriously, to Sarah's great relief. Sarah thought she heard Mrs. Burke sigh with relief of her own. "That will make us seven at the table. A lucky number." She continued to stare at Sarah for a long moment, until Sarah began to feel uncomfortable. Then she said, "I sense that you don't believe in the power of the spirits."

Someone made a small sound of protest, probably Mrs. Burke, but Sarah refused to contradict her. "I'm skeptical," she admitted.

Madame nodded knowingly. "But you came because your mother asked you," she guessed, although she didn't sound the least bit unsure about her assumption.

"Will her presence hinder you in any way?" Mr. Sharpe asked with some concern.

Madame released Sarah from the power of her gaze and

turned it on Sharpe. "Not at all. I am not a consideration, in any case. I am merely a tool the spirits use to communicate. If the spirits choose to speak, they will speak. If they do not choose to speak, they will not." She looked around again, as if making sure everyone was present. "Shall we move into the other room?"

Without waiting for a response, she turned and was gone, as if she were a spirit herself and could vanish at will. Mr. Cunningham stepped aside so the ladies could pass, although Sarah sensed he wished propriety didn't constrain him from following at Madame's heels.

"This way," the Professor said from where he had been waiting outside the parlor door, and led them down the hall. The room they entered was in the rear of the house. It was smaller than the parlor and had no windows. A gas jet burned in a sconce on the wall as the one source of illumination. The only furniture in the room was a round table in the center and a large wardrobe against the far wall. Seven chairs had been placed around the table, and a black tablecloth hung nearly to the floor.

Madame Serafina directed everyone where to sit. Mrs. Decker was to sit to her right, then Mr. Sharpe, then Sarah, then Mrs. Gittings, then Mr. Cunningham, and lastly Mrs. Burke on her left. When everyone was settled, Madame took a moment to look at each person in turn, her dark eyes seeming to penetrate their very thoughts. At least Sarah thought they could when Madame was looking at her. If so, she knew that Sarah was on the verge of bolting from the room. What had ever possessed her to do something so ridiculous?

"Because we have some new guests with us today, I will explain what will happen," she began, her voice sounding even more hypnotic in the stillness of the dimly lit room.

"Before we begin, we will hold the hands of the person on either side of us. This creates a bond between us and makes it easier for the spirits to communicate with us. Then I will turn out the light and close the door. The room will be very dark. When I have taken my seat again, I will call on my spirit guide, Yellow Feather. He was an Indian warrior who died in battle many years ago, and he is the one who actually speaks to the spirits, not I. In fact, he speaks through me. If he chooses to appear today, he will actually take over my body. You will know because you will hear his voice and not mine when I speak. If any of the spirits have a message for someone here, they will convey it to Yellow Feather. Do you have any questions?"

Sarah had a million questions, but she didn't want to speak any of them aloud. Her mother had no such hesitation. "Should we tell you if there's a particular person we want to contact?"

Madame smiled kindly. "It's usually better if I do not know. In fact, I won't even be conscious during the séance. But you may ask Yellow Feather questions, if you wish, and answer his. Is there anything else you wish to ask?"

Mrs. Decker couldn't think of anything, so Madame showed them how they should hold each other's hands. Each person in the circle would use his left hand to grasp the right wrist of the person next to him. Mrs. Gittings readily took hold of Sarah's right wrist, but Mr. Sharpe gave Sarah an apologetic glance when he offered her his own wrist. She took his right wrist gingerly in her left hand, finding it oddly uncomfortable to be practically holding hands with a man she'd only just met, but no one else seemed concerned with the arrangement. They had done this before, after all.

When everyone was properly clasped together, Madame disengaged her own hands and rose from her chair. "I'm going to put out the light now and close the door and then return to my seat. The room will be completely dark. Then I will call for Yellow Feather."

Moving almost silently, she crossed to the door and put out the light. Then she pushed the door shut. More than one person made a small sound of surprise as the room plunged into total darkness. Sarah closed her eyes and opened them again but could see no noticeable difference. She thought she would get used to the dark after a few minutes, but that didn't happen. She couldn't even see any light coming through the cracks from where she knew the door to be. A slight rustling told her Madame had returned to her seat. Could those amazing eyes see in the dark, too? Or maybe she just knew the layout of the room from memory.

They sat for a minute or two with nothing to hear but the sound of their own breathing, and then Madame's voice broke the silence.

"Yellow Feather, are you there?" she called. "Yellow Feather, if you're there, come to me now. I have some seekers here. They are searching for their loved ones. Yellow Feather, can you hear me?"

Mrs. Gittings's fingers tightened their grip as they waited in the silence, and Sarah wondered if she was doing the same thing to Mr. Sharpe. Time seemed to be frozen, and Sarah had no idea how long they waited in the silence.

"Yellow Feather, someone needs to speak with you. Someone needs to contact a loved one."

Another long silence. Sarah heard a low humming sound, although she couldn't tell exactly where it was coming from or even if it came from a human throat. The air in the room seemed to be vibrating with it, or maybe it was just the vibration she sensed and not a sound at all. Then she heard a strangled sound, as if someone were choking.

Was someone ill? Mrs. Gittings's fingers tightened again, and Mr. Sharpe's wrist tensed beneath Sarah's hand.

"This is Yellow Feather," a deep voice proclaimed, and Sarah's breath caught in her throat. The sound came from where she knew Madame Serafina sat, but the voice was a man's. "I sense a stranger's presence, someone who does not believe."

Sarah stiffened, instinctively feeling guilty and feeling angry for feeling that guilt.

"Don't pay her any mind, Yellow Feather," Cunningham pleaded. "Please, is my father with you today? I need to speak with him."

"Many spirits are here with me, but not all of them wish to speak. Some are very sad and others are angry."

"Is my father angry?" Cunningham asked, his voice shrill with alarm. "I did exactly what he told me to do! It wasn't my fault that it didn't work out!"

"Someone is here," Yellow Feather's voice said. "She has a rose."

Sarah could feel a tremor go through Mr. Sharpe's arm. "Harriet," he breathed. Then louder, "Harriet?"

"She has a red rose. This has some special meaning."

"Yes, I always gave her red roses on our anniversary," Mr. Sharpe said, his voice trembling. "Harriet, can you hear me?"

Sarah found herself holding her breath, infected by his tension. She could almost imagine she smelled roses.

"She wants to tell you something," Yellow Feather said, "but the message isn't clear. She's afraid for you."

"Afraid? Why is she afraid?"

"You are trying to make a decision."

"Yes, yes," Mr. Sharpe said. "What does she want me to do?"

The scent of roses was stronger now. Sarah was sure of it.

"There is danger," Yellow Feather said. "Someone is in danger."

"No, there's no danger," he insisted.

"You must protect someone from this danger."

"How? How can I do that?"

The humming sound returned, louder now, almost audible but not quite. A long minute passed, and then another. Sarah felt Mr. Sharpe's tension. It was radiating through her now. The smell of roses filled her throat.

"Tell me!" Sharpe begged. "Tell me what to do!"

The humming stopped, and Yellow Feather made a groaning sound, as if he were in pain. "You know the answer. Follow your heart."

"I can't!" Sharpe protested.

"Follow . . ." Yellow Feather said on a soft moan. "Follow . . . your . . . heart."

Sharpe drew a breath and let it out on a sigh of surrender.

"Father," Cunningham tried again. "Father, are you there?"

"Opal is here," Yellow Feather said, ignoring Cunningham.

"Opal!" Mrs. Burke said in surprise. She didn't sound happy.

"She wants to tell you something. Something important. Something you need to know."

"I did what you told me!" Mrs. Burke said anxiously. "But it wasn't enough."

"She says . . . Someone else is here."

"Who? Who is it?"

"Father?" Cunningham interrupted. "Father, are you there?"

"Someone Opal loves." Yellow Feather sounded impatient. "Someone you both love."

"Mother?" she asked in surprise. "Mother, are you there?"

Yellow Feather moaned. "I'm tired, so tired . . ."

"No, no!" Mrs. Burke nearly shouted. "You must tell me what my mother is saying!"

"The message is unclear," Yellow Feather complained, sounding oddly petulant. "She's fading."

"No, please! I have to know! What is she saying?"

"Something . . ." Yellow Feather sounded as if he were struggling. "Something she gave you."

"What? What is it? She gave me so many things!"

"Something special . . ." Yellow Feather paused. "What? I can hardly hear her."

"Please, what is it?" Mrs. Burke nearly sobbed.

"Something . . . valuable."

"The brooch?" she asked in surprise. "Not the diamond brooch!"

"I don't know . . . Wait, yes . . . Yes, she says it's all right," Yellow Feather reported, slightly puzzled. "Do you know what she means?"

"But it's been in the family forever!" Mrs. Burke protested.

Yellow Feather moaned. "She's fading."

"Are you sure it's the brooch?" Mrs. Burke pressed frantically. "And she said it's all right?"

"Yes, it's all right," Yellow Feather confirmed faintly.

Mrs. Burke made a sound that could have been a sob.

"I'm tired, so tired . . . but someone else is here, a spirit I've never seen before." More moaning. "Pain," Yellow Feather said. "Someone in pain. A child."

"Abigail?" Mrs. Gittings called out desperately.

"A baby," Yellow Feather said, his voice thick. "A tiny baby, just born."

Mrs. Decker gasped.

"Mother, don't," Sarah said before she could think.

"A tiny baby," Yellow feather said, his voice stronger now, as if to overpower Sarah's protest.

"It's Maggie's baby!" Mrs. Decker cried.

"Too small to speak, but pain, I feel so much pain."

"Is Maggie there?" Mrs. Decker called. "Maggie, can you hear me?"

Fury boiled up in Sarah's chest. It wasn't Maggie, it couldn't be!

Yellow Feather moaned. "Someone is here, but she will not speak. She is too angry."

"Maggie, I'm sorry!" Mrs. Decker cried. "I'm so sorry! I didn't know!"

Sarah opened her mouth, ready to stop this farce, but a new sound shocked her, and the words died in her throat. At first she didn't know what it was or where it was coming from. It began like a screech from a poorly played violin and then broke into a more familiar sound, a sound Sarah heard so often that she couldn't mistake it, but she still couldn't believe it. A baby's cry. A newborn baby's cry!

"My God," Mr. Sharpe said beside her.

No! Sarah wanted to scream, but she could form no words. Her throat seemed paralyzed. Tears flooded her eyes. This was too cruel! Too horrible to bear!

Someone was sobbing. "Maggie!" the sobbing voice choked.

"Stop it!" Sarah said and tried to break free, but Mrs. Gittings's fingers tightened on her wrist, refusing to let go, and when Sarah released Mr. Sharpe's wrist, he grabbed hers in a bruising grip.

The baby's cry stopped abruptly.

"She is too angry," Yellow Feather's deep voice proclaimed solemnly. "She can't forgive you."

"Sarah," her mother's voice pleaded. "She'll talk to you!"

"No!" Sarah felt the tears rolling down her cheeks. She wouldn't let herself be drawn into this nightmare.

"Please," her mother begged. "She'll talk to you. Tell her, Sarah. Tell her I'm sorry!"

"Sarah doesn't believe," Yellow Feather said sadly.

"Yes, she does!" Mrs. Decker insisted wildly. Sarah could hardly believe it was her mother's voice. "Sarah, tell him! Tell him you believe! Talk to Maggie for me. Tell her!"

Mrs. Gittings shook Sarah's arm. "Tell her!" she commanded.

"For God's sake, tell her!" Cunningham's voice begged.

Sarah's mouth was so dry, she could hardly force her tongue to work. "Mag . . . Maggie?" she tried, hating herself, hating all of them.

Yellow Feather moaned.

"Maggie, they . . ."

Yellow Feather moaned more loudly, as if his heart were bursting in his chest.

Sarah tried to swallow and then forced the words past her reluctant lips. "They didn't mean to hurt you!"

Yellow Feather's voice exploded in a piercing shriek that froze Sarah's blood in her veins and then someone else screamed.

"Madame Serafina!" Mrs. Burke cried. "She's fainted!"

3

Mrs. Gittings and Mr. Sharpe released Sarah's wrists, and she jumped to her feet, not really certain what to do next but knowing that she must do something. Someone had managed to find the door in the dark and opened it, letting in enough light to see that Madame Serafina had slid out of her chair and fallen to the floor in a heap. Sarah's mother seemed to be fine. She was still in her chair, staring down at Madame Serafina in alarm.

"Professor!" Mrs. Gittings was calling out into the hall. She was the one who had found the door. "Madame fainted!"

The man ran into the room. "Don't touch her!" he commanded. "Is there any ectoplasm?"

"No," someone said.

"We didn't see any," someone else confirmed.

He knelt down on one knee, pulled the stopper from the

small bottle he carried, and passed it under Madame's nose. Sarah could smell it from here. Smelling salts. Madame stirred, instinctively recoiling from the harsh odor.

"Madame, are you all right?" he asked.

Her eyelids fluttered open, revealing those magnificent eyes. "What happened?"

"You fainted," Mrs. Burke said, wringing her hands nervously.

"*She* did it," Cunningham said angrily, pointing at Sarah. "It's all her fault. She doesn't believe!"

Sarah resisted the absurd impulse to apologize. She'd done nothing wrong.

"You were the one who told Yellow Feather not to mind her," Mrs. Gittings reminded him fiercely. "Madame, are you all right?"

The Professor was helping her sit up. She looked dazed, her eyes not really focusing. "I think so." She looked at Cunningham with concern. "Was it your father?"

"No! He didn't even speak to me," Cunningham reported indignantly. "It's all her fault." He glared at Sarah again.

"Can you try again?" Mrs. Decker asked to Sarah's surprise. "My daughter . . . I need to speak to her."

Madame Serafina looked at Mrs. Decker, studying her face as if trying to look into her soul. "Did Yellow Feather contact her?"

"Yes, she was there," Mrs. Decker said with a certainty that pricked Sarah's heart. "Don't you remember?"

Madame smiled sadly. "I never remember anything that happens when Yellow Feather is speaking through me. But perhaps I can summon him again." She took the Professor's arm and let him help her to her feet, but as soon as he released her, she swayed dangerously.

He caught her and lowered her into the chair she'd occupied previously. "She can't possibly do another session now," he said. "It would be far too dangerous. Can't you see how weak she is?"

She did look weak, which was just fine with Sarah. She had to get her mother out of there.

"I'm very sorry if I caused any trouble," Sarah said just the way she had been taught to as a child—say you're sorry even if you don't mean it.

Madame looked up at her in surprise, her dark eyes unreadable. "You still don't believe?" she asked in amazement.

Sarah didn't want to lie, and she didn't think she needed to. Madame seemed to already know the answer. "Mother, we should go so Madame Serafina can rest."

"Oh, yes, of course," her mother said, suddenly remembering her manners. She rose from her chair, and Sarah was alarmed to see that she also looked a bit unsteady. Mr. Sharpe solicitously took her arm, but she didn't even notice. She was looking at Madame Serafina. "Thank you so much. I'm very grateful."

"I hope I was able to help," Madame said with apparent sincerity.

Sarah pushed past Mr. Sharpe and took her mother's other arm. "Let's go now," she said, and her mother followed her meekly out into the hallway, leaving Sharpe and the others behind. They could hear Cunningham complaining again that his father hadn't even spoken to him.

"Are you all right, Mother?" Sarah asked.

"I'm not sure," Mrs. Decker said with a degree of wonder. "I've never had an experience like that before. It was extraordinary."

"Yes, it was," Sarah readily agreed. *Extraordinary* was one way to describe it.

The Professor had followed them out and hurried to open

the door for them. "Thank you for coming, Mrs. Decker. I hope you were satisfied with the sitting."

"Yes, thank you," she said vaguely.

"You are welcome to return at any time," he said. Sarah noted that he did not include her in the invitation.

"Thank you," Mrs. Decker said as Sarah maneuvered her out the door.

They paused on the front steps. Sarah was almost surprised to see that the world had gone on its ordinary way all the time they'd been conversing with the dead. She would not have been surprised to see that the sky had turned green or something. But the sights and sounds of the city were exactly the same as they'd been an hour ago when they'd entered this strange house.

Sarah looked up and down the street and saw the Decker carriage where the driver had found a spot to pull over. She waved and caught his eye. He quickly slapped the horses into motion and deftly maneuvered the carriage out into the street and up to where they waited.

Although the task took only a few minutes, the wait seemed like hours as Sarah kept checking to make sure her mother was all right. She was still rather pale, and she hadn't said a single word since they'd left the house. She also hadn't looked at Sarah even once.

When the carriage reached them, the driver stopped and jumped down to assist them. Only when they were safely inside and the vehicle was moving did Sarah break the silence. "Are you going to be all right, Mother?"

She looked at Sarah in surprise, as if she'd forgotten she was there. "Of course I am," she replied with some annoyance. "Stop asking me that." She looked away again, out the window, although Sarah was sure she wasn't seeing anything.

"I didn't believe it was possible. Not really, I mean. I didn't believe she could really speak to the dead."

"Mother——" Sarah tried, but her mother was having none of it.

"I know you don't believe, but how else can you explain it? She knew about Maggie's baby."

"I don't know," Sarah admitted, "but I'm sure there's some explanation."

"No one knew about the baby," Mrs. Decker reminded her. "No one. Everyone thinks Maggie died of a fever in France."

"Yes, but——"

"No one knew, outside of our family," Mrs. Decker went on relentlessly. "She *must* have been talking to Maggie. Did you . . . did you hear the baby cry?" she asked, her voice breaking.

Sarah instinctively took her hand. "Mother, please . . ."

Mrs. Decker's fingers closed around hers like a vise. "You heard it, didn't you? A baby was crying."

"Yes, I . . . I heard something that sounded like a baby crying," Sarah admitted.

"You see? And what about those other messages? The one that Kathy got, and Mr. Sharpe? They knew the spirits who were speaking. They understood the messages."

Sarah had no explanation, but she still wasn't convinced. "So it seemed."

"*Seemed?* Kathy was *certain.* I must ask her what it meant, the information about a diamond brooch. I know she understood it, though. That was obvious."

"She appeared to," was all Sarah could manage.

Mrs. Decker turned to look out the window again. The carriage moved slowly through the crowded streets. People walked past on the sidewalk, giving them hardly a glance. "Maggie was there," she said softly after a few moments.

Sarah closed her eyes and bit her tongue. She mustn't say what she was thinking. Her mother was as stubborn as she, and Sarah would never give up on something just because her mother advised her to. In fact, she'd be more likely to persevere if her mother advised her to stop. She swallowed down her frustration and willed her voice to steadiness. "If you believe Maggie was there, then she heard you say you were sorry," she pointed out reasonably. "You accomplished your purpose." This was the only reason she had agreed to go with her mother in the first place.

Mrs. Decker looked at her sharply, as if trying to judge her sincerity. "That's true."

Sarah felt the knot of tension in her stomach ease a bit. "I know that must be a great burden lifted from you. I may not approve, but if this . . . what happened today . . . If this gives you peace, then I'm happy for you."

"Thank you, Sarah. That means a lot to me."

"But I hope this will be the end of it." Her mother stiffened in silent resistance, but Sarah hurried on, determined to follow Maeve's advice not to allow Mrs. Decker to be taken advantage of. "Did you notice that Mrs. Burke didn't seem very happy with the message she got today? Neither did Mr. Sharpe. I have a feeling that you might not always be pleased with what you hear."

"I wasn't pleased today," her mother reminded her.

"Exactly. If all you wanted was an opportunity to tell Maggie you were sorry, you got that today."

"But she didn't forgive me," Mrs. Decker reminded her.

"And what if she never does?" Sarah asked ruthlessly. "What if she curses you or says hurtful things? Would you be able to bear it?"

"I—"

"I know you've suffered all these years, Mother, but it could be even worse. I beg you to stop now. You've asked for Maggie's forgiveness. That's all we can ever do when we've wronged someone. I think she would have forgiven you in life, if she'd had the chance. We have to believe she would also forgive you in death."

"If only I could be sure," Mrs. Decker said, her voice catching on tears.

"*I'm* sure," Sarah said. "Mother, don't do this to yourself again. Let Maggie's spirit rest in peace."

Her mother drew an unsteady breath. "I suppose you're right."

"I am, I promise you."

"I feel sorry for that poor girl."

"Who?" Sarah asked in surprise.

"Madame Serafina."

"Why?"

"That must be so difficult for her. You saw her afterwards. She was exhausted."

Or pretending to be, Sarah thought. If she was too tired to continue, the clients would have to pay to come back another time to finish the session, just like Maeve had predicted. Poor Mr. Cunningham had gotten nothing at all for his fee today. Or Mrs. Gittings either. "She seems very young to be involved in all this," Sarah said.

"Mrs. Burke told me she's been doing it since she was a child. It's something you're born with, she said."

"Really?" Sarah couldn't imagine a child suddenly realizing she could commune with spirits. "That's amazing."

"Yes, it is," Mrs. Decker agreed vaguely. She was looking out the window again, thinking.

Sarah didn't want her thinking about the séance anymore,

but she knew better than to say so. She was wracking her
brain for a neutral topic when the carriage came to a stop,
and Sarah realized they were in front of her house. "You're
coming in for a while, aren't you?" Sarah asked. "I told Catherine you would."

"Oh, dear, I'm sorry, Sarah, but I just can't. I'm . . . Well,
I'm as exhausted as Madame Serafina, I'm afraid. Tell her I'll
come tomorrow and bring her something nice."

"Perhaps that's best. You do look worn out. Try to get
some rest and put all of this behind you," Sarah advised.

Mrs. Decker managed a small smile. "Of course I will.
Thank you again for coming with me, my dear. I can't imagine how I would have managed without you."

"I'm glad you asked me. Get some rest now, and I'll see
you tomorrow," Sarah said as the coachman opened the door.

Catherine was disappointed when Mrs. Decker didn't
come in for a visit, but Sarah's promise that she would come
tomorrow and bring a present mollified her a bit. Their el-
derly neighbor, Mrs. Ellsworth, had spend the morning with
the girls, making cookies, and Sarah had to taste them. Even-
tually, Maeve took Catherine upstairs to play, leaving the two
women alone in the kitchen, lingering over their coffee.

"Maeve tells me you went to a séance this morning," Mrs.
Ellsworth said casually, but she didn't fool Sarah one bit.
Mrs. Ellsworth had been the foremost authority on everyone
else's business since long before Sarah had moved to Bank
Street. She'd spent many years of her life sweeping her front
steps so she could keep her eye on everyone's comings and
goings, and nothing was too insignificant to escape her notice. Her keen observations had saved Sarah from disaster
more than once, so she had long since forgiven her for being
perhaps a bit too interested in Sarah's business. And since
Sarah had taken Catherine to live with her, Mrs. Ellsworth

had proven herself more than a good friend to all of them, turning her full energies to teaching the girls housewifely skills instead of minding other people's business.

"Have you ever been to a séance?" Sarah asked her.

"Heavens, no!" she exclaimed, surprising Sarah.

"Really? I would have thought . . ." She let her voice trail off awkwardly.

"Because I'm superstitious?" Mrs. Ellsworth guessed slyly. Her superstitions were legendary. "There's a big difference between throwing salt over your shoulder and talking to the dead."

"I guess you're right," Sarah admitted a bit sheepishly.

"What was it like?" she asked, leaning forward eagerly. "I've always wondered."

Where to begin? "I know it's all fake, of course, but—"

"Are you sure?" Mrs. Ellsworth challenged, quite seriously.

"Of course it is. Nobody can talk to the dead."

"Are you *sure*?" she repeated. "I've heard stories from people . . . regular people, not the ones who set themselves up in business, mind you, but people like us. An old friend of mine, her mother who'd been dead more than twenty years appeared one day and warned her that her daughter was involved with a terrible man. She was, too. My friend put a stop to it just in time."

"I know things sometimes happen that we can't explain," Sarah said. "But your friend didn't try to contact her mother, did she? She didn't sit down in a dark room with a bunch of strangers and try to summon her spirit."

Mrs. Ellsworth tapped her upper lip with her finger thoughtfully. "It does sound odd when you say it like that."

"It was more than odd, I assure you." She told Mrs. Ellsworth about arriving at the house and meeting the other people gathered there and then seeing Madame Serafina for the first time. "She didn't look like she was more than twenty."

"I would've expected a much older person."

"She was a lovely girl, too. I can't imagine how she became involved in this."

"How does she contact the spirits?"

Sarah told her about going into the other room and sitting down around the table. "Then we all held hands around the circle, and she turned out the light."

"You were in total darkness?"

"Oh, yes. I couldn't see a thing. Then she calls for the spirits."

"Just like that?" Mrs. Ellsworth asked in surprise.

"Well, I should have said that she calls for her spirit guide, Yellow Feather."

"Yellow *what*?"

"Yellow Feather. He's an Indian warrior who died in battle," Sarah explained with a smirk.

"How very odd!"

"He's her spirit contact or something like that. The other spirits speak to him and he passes along what they say and asks them questions."

"And she's the only one who can hear him?"

"Oh, no, I forgot to tell you, he speaks through her."

"How does he do that?"

"I'm not exactly sure how it works, but his voice comes out of her mouth, as if he were using her body."

"How do you know it's his voice?" Mrs. Ellsworth asked, thoroughly confused now.

"Oh, it sounds like a man's voice. I could hardly believe my ears at first. Her voice changed completely. And when it was all over, she claimed she didn't remember anything he'd said. When he's speaking through her, she's not really conscious, I suppose. That's how she explained it anyway."

"Good heavens. I never heard of such a thing."

"Neither had I," Sarah assured her.

"Why on earth did your mother want to attend this séance in the first place?"

Sarah sighed wearily. "She wanted to contact my sister."

"Your sister? I didn't know you had a sister."

"She died long before I met you," Sarah said, wishing she hadn't mentioned Maggie. She hated telling her story, even to kindly Mrs. Ellsworth. "She . . . she married a man my parents didn't approve of," she said, keeping to the bare facts.

"Just as you did," Mrs. Ellsworth reminded her with a puzzled frown.

"She did it long before I did, and they disowned her for it," Sarah said, the words paining her even now. "And then she died in childbirth. My mother has carried that guilt all this time."

"And I suppose she wanted to ask for forgiveness," Mrs. Ellsworth said. "Poor thing. We tend to think that people who have a lot of money don't have any troubles, but that isn't true, is it?"

"No, it isn't," Sarah confirmed, remembering all the wealthy people who had been involved in murders that she had investigated with her friend Detective Sergeant Frank Malloy of the New York City Police. "They don't have to worry about putting food on the table or keeping a roof over their heads, but they have the same kinds of losses and disappointments that everyone else has."

"I guess that explains why your parents didn't protest too much when you married Dr. Brandt."

"They weren't happy about it," Sarah recalled with a pang, "but they accepted it, just as they accepted my becoming a midwife."

"Even though they would have been much happier if you'd given it up and returned to your rightful place in society after Dr. Brandt died," Mrs. Ellsworth guessed. Sarah's husband, Tom, had been murdered four years earlier.

"I think they've finally accepted the fact that I never will."

"And do you think your mother was satisfied with the séance?"

Sarah had almost forgotten the original subject of their conversation. "I hope so. I reminded her that she's wanted to apologize to Maggie and she did that at the séance. I don't believe for a moment that Maggie's spirit was there to hear it, but my mother believes it was, and so she thinks she accomplished her purpose. I hope that will satisfy her."

"You don't sound very sure," Mrs. Ellsworth said.

"Those other people at the séance, they've all been to see Madame Serafina more than once. They seemed well acquainted with each other, and I got the impression this was a regular event in their lives."

Mrs. Ellsworth frowned. "I guess I could understand that, if I believed this Madame what's her name could contact my dead loved ones. I've always wanted to ask my husband where he put his pocket watch. I wanted to give it to Nelson after he died, but I never found it."

Sarah smiled in spite of herself. "Maybe you should go see Madame."

"I can't imagine what else I'd ask him, though," she mused. "I'd think one visit would be enough."

Sarah tried to recall what the others had been asking. "They seemed to want guidance about making decisions. As if they came back regularly to ask about something new."

"Oh, dear, how tiresome," Mrs. Ellsworth said. "Why can't they just make up their own minds? Or at least ask somebody who's easier to contact, like a living relative, for instance?"

This really made Sarah smile. "I'm sure I don't know. But some people just don't seem to be able to stop. I don't want my mother to become one of them."

"Oh, I'm sure your father would soon put a stop to it if she did," Mrs. Ellsworth said.

Sarah wasn't so sure. Felix Decker was one of the richest, most powerful men in the city, but he was completely powerless to manage his wife, particularly if he had no idea what she was doing. "Let's hope it doesn't come to that," Sarah said and tried to change the subject. "Is that the newspaper?"

Mrs. Ellsworth glanced over to where the paper lay folded on the end of the table. "Oh, yes, I brought it over for you to see. I don't suppose you've heard the news yet," she added with a frown.

"What news?"

"About Mr. Roosevelt."

"Oh, dear," Sarah said, reaching for the paper. She unfolded it to reveal the headline, ROOSEVELT RESIGNS. She quickly scanned the story. Her old friend Theodore Roosevelt had resigned as police commissioner to accept a job in Washington, D.C. "Just as my father predicted."

"Your father knew that President McKinley was going to offer him a position in Washington?" Mrs. Ellsworth asked in amazement.

"I'm sure he didn't know exactly what it would be, but politicians always pay their debts, and Mr. Roosevelt campaigned very vigorously for McKinley. The president will be giving out hundreds of political patronage jobs to his supporters to reward them."

"Assistant secretary of the Navy doesn't sound like a very important job," Mrs. Ellsworth observed.

"I'm sure Theodore will make the most of it," Sarah said, recalling her old friend's ambition fondly, "although this probably isn't good news for the police department."

"What do you mean?"

"Mr. Roosevelt made a lot of changes in the department. He hired men on merit instead of political patronage. He promoted men who were good at their jobs instead of those who could afford to pay a bribe to get a better position. He even hired officers who weren't Irish."

"But surely they won't go back to the way things were before just because Mr. Roosevelt leaves," Mrs. Ellsworth protested.

"Mr. Malloy is afraid they will," Sarah said, recalling what he had told her. "That's why he was in such a hurry to solve Tom's murder. He knew Roosevelt was going to resign soon, and then he might not be allowed to work on the case anymore."

"Oh, my," Mrs. Ellsworth said with a frown. "Is he afraid he might lose his job?"

Sarah knew that was a possibility. Roosevelt had singled Malloy out several times to work on cases involving wealthy murder victims. Some in the department would be envious of that special treatment, and they could hold it against him. But Sarah thought that wouldn't be the worst thing that could happen. "He might be, but I think he's more afraid of having to go back to the way things were before all the reforms."

Mrs. Ellsworth nodded. "He's changed a lot since he met you."

Yes, he had, Sarah thought, and she had changed, too. She'd never thought she'd be able to love again after losing

Tom, and she'd certainly never thought she could love a policeman.

MAEVE HAD OBVIOUSLY WANTED TO HEAR ALL ABOUT THE séance the moment Sarah had walked in the door, but she knew better than to discuss it in front of Catherine. She had to wait until Catherine was tucked snuggly into bed and she could slip downstairs to find Sarah in the kitchen, still cleaning up after supper.

"I'll do that," Maeve said, taking the dishtowel from Sarah's hand. "Sit yourself down and tell me everything that happened!"

Sarah did. Maeve listened attentively, asking only the occasional clarifying question. When Sarah was finished, Maeve sat down across from her at the kitchen table and considered what she had heard for several moments.

"Well?" Sarah prodded after a while.

"Well, what?" Maeve asked in surprise.

"What do you think? Was any of it real?"

Maeve shrugged. "It's easy enough to change your voice and pretend you're somebody else."

"But she sounded like a *man*," Sarah protested.

"Like I said, actors change their voices all the time."

"What about the baby crying?"

"I don't know. I'd have to see the room. There's ways to do that, though. Have you ever seen a magician?"

"Yes, I have."

"Do you think he really makes things appear out of thin air?"

"Of course not. It's a trick."

"Madame Serafina probably knows some tricks, too."

Sarah frowned. "I'm sure she does. The truly amazing thing

wasn't that we heard a baby cry but that she knew about the baby in the first place, or rather that Yellow Feather or whoever it was knew about it."

"Did you talk about Maggie and her baby while you were waiting with the other people?"

"No, I'm sure we didn't. Why would that matter?"

"She might be able to overhear what people are talking about while they're waiting. That would be a good way to get private information about them."

"She wouldn't have heard us talking about Maggie. In fact, my mother even asked Madame Serafina if she needed to know who we wanted to contact. Madame said no, so she knew nothing about us before we arrived."

"I doubt that," Maeve scoffed. "People know a lot about Mrs. Felix Decker."

Sarah hadn't thought of that. "I suppose that's true."

"And didn't you say your mother's friend was the one who told her about this and invited her to come? She probably told Madame everything she knew."

"But she didn't know about Maggie's baby. Nobody knows that except our family."

"*I* know," Maeve reminded her.

Sarah laid a hand on Maeve's arm where it rested on the table. "You're family," she said, remembering how Maeve had recently risked her life to help solve the mystery of Tom Brandt's murder.

Maeve blinked at her in surprise. "Oh," was all she could manage for several seconds.

Sarah hurried on before Maeve's emotions got the better of her. "So you see, Madame couldn't have known about Maggie's baby."

"Maybe it was a lucky guess. Lots of babies die. I'm sure

somebody else in the room could've thought it was a baby in their family, too, if your mother hadn't spoken up first."

Sarah hadn't thought of that. "You're probably right."

"I wish I knew more about this séance business. I could explain to Mrs. Decker how they do it, and she'd be cured of ever wanting to go back."

"I'm hoping she's already cured."

"Well, if she's not, ask her to take me along next time. At least I could pretend I believe in it."

"I could've pretended I believed in it if I'd wanted to," Sarah protested, pretending to be insulted.

But Maeve was shaking her head. "You're an awful liar, Mrs. Brandt."

"Some people would consider that a compliment," Sarah reminded her.

"Yes," Maeve agreed with a grin. "Some people would."

MRS. DECKER ARRIVED THE NEXT DAY WITH A NEW PIC-ture book for Catherine. She didn't mention Maggie or the séance, and Sarah believed she had put it all behind her. The next two weeks passed uneventfully. Sarah delivered a few babies, and her mother chanced to visit when she was out, so they hadn't seen each other again. Then one day, her doorbell rang.

Catherine and Maeve hurried to answer it. Sarah thought it would be a summons to another delivery until she heard Maeve call.

"Mrs. Brandt, there's a policeman here to see you."

She didn't sound alarmed, but Sarah knew this couldn't be good news. She hurried out of the kitchen and through the front room that served as her medical office into the entry hall. She found the girls staring at a handsome young man in a blue uniform. He held his hat in both hands in front of his chest, and he was staring at Maeve with more than a little interest.

"Officer Donatelli?" Sarah asked in surprise.

He looked up. "Good afternoon, Mrs. Brandt," he said, suddenly all business. "I'm sorry to bother you, but Detective Sergeant Malloy sent me to fetch you."

"What for?" she asked in surprise. She hadn't heard from Malloy for weeks and she knew he'd never send for her unless it was something very serious.

"There's been some trouble . . ." He glanced meaningfully at Catherine, who was listening intently to every word.

"Maeve, would you take Catherine upstairs?" Sarah asked, worried herself now.

Plainly, neither girl wanted to miss hearing Officer Dona- telli's news, but they obediently marched up the stairs. When they were safely out of earshot, Sarah asked urgently, "Is Mal- loy all right?"

"Oh, yes, ma'am," he hastened to assure her. "He just . . . Well, it's your mother, you see."

"My mother!" she echoed in alarm. "Has she been in- jured?"

"Oh, no, I'm sorry! I didn't mean to scare you. She's fine, just fine. It's just . . ."

"What is it!" she demanded impatiently when he hesi- tated.

"Well, I'm sorry to say that there's been a murder."

"Who was murdered? Someone I know?"

"I don't know if you do or not, but it happened at a sé- ance."

"A séance! At Madame Serafina's?"

"Yes, ma'am, that's it, on Waverly Place."

"And my mother was there?" Sarah asked, almost wailing in despair.

"I'm afraid she was. That's why they called for Detective Sergeant Malloy. She asked for him special."

Of course she had. She knew he would handle everything with the utmost discretion. If he could. If anyone could. What would happen when the press found out that someone had been murdered at a séance attended by a half-dozen socially prominent citizens, one of them Mrs. Felix Decker?

"And he sent me to get you," Officer Donatelli was saying. "He wanted you to make sure your mother gets home all right."

Sarah sighed wearily. "I'll get my things."

4

DETECTIVE SERGEANT FRANK MALLOY COULDN'T BELIEVE it. He'd managed to keep Sarah Brandt from becoming involved in a murder investigation for weeks, and now she was summoning *him* to one!

At least that's what he'd been told. They'd sent a uniformed officer out to track him down where he was investigating a warehouse robbery over near the docks this morning. They'd told him somebody'd been murdered at a séance, and Sarah Brandt was there and demanding he be brought in to investigate. That sounded like Sarah. Imagine his surprise when he arrived at the house to find not Sarah at all but her mother, Elizabeth Decker.

"I couldn't give the police my real name," Mrs. Decker explained to him the moment they were alone. He'd immediately taken her to what appeared to be some sort of office to interrogate her in private. "Do you know what the newspapers would do if they found out I was present at a murder?"

"But nobody would think twice about your daughter being at one," Frank said with a weary sigh.

"Exactly." Mrs. Decker gave him an approving smile. "And she'd already been here with me the first time I came."

Why was Frank not surprised? "Tell me what happened here," he said, not feeling at all like smiling.

Mrs. Decker sobered instantly. "We were having a séance in that room where the . . . the . . ."

"The body," he supplied when she couldn't bring herself to do it.

"Yes, where the body is. We were seated around the table, holding hands."

"Holding hands?" he echoed in surprise. He had seen the room with the table where the body was, but nobody had mentioned holding hands.

"Yes, it increases the bond to help the spirits communicate with us."

"Maybe we should sit down," he suggested, feeling a headache starting to form behind his eyes.

"Oh, thank you, Mr. Malloy. I'm afraid I'm still suffering from the shock of seeing her lying there—"

"Over here," Frank said, taking her elbow and directing her to one of two straight-backed chairs that had been placed in front of the desk that sat in the center of the room. The top of the desk was bare and slightly dusty, as if no one ever actually used it. He seated Mrs. Decker and took the other chair, turning it to face hers. "You were sitting around the table holding hands," he reminded her.

"Well, I guess we weren't exactly holding hands," she clarified. "We were holding each other's wrists, but it has the same effect, doesn't it? In any event, Madame Serafina—she's the spiritualist—she was talking with the spirits, or rather Yellow Feather was talking with them—"

"What's Yellow Feather?" Frank asked, confused already.

"He's Madame's spirit guide. He's an Indian warrior who died in battle over a hundred years ago."

Frank was having trouble following all this. "Is he some kind of ghost?"

"No, I told you, he's a spirit guide. He comes when Madame calls him, and then he speaks through her."

"What do you mean, he speaks through her?"

"He uses her body. It's his voice, though, very obviously. Her body speaks but a man's voice comes out."

Frank had a lot of questions about that, but he decided to save them for later. "All right, so this Indian spirit is talking through her. Then what happened?"

"We were all asking questions, and Yellow Feather was getting very agitated. He was shouting, and there was some music—"

"Music?"

"Yes, we could hear music playing, although I confess I wasn't paying much attention to it. I was too distracted by what Yellow Feather was saying."

"But there was a lot of noise in the room?"

"That's right, so we didn't notice . . . Or at least I didn't notice anything out of the ordinary until Mrs. Burke screamed."

Frank gaped at her. She had been sitting in a room, practically holding hands with perfect strangers and talking to ghosts, and she didn't notice anything out of the ordinary? He was really beginning to understand where Sarah had inherited her intrepid disposition. "Didn't anybody notice somebody going up behind this woman and sticking a knife into her back?" he asked in amazement.

"How could we? It was pitch dark."

"All this was going on in the dark?"

"Oh, yes. The room must be dark to decrease distractions when you're contacting the spirits."

Frank stared at her for a long moment, trying to judge her sincerity. Plainly, she was telling the absolute truth, no matter how ridiculous it sounded to him. "Then that would explain how someone could sneak into the room."

"Oh, no, it couldn't," Mrs. Decker protested. "There's only one door to the room, and it was closed tightly the entire time. We would have noticed immediately if someone opened it because light would have come in."

That was good. The number of suspects would be limited to those in the room. "So one of the . . ." He couldn't think of what people attending a séance would be called. "One of the other people in the room killed her, then."

"Oh, no, that's impossible," she assured him confidently.

"Why is it impossible?"

"Because," she reminded him, "we were all holding each other's hands. No one could move without someone else noticing."

Frank definitely had a headache now. He rubbed the bridge of his nose. "I see."

"Mr. Malloy," Mrs. Decker said, leaning forward and looking him straight in the eye. "I'm very much afraid that Mrs. Gittings was killed by one of the spirits."

FRANK LEFT MRS. DECKER IN THE OFFICE, JUST IN CASE some reporters showed up to nose around. He was surprised they hadn't gotten the scent of this already. It had all the makings of a scandal. High-society ladies and gentlemen attending a séance with a beautiful spiritualist and one of them ends up murdered. Frank could probably write the story himself, if he'd been so inclined. But he was more inclined to keep Mrs. Decker's name out of the newspapers if at all possible. He didn't like *Mr.* Decker much, but he owed the man for helping him solve Tom Brandt's murder, and he genuinely liked Mrs. Decker. He'd have to send for Sarah, though. If the cops who'd been called in to investigate before he got here told any reporters who was present at the séance, they'd give Sarah's name. It would be a good idea if she was actually here, and then she could get her mother out without drawing suspicion to Mrs. Decker. He'd send Gino Donatelli, the one patrolman he could trust not to talk to the press.

"So that's the famous Mrs. Brandt," one of the officers standing in the hallway said when Frank came out of the office and closed the door behind him. "She's a little long in the tooth, isn't she?"

Frank gave him a murderous glare. Did every cop in the city know he was friends with Sarah Brandt?

"Sorry," the cop said hastily. "I just thought . . . Well, she's still a fine-looking woman for all of that."

"Make sure nobody bothers her unless I say so," Frank said. "And find the nearest call box and get Officer Donatelli over here for me."

"The wop?" the cop asked in surprise.

The New York City Police Department had only recently begun hiring officers of any ethnicity besides Irish, and few of the old guard trusted them. "That's right. Any more questions?" Frank added in a tone that said there better not be.

"No, sir. I'll get Donatelli for you."

Frank sighed and went back into the room where the body still lay. He'd done no more than glance around the first time to see who the victim was. He'd been in too much of a hurry to get Mrs. Decker out of sight.

The ward detective who'd been called to the scene first was still in there, waiting for Frank to finish with "Mrs. Brandt."

"How's the lady doing?" he asked politely.

"She'll be fine," Frank snapped, walking over to get a better look at the body.

"We already sent for the medical examiner," Detective Sergeant O'Toole informed him.

Frank nodded. He hunkered down next to the woman. She looked to be middle-aged. Nothing unusual about her. Well dressed. She'd apparently been sitting in one of the chairs, and someone had slipped a stiletto between her ribs. He couldn't see the blade, but he could tell by the design of the handle protruding from her back that it would be long, thin, and diamond shaped with a needle-sharp point. The kind of knife made popular by the Italian secret society, the Black Hand. Her body lay as if it had just slid off the chair of its own weight. When he touched her hand, it was only slightly cool and still flexible.

He pushed himself back to his feet and turned to where O'Toole still waited. "What do you figure happened here?"

"Can't get much sense out of those people in there," he said in disgust, nodding toward the front room, where the séance participants had been gathered. "Something about talking to ghosts or something."

"Spirits," Frank corrected him. "They were sitting around the table holding hands or wrists or something?"

"That's what they said. Six of them, including that girl they call Madame, although she ain't like no madam I ever saw."

"In the dark," Frank said.

"So they said."

"Close that door," Frank said. "Let's see how dark it really is."

O'Toole closed the door. He had to use some force. It fit very tightly in its frame. Frank reached up and turned off the gas jet.

O'Toole swore softly. "Can't see my hand in front of my face."

He was right. Whatever happened here, no one else would have seen. "Open the door."

Frank found a match and lighted the gas again. He looked around once more, this time taking in all the details of the room. "There's no window in here."

"No," O'Toole confirmed. "This here's a false wall." He indicated the wall opposite the door. "There's a space about four feet deep between it and the outside wall of the house. Looks like that's where they store stuff. A lot of junk in there."

A large cabinet sat against the false wall. "What's in there?"

"Nothing," O'Toole reported. "Just an empty cabinet."

Frank wondered why they had an empty cabinet in the room, but before he could figure it out, he heard a woman start to scream hysterically. Muttering a curse, he went back out into the hallway and into the front parlor. The cops O'Toole had set on guard were just staring helplessly as one of the women was having a fit. Frank had half expected it to be the young one, the spiritualist, but it was the other one. She was a woman about Mrs. Decker's age and dressed like she had money and lots of it.

The girl was talking to her, holding her hands and trying to calm her down, and by the time Frank got there, she wasn't screaming anymore, just sobbing uncontrollably. The door to the office opened and Mrs. Decker stuck her head out. Naturally, she'd want to see what was going on.

"Get back in there," he commanded her in a voice very few people had ever disobeyed.

Her eyes widened in surprise, but she had the good sense to do what he told her. Everyone in the front parlor had looked up when he shouted at her. The three men who had been waiting there instantly all began talking at once.

"See here, you can't keep us here like this!"

"I have an appointment this afternoon!"

"What's going on? I have to see Mrs. Gittings!"

"Quiet!" Frank shouted, and they all fell silent, even the hysterical female, who looked absolutely terrified. "I've got to ask each of you a few questions, and then you can go. Is there another room where I can meet with you in private?"

"The dining room," the tall man who'd wanted to see Mrs. Gittings said.

"Do you live here?" Frank asked.

"Yes, I . . . I work for Madame Serafina. I'm Professor Rogers." He was very pale and he was clutching his hands together in front of him, as if trying to keep them from trembling.

"I'll talk to you first," he said, indicating the hysterical woman. "And then you can go home."

"But I don't know anything!" she protested tearfully. "I didn't see anything. None of us did."

"Then it won't take long for you to answer my questions," he said reasonably. "Come along."

"You'll be fine," the young woman assured her. She seemed very calm for having just witnessed a murder, Frank thought.

The older woman rose uncertainly.

"Come with me, please, Mrs. Burke," the Professor said, and he escorted her out into the hallway toward the room where the dead woman lay.

She balked, but he took her elbow. "This way," he said, and steered her toward the room across the hall. Sliding pocket doors led to a large empty room. Dust motes danced in the sunlight streaming through the large windows. Plainly, Madame Serafina had felt no need for formal dining. A chandelier hung forlornly from the center of the ceiling. It was an old one that had been converted to gas. Fortunately, the sunlight made artificial light unnecessary, at least in here.

"Get some chairs, will you, Professor?" Frank said.

He disappeared and returned with two straight-backed chairs that he'd probably fetched from the kitchen. O'Toole wouldn't have let him into the séance room. Then the Professor closed the doors behind him and was gone.

Mrs. Burke sat down on one of the chairs, and Frank placed the other so he could face her. "I know this has been a shock, Mrs. . . . I'm sorry. What was your name?"

"Mrs. Burke," she said, her voice a little steadier. "Mrs. Philip Burke."

Frank pulled a notebook and pencil from his pocket and jotted it down, along with the address she gave him. She was a near neighbor of Mrs. Decker's on the Upper West Side and a long way from home down here on Waverly Place. "Tell me what happened or at least what you remember happened."

"Where shall I start?"

"Right before Mrs. Gittings . . ." He made a vague gesture with his hand.

She nodded and drew a steadying breath. "We were sitting around the table."

"In the dark, I know. Holding hands. Talking to the spirits."

"That's right," she said with some surprise.

"Who were you holding hands with?"

"Not holding hands exactly," she corrected him. "We hold

each other's wrists. Madame Serafina was holding mine and . . ." She had to stop and swallow before she could finish. "And I was holding Mrs. Gittings's."

Frank nodded encouragingly. "And what was happening just before you noticed something wasn't right with Mrs. Gittings?"

She gave a little shudder and for an instant Frank was afraid she would start screaming again, but she got hold of herself and went on. "Mrs. Decker was . . . Oh, dear! I mean, Mrs. Brandt . . ."

"I know who Mrs. Decker is," Frank told her. "I won't tell anyone. Go on. What was Mrs. Decker doing?"

"She was trying to get her daughter to speak to her."

"Her daughter?" Frank echoed in surprise, wondering why Mrs. Decker would need a séance to talk to Sarah.

"She has a daughter who died," Mrs. Burke clarified. "She wanted to contact her."

"Oh, right," Frank said, remembering now. "Go on."

"As I said, Mrs. Decker was trying to get her daughter to speak to her, but there was a lot of confusion, and Yellow Feather couldn't understand the message. Yellow Feather is—"

"I know, the spirit guide," Frank said, managing to keep the sarcasm from his voice. "What did you hear?"

"Yellow Feather was shouting and there was some music," she remembered with a frown. "I don't think it was really a song exactly, just notes, discordant. There was so much noise, and we were all listening to find out what Mrs. Decker's daughter would say to her."

"What *did* she say?"

"Nothing," she admitted sadly. "Or at least nothing I could understand. I was distracted, you see. I was holding Mrs. Gittings's wrist." She held up her left hand and looked at it in wonder.

"How exactly do you do that?" Frank asked, trying to picture it in his mind. "Hold each other's wrists, I mean."

"Oh, well, you hold the wrist of the person on your left, and the person on your right is holding your right wrist."

Frank nodded, understanding at last. "All right, go on. You were holding Mrs. Gittings's wrist."

"Yes, and she was very still, although I didn't think about that at the time. But then she leaned over toward me, or at least I thought that's what she was doing. Her shoulder touched mine." She instinctively grabbed her left shoulder with her right hand, as if she could still feel the pressure from the dead woman. "And then . . . and then . . . she just kept coming." Her voice caught on a sob and she was weeping again, her shoulders shaking as she bawled into a fine, lace handkerchief.

Frank sighed and sat back, letting her cry for a few minutes. "I'm sorry to put you through this, Mrs. Burke, but I only have a few more questions and then you can go," he said when she'd slowed down a bit.

She looked up, her eyes red-rimmed and full of horror. "She fell on me! I'll never forget how that felt. I tried to catch her, but she was too heavy."

"And then you screamed," Frank said.

"I did?" she asked in surprise. "I don't remember. I was just trying to tell everyone she fainted, trying to make myself heard over the din."

"What happened next?"

"I don't know . . . Someone opened the door, I guess. I didn't see who. Then I could see her lying there, in the light that came in from the hall. Her face . . . She looked surprised. Her eyes were open, and she just seemed surprised. I asked her if she was all right," she remembered with another shudder.

"What happened then?"

She tried to remember. Frank could see her making the effort, picturing the scene. "Everyone was talking at once. Someone . . . Mr. Sharpe, I think, he knelt down to help her. Madame was calling for the Professor to bring smelling salts. We thought she'd fainted, you see. Then someone said, 'My God! Look at her back.' "

"Do you remember who that was?"

"I . . . No, I'm sorry. I looked at her back, and I saw . . ." She shuddered again. "And then everything is all confused. I just wanted to get *away*. The next thing I remember clearly, we were all in the parlor, and the Professor told us to wait there while he got the police."

"This Mrs. Gittings, was she a friend of yours?"

"Oh, no, not at all," she said too quickly. "I met her here. She was at the first séance I attended."

"Do you know anything about her?"

Mrs. Burke had to think about this. "I believe she was trying to contact someone in her family, but I can't think who. Isn't that strange? I know who everyone else in the group wanted to contact."

"You don't know where she lived?"

She bit her lip, and Frank realized she was lying, although he couldn't imagine why. "No, I don't. I'm sorry. I'm sure Madame or the Professor could help you."

"Thank you, Mrs. Burke."

"May I go now?" she asked eagerly.

"Yes, you can. Do you have a carriage waiting for you?"

"Yes, I do."

"Stay right here. I'll have the Professor escort you out." She looked as if she might not even be able to walk back to the parlor, and if she did faint, Frank wanted no part of it.

The Professor was only too glad to do Frank's bidding.

Frank returned to the parlor to select the next witness. Once again, everyone looked up when he walked into the room. The two remaining men had been conferring in the corner, and they both started toward him. Frank instantly chose the older man as the one most likely to have power and influence and therefore the most likely to cause him trouble.

"I'll see you next," he said and turned away before the other one could argue. As he'd expected, the older gentleman followed him. They passed Mrs. Burke and the Professor on their way out.

"Are you all right, Mrs. Burke?" the man asked solicitously.

"Yes, thank you, Mr. Sharpe."

"If you need help getting home—"

"Oh, thank you, but my carriage is waiting outside. I'll . . . Well, good-bye."

"Good-bye," he replied and watched until the Professor had gotten her out the front door before following Frank to the empty dining room. Frank closed the doors and indicated he should take a seat.

Sharpe was well dressed and well groomed, the masculine equivalent of Mrs. Decker and Mrs. Burke. He could probably have been welcomed into Felix Decker's home and conducted himself well.

"I don't know why you've detained all of us," Sharpe was protesting even before Frank had a chance to sit down himself. "You can't think any of us were responsible for what happened to Mrs. Gittings."

"Somebody stuck a knife into Mrs. Gittings's back," Frank reminded him. "If it wasn't one of the other five people in that room, who was it?"

"I . . . I'm sure I don't know," he sputtered. Plainly, he hadn't thought of it in those terms.

"I don't know either," Frank said, keeping his voice respectful so the man would have no reason to take offense. He reached into his pocket and pulled out the notebook and pencil. "What is your name, sir?"

He didn't like this one bit, but he said, "Sharpe. John Sharpe." He gave his address with equal reluctance, indicating that he, too, lived on the affluent Upper West Side.

Frank wanted to know what a man like Sharpe was doing at a séance in Greenwich Village, but he refrained from asking. There would be time for that later. "I'd like to know what you remember about what happened in there." Frank nodded in the direction of the room where the dead woman lay.

"We were sitting around the table," he said as if the words were being pulled from him like so many aching teeth. He must have been embarrassed to be caught in such a situation, and he hated having someone like Frank know about it. Like most people of his social class, he'd consider the police little better than the criminals they arrested.

"I know that part. You were holding each other's wrists, trying to talk to the spirits, and there was a lot of noise and confusion. What did you hear?"

"Yellow Feather, that's Madame's spirit guide, he was shouting. A lot of spirits were trying to get his attention, and he couldn't make sense out of what they were saying."

"What else did you hear?"

He tried to remember. "Noises, very strange noises, like music but more like an orchestra warming up than a real melody."

Frank nodded encouragingly. "Who were you holding hands with?"

"We don't hold hands," Sharpe reminded him stiffly. "We clasp each other's *wrists*."

"All right, whose *wrists* were you clasping?" Frank asked, managing not to sound annoyed.

"I was clasping Mrs. . . . . Mrs. Brandt's wrist with my left hand, and Mrs. Gittings was holding my right one."

Sharpe had won some points with Frank for trying to protect Mrs. Decker's identity.

"When did you notice something was wrong with Mrs. Gittings?"

He gave this a moment of thought. "I wasn't really paying close attention to her. I was listening to Yellow Feather and trying to make some sense out of what the spirits were saying."

"Did you hear her say anything or make any kind of sound?"

"I've been asking myself that question. If someone stabbed her, surely she cried out, but I have no recollection of it. I didn't notice anything at all until she let go of my wrist."

"How soon was this before Mrs. Burke screamed?"

"A few seconds, no more. I probably didn't really notice until Mrs. Burke screamed, I was so intent on . . . on Yellow Feather."

Frank managed not to smirk. He wouldn't get very much further with Sharpe if he let his true feelings about the séance show. "What did you do when she screamed?"

"I . . . Nothing at first. I didn't know what had happened, but then Mrs. Burke started yelling that Mrs. Gittings had fainted. Someone opened the door and started calling for the Professor to bring smelling salts. Madame was the one calling, so she must have opened the door. I could see because of the light from the hallway that Mrs. Gittings was on the floor."

"At what point did you let go of Mrs. Decker's wrist?" Frank asked, forgetting to use the wrong name.

Sharpe didn't notice. "I'm not sure."

"Were you still sitting down when the door opened?"

"Oh, yes. No sense getting up and stumbling around in the dark, is there?"

Frank supposed there wasn't. "Had you let go of Mrs. Decker's wrist by then?"

He shook his head. "Probably, but I can't be sure. What does it matter? You don't think she stabbed Mrs. Gittings, do you?"

Frank didn't bother to answer him. "When you saw Mrs. Gittings on the floor, what did you do?"

"I . . . I knelt down beside her."

"Why?"

He seemed surprised at the question. "To see if I could help. I didn't touch her. One doesn't lay hands on a woman in a situation like that, of course, especially a woman who's practically a stranger."

"You didn't know her well?"

"No. I met her at my first séance."

"Was she always here when you attended a séance?"

"Yes, she was."

"Do you know who she was trying to contact in the spirit world?"

"What does that have to do with anything?" he snapped.

Frank supposed Mr. Sharpe didn't share Mrs. Decker's view that a spirit had murdered Mrs. Gittings. "I'm just trying to find out more about her," Frank explained mildly, although he was actually trying to find out how well Sharpe knew the victim. "When did you realize she'd been stabbed?"

"I . . . Not until someone, Cunningham, I think, said something. 'Look at her back,' or something like that. That's when I saw the handle of the knife and the . . . the blood."

"Did you try to help her when you saw she'd been stabbed?"

"What could I do? I'm not a doctor," he protested. "Besides, she . . . she wasn't moving, and her eyes were open, staring." He looked away, and Frank noticed his finely manicured hands were knotted into fists. Not a man accustomed to sudden death.

"Whose idea was it to leave the room?"

"Mine, I'm sure," he said, although Frank thought he might be making the claim to make himself look better. "Mrs. Burke was already hysterical. We had to get the ladies out of there."

"Did the Professor bring the smelling salts?"

"What?"

"You said Madame called for him to bring the salts. Did he bring them?"

"I don't remember."

"Did you see him at all?"

"I . . . Yes, he was in the doorway when we started out of the room. Someone told him Mrs. Gittings had been stabbed."

"What was his reaction?"

"His reaction? What do you mean?"

"Was he surprised, shocked, angry, frightened?"

"How should I know? I was concerned about getting the ladies out of there."

"And whose idea was it to get the police?"

"Not mine," Sharpe told him, not bothering to hide his contempt. "Before I had a chance to settle the ladies, an officer was here taking everyone's name and telling us not to leave."

"So you didn't see anyone enter or leave the room once the six of you were inside for the séance?"

"Of course not. The room only has one entrance, and if

anyone opened the door, we would have noticed immediately."

"Even with all the noise and confusion?"

"We would have noticed if the light came in," he insisted. "We couldn't see a thing until after Mrs. Burke screamed and Madame opened the door. Now if you're finished with me, I have an appointment."

"Yes, that's all for now," Frank said, but Sharpe was already on his feet and heading for the door.

After Sharpe left, Frank waited a few moments, going over in his mind what he'd learned so far. Odd how no one seemed to know anything about the victim. One of the five would have had to kill her, and so far three of them professed to know nothing about her. He was starting to think that when he found the one person who'd known her, he'd have the killer. Could it really be so simple?

The sound of a disturbance distracted him, and he hurried out into the hallway to see what was going on. The noise was coming from the back of the house, and when he opened the door that led into the kitchen, he saw Officer Donatelli scuffling with a slender young man.

"What's going on?" Frank demanded.

The young man looked up, startled, and the distraction was enough to give Donatelli the advantage. In an instant he had the fellow sprawled facedown on the floor with his knee in the middle of his back. Donatelli looked up, grinning with satisfaction. "I just got here and found this fellow trying to sneak out the back."

5

"LET GO OF ME! I DIDN'T DO ANYTHING!" THE FELLOW WAS complaining.

Frank reached down, grabbed him by the back of his shirt, and hauled him to his feet when Donatelli obligingly removed his knee. "Who do we have here?"

The young man was plainly Italian and just as plainly terrified to find himself in the hands of the police. "I was making a delivery! I have to be on my way or I'll lose my job," he bluffed.

Frank looked him over. He was dressed all in black close-fitting clothes and soft slippers that were obviously not meant for the street. "What were you delivering?"

"I . . . I . . ." He looked around wildly, as if trying to find the answer hanging on one of the kitchen walls. "Eggs," he finally decided.

Frank glanced around the pristine kitchen. "I don't see any eggs."

"And what were you carrying them in, *paesano*?" Donatelli asked cheerfully. "Your pockets?"

"I . . . I left my basket outside. I'll go get it!"

He lunged toward the back door, but Frank still held him by the shirt, and he pulled him back with a jerk. "Not so fast. Now tell me again what you're doing here, and this time, it better be the truth."

The young fellow glanced up at Donatelli, who nodded grimly.

"I . . . I work here," he admitted reluctantly.

"What do you do?" Frank asked skeptically. He didn't know any Italian house servants.

"I . . . I fix things."

The kitchen door opened again and this time O'Toole stuck his head in. "What's going on here?"

"Officer Donatelli caught this fellow trying to sneak out the back door," Frank reported.

"Sneak *out*?" O'Toole asked. "That's impossible. We searched the whole house when we got here, and he wasn't in it. He must've been sneaking *in*."

Frank looked questioningly at Donatelli.

"He was definitely inside when I got here. I caught him just as he slipped out the back door," the officer insisted.

Frank turned back to the young man. "Which is it? Were you inside or out?"

The fellow's dark eyes darted to O'Toole and back to Frank again. He'd chosen Frank as the more dangerous adversary. "I was inside. Hiding," he added when O'Toole started to protest.

Before Frank could reply, they could hear shouting coming from the front of the house. The young man Frank had left in the parlor was starting to demand his right to leave the premises. He was likely to get away if Frank didn't tend to him immediately.

"O'Toole, would you look after this fellow for me while I take care of that loud gentleman?" He passed the young man to O'Toole, who dragged him out as he demanded to know where he had been hiding himself. Frank turned to Donatelli, who asked, "What's going on here?"

Frank told him as briefly as he could.

"Talking to spirits?" Donatelli asked in amazement.

"That's not the worst of it. Mrs. Brandt's mother is here."

"Mrs. Brandt?" Donatelli worshipped Sarah Brandt.

"That's right. She's a rich society lady, and we don't want her name to get in the newspapers. She told the cops who got here first that she's Sarah Brandt, so I want you to go get Mrs. Brandt and bring her here so she can take her mother home. Can you do that?"

"What if she's off delivering a baby or something?"

"Then find her."

"Yes, sir."

Donatelli was gone in an instant, and Frank turned his attention back to his suspects. The well-dressed young man was still shouting when Frank found him in the parlor. He had the grace to stop when he saw Frank glaring at him.

"I . . . I demand to be released," he tried.

"Just as soon as you've answered some questions. Come with me." As he waited for the young man to join him, Frank glanced at the two remaining occupants of the parlor. Madame Serafina was beginning to look a little less composed than she had before, and the Professor was positively ashen. He was standing by the door, as if on guard, although there were two patrolmen standing right outside in the hallway.

"You, sit down someplace," Frank told him, and then he pointed the young man to the dining room.

When they were seated with the door safely shut, Frank asked him his name.

"Albert Cunningham," he said, less sure of himself now that he was alone with Frank. He was younger than Frank had initially guessed, maybe not even twenty-one or -two, but just as neatly groomed and well dressed as Sharpe. He might be considered handsome in a few more years, when life had etched some character into his well-formed face. Now he was merely young. He gave an address not quite as fine as the other séance attendees boasted, but still in a very good neighborhood of the city.

"What were you doing here today, Mr. Cunningham?" Frank asked without expression.

Cunningham was instantly suspicious or perhaps just a bit guilty. "What do you mean?"

"Just what I asked. What were you doing here? The others said they were trying to contact some dead relatives."

"I . . . I wanted to speak with my late father," he admitted reluctantly.

"Did you?"

"Well, no, not today."

"Have you spoken to him before?" Frank asked curiously.

"Yes, a number of times," he reported somewhat defensively.

"So you've been here many times in the past?"

"I . . . I suppose you could say that."

"And you knew Mrs. Gittings very well?"

"No, not well . . . at least, not *very* well. I . . . she's always here, of course, but we don't . . . I can't say we're exactly acquainted."

Frank nodded. This was what he'd been expecting. Nobody, it seemed, knew the mysterious Mrs. Gittings. "Tell me what happened today."

Cunningham ran a hand nervously over his well-oiled hair. "Well, let's see, we were all in the séance room . . ."

"Sitting around the table, trying to contact the spirits," Frank supplied. "Who were you holding hands with?"

"We don't hold hands—"

"I know, you hold wrists," Frank corrected himself, annoyed. "Whose wrist were you holding?"

"I was holding Madame's wrist, and Mrs. Decker was holding mine."

Frank frowned. "Don't you mean Mrs. Brandt?"

"Who?" Cunningham asked in genuine confusion.

"Mrs. *Brandt*," Frank repeated. "The lady who was holding your wrist."

Cunningham finally remembered. "Oh, yes, Mrs. Brandt," he hastily confirmed.

"Don't forget again," Frank warned him and was gratified to see Cunningham swallow nervously. He quickly got back to the subject at hand. "What was happening just before Mrs. Burke screamed?"

This time Cunningham passed a hand over his mouth, then twisted his soft, young hands in his lap. "We were . . . Yellow Feather was trying to contact the spirits for us. He had quite a crowd of them, which is very unusual. Sometimes he can't get even one! But today . . . Well, he was getting messages from all of them, and he couldn't make out what they were trying to tell him."

"There was a lot of noise?"

"Oh, yes, we were all shouting out questions, in case someone had a message for one of us."

"I thought Mrs. Decker was the one asking questions."

He didn't notice that Frank had used her real name. "She was, but when Yellow Feather said so many spirits were there, we . . . I'm afraid we weren't very polite. We all started shouting at once."

"What else did you hear?"

"Hear? I . . . I don't know. Oftentimes we hear noises, but I'm not sure if I heard anything like that today. It was so confusing."

"Did you hear Mrs. Gittings asking questions?"

His smooth brow furrowed at that as he tried to recall. "I can't say if she did or not. Like I said, we were all—"

"Being rude, yes, I know," Frank said. "When did you realize something was wrong?"

"When Mrs. Burke screamed, of course. That's when we all realized something was wrong."

"What did you do when she screamed?"

"I . . . I jumped up, I know."

"Did you let go of Madame's hand?"

"I suppose I did. I don't remember, but I must have."

"Did you open the door?"

"No, Madame opened it. She was calling for the Professor to bring smelling salts."

"What did you do then?"

"Nothing, I . . . I looked over, across the table, to see what was wrong with Mrs. Gittings. Mrs. Burke was screaming that she'd fainted."

"What did you see?"

"I saw . . ." His face suddenly went white as he recalled what he had seen.

Frank jumped up and forced Cunningham's head down between his knees. "Take a deep breath, that's right, again, keep breathing . . . you'll be fine now."

After a minute or two, Cunningham was sputtering in outrage, and Frank released him. He sat upright again, bright red spots burning in his cheeks. "What'd you do that for?"

"You were going to faint," Frank told him with a hint of disgust.

"The hell I was!" he protested, gathering his pride together as a shield.

Frank didn't bother to argue. "So you looked down and saw Mrs. Gittings," he reminded him when he'd taken his seat again.

Cunningham swallowed loudly. "I saw the . . . I saw it sticking out of her back. And the blood on her dress. At least, I realize now it was blood. I couldn't tell the color. The light was bad and her dress is dark and I just saw . . . Well, I saw the knife," he added, his courage returning now.

"Did you say anything?"

He wasn't sure about that. "I may have. I guess I did. I told them to look at her back or something. They still thought she'd just fainted."

"Then what happened?"

"Mrs. Burke started screaming again. I . . . Someone said we should get out, get the ladies out, I think."

"Who was it?"

"Sharpe, probably. He'd think of that."

"So you left the room?"

"I took Madame Serafina's arm. I was concerned about her, that she'd be upset. I wanted to make sure she was all right. We all went to the parlor."

"Who sent for the police?"

"I don't know. When we got to the parlor, everybody was talking at once, and Mrs. Burke was crying, and then a patrolman came in and told us all to stay where we were."

"Did you see Professor Rogers when you came out of the séance room?"

Cunningham frowned. "I don't remember."

"You said Madame called for him to bring the smelling salts," Frank reminded him.

"She did."

"Did he bring them?"

"I don't know. If he did, I didn't see him."

"When *did* you see him next?"

Cunningham frowned, trying to remember. "He brought the policeman in. I don't remember seeing him before that. He must have gone out into the street and found him or something. What's going to happen now?"

"What do you mean?" Frank asked.

"I mean, what's going to happen to Madame? This wasn't her fault, you know."

"I don't know anything right now," Frank informed him. "So I don't know what's going to happen to her."

"You can't arrest her!" he said, the red spots blooming in his cheeks again. "She didn't do anything. I know because I was holding her wrist the entire time. She couldn't have stabbed Mrs. Gittings."

Which conveniently gave Cunningham an alibi, too, Frank mused. "Did you hear anybody else come into the room during the séance?"

"No, of course not. Nobody could come in unless they came in by the door, and we would have known immediately if anyone opened it."

"Then that means someone at the séance killed Mrs. Gittings."

"Why would they do that?" Cunningham asked reasonably. "Why would *anyone* want to kill her, come to that? Besides, we were all holding each other's hands. Nobody could have stabbed her without someone else knowing it."

"Then who do you think did it?" Frank asked with interest.

"I have no idea!" Cunningham said, insulted at being asked. "That's your job, isn't it? Now, I'd like to leave. I must be home soon. My mother is expecting me."

"Yes, you can go now," Frank said wearily.

Cunningham was on his feet and out the door before Frank could even rise from his chair, but when he got back to the parlor, he was surprised to see Cunningham was still there. He was standing over where Madame Serafina still sat on one of the sofas, holding her hand in both of his and speaking to her very earnestly. She stared up at him with her large, dark eyes, her expression guarded and maybe a little frightened. But she was nodding at whatever he was saying.

"Thank you, Mr. Cunningham," she said when he'd finished. "I'm sure I'll be fine."

He straightened and then, noticing Frank in the doorway, added more loudly, "And don't allow the police to bully you. You've done nothing wrong. And you must send for me if you need anything at all."

"I will, thank you." She gave him a wan smile.

He took his leave, and when the front door had closed behind him, Frank turned to one of the cops still standing guard in the hallway. "Where's O'Toole?"

"He took the little wop upstairs."

"Go get them both and bring them down here."

The cop took the stairs two at a time while Frank waited, trying to decide what to do next, when he remembered Mrs. Decker was still waiting. She must be going crazy trying to hear what was happening, he thought. He tapped on the office door and entered to find her sitting behind the desk, going through the drawers. She looked up in surprise.

"Oh, dear," she exclaimed, laying a hand over her heart. "You startled me."

"What are you doing?" he asked in dismay.

"Searching the desk," she replied without a hint of guilt. "Nothing in it appears to belong to anyone in this house, though. I think it may have been left by a previous occupant."

Frank closed his eyes and tried to think of a nice way to tell Mrs. Felix Decker that she should mind her own business. When he opened them again, he still hadn't thought of anything. "Mrs. Decker, I've sent for your daughter. I'll let you know when she gets here."

"Oh, thank you, Mr. Malloy. I'm sorry to be so much trouble for you. I know you already have your hands full with a murder without having to worry about me."

Someone was knocking on the front door, and Frank decided he'd better make sure it wasn't the press trying to barge in. He hurried out to close the parlor door just in case. To his relief, the cop guarding the door admitted Dr. Haynes, the medical examiner. Frank greeted him just as footsteps alerted him that O'Toole was bringing the Italian boy downstairs.

"What have you found out about him?" Frank asked O'Toole, noting that the boy seemed a little the worse for wear.

"Not much. He says he lives here and works for Madame Serafina doing odd jobs. Can't get nothing else out of him." He'd obviously been using a bit of force in his efforts, too. The boy stared defiantly back at them both.

"Would you take Doc Haynes back to see the body, and I'll take him off your hands?" Frank asked.

"Gladly," O'Toole replied, handing the boy off to Frank.

The boy glared at him balefully, but Frank ignored him and dragged him over to the parlor door, throwing it open and shoving him inside.

"Nicola!" Madame exclaimed, jumping to her feet. For the first time today she looked truly distressed. The Professor had been sitting in one of the chairs, and he jumped up as well.

The boy caught himself and stiffened instantly, shaking his head at her in silent warning.

"You know this fellow?" Frank asked. "Because if you don't, I'm going to arrest him for killing Mrs. Gittings."

"No!" she cried just as Nicola said, "I didn't kill anyone!"

"Then what are you doing here?" Frank demanded.

"I already told that other cop, I live here. I work for Madame Serafina," he said, as if reciting something he'd memorized.

"That true?" Frank asked her.

"Yes, it's true," she confirmed almost desperately. "He . . . he isn't involved in this. He wasn't even here when it happened."

"Where was he then?" Frank was genuinely curious. O'Toole and his men had searched the house, but they hadn't found Nicola, yet Frank knew he'd been here.

"He was out," Madame said before he could answer. "He always leaves the house when we have a sitting."

"A sitting?" Frank asked.

"That's what we call it, when people come for a séance."

"He was hiding."

The three of them looked up in surprise at the Professor. They'd forgotten he was there. He was staring at Nicola with open dislike.

"I was not hiding!" Nicola protested.

"He killed her," the Professor said. "It had to be him."

"I didn't kill anybody!" Nicola insisted. "Why would I?"

"Because she wanted to send you away," the Professor said, his voice oddly flat, as if he were trying desperately to hold himself together.

"You don't know what you're saying," Madame Serafina said, hurrying to his side. "You're just upset. Nicola would never kill her. Please, sit down, Professor. Nicola, get him some brandy."

Nicola started for the door, but Frank grabbed his arm, stopping him dead. "Nobody's going anywhere. Why would Mrs. Gittings want to send you away?" he asked the boy.

His eyes widened in fright, and he glanced at Madame as if for guidance on how to answer.

The Professor answered for him. "He was a distraction. He's in love with Madame and wants her to run away with him."

"She was mine long before you ever saw her," Nicola replied angrily.

"Nicola, please," Madame cautioned with a hint of desperation. "You're both upset. Don't say something you'll regret," she added with a meaningful glance at Frank.

"I won't regret telling the police he killed her," the Professor said.

None of this was making any sense. "What does Mrs. Gittings have to do with any of you?" Frank asked.

All three of them froze, staring back at him like cornered rats. Suddenly, Frank realized he'd been wasting his time talking to the others, who'd known nothing useful at all. These three knew who Mrs. Gittings was and probably why she'd been killed.

"You," he said to one of the cops in the hallway. "Take this one back upstairs and keep him there until I send for him." He shoved Nicola into the cop's arms. Nicola made a few attempts at resistance until the cop cuffed him a good one, and then he went along quietly.

Frank noticed that Madame winced when Nicola got slugged, but she made no attempt to intervene. She just stood where she was, wringing her hands and glancing apprehensively at the Professor.

"You," Frank said to the Professor. "Come with me."

The man followed him obediently to the dining room and took the chair Frank indicated. "What's your name?" Frank asked, taking out his notebook.

"Professor Ralph Rogers." The Professor was a man of middle years who'd undoubtedly worked hard to make his way in the world. His hands were clean and well manicured but bore the marks of manual labor performed in the distant past. He'd probably been considered plain in his youth, but the years had added some interesting character to his face. His hair was well barbered and neatly combed. He carried himself well and his voice was cultured. Frank thought he looked like an actor playing the role of a butler. Maybe he was.

"Where do you teach, Professor?" Frank asked idly.

Rogers blinked, but he didn't back down. "It's a courtesy title."

Frank let that pass. "What's your job here?"

"I serve Madame."

"Doing what?"

"Whatever she requires."

Frank didn't let his irritation show. "Like bringing smelling salts?"

"If that's what she requires."

This was getting him nowhere. "Tell me what happened here today."

"We were having a sitting," he said.

"Yeah, all those people were in the room, holding hands

in the dark, talking to the spirits," Frank said, not bothering
to hide his sarcasm. "What were you doing?"

"I was waiting in the kitchen."

"That's what you do when there's a sitting?"

"Yes. My job is to greet the clients and make sure they're
comfortable. Then I stay close by during the sitting, in case
I'm needed."

"How do you know if you're needed?"

"Madame calls for me."

"Where were you when she called for you today?"

"In the kitchen, as always."

"Why didn't you come then?"

His eyes widened in surprise. "I came!"

"Nobody saw you," Frank said, stretching the truth a bit.
Nobody remembered seeing him, at least.

"I came immediately," he insisted, a bit defensive.

"And what did you see?"

"I saw . . ." His voice trailed off, and he swallowed audi-
bly. "I saw her on the floor."

"What did you think when you saw her?"

He made a visible effort to control himself. "I thought
she'd fainted. That's what Madame said. She wanted smelling salts because someone had fainted."

"When did you know she'd been stabbed?"

"I . . . Someone said it, I think. Then I saw the . . . I saw
it. And she wasn't moving."

"What did you do then?"

"Everybody started running out of the room. The gentlemen were getting the ladies out. I . . . I went to see if . . . if I
could help."

"You tried to help Mrs. Gittings?"

"Yes, I went to her, but . . . Well, I could see it was too
late. Her eyes . . ." His voice caught, and he closed his eyes.

"Are you all right?"

"Yes," he said in a near whisper. "It's just . . . The shock."

"How did you know she was dead?" Frank prodded mercilessly.

"Her eyes," he said raggedly. "They were open."

"What did you do then?"

His eyes flew open and he stared at Frank as if just remembering he was still there. "I went out to find a policeman."

"Why did you do that?" It was a reasonable question, considering that Madame Serafina would most likely not want any scandal associated with her business, certainly not with her wealthy clients there, and involving the police was the surest way to cause a scandal.

The Professor's expression hardened. "Because I wanted to be sure that whoever killed her was caught."

"And you think Nicola killed her?"

"He's the only one who had a reason."

"And what is that reason?"

"I told you, she wanted to send him away."

Frank was confused again. "Mrs. Gittings wanted to send Nicola away?"

"That's right."

"Because he was a distraction," Frank remembered.

"Yes."

"But why would Madame Serafina have to do what Mrs. Gittings wanted?"

"Because . . ." The Professor caught himself, sitting up straight and staring at Frank again. "Hasn't anyone told you?"

"Told me what?"

"This is her house."

"Whose house?"

"Mrs. Gittings. This is her house. She is Madame's sponsor."

Suddenly, everything made sense. That was why Mrs. Gittings was at every séance. That was why nobody knew anything about her. *Sponsor* was a nice word. Mrs. Gittings was really the brains behind the whole séance scam. They all worked for her.

Frank nodded his understanding. "How long has this been going on?"

"Almost a year. Madame's talent was beginning to draw the attention of some important clients."

Frank thought of Mrs. Felix Decker. "And starting to bring in a lot of money," he guessed.

"Madame cares nothing for that," the Professor insisted. "She only wishes to help others."

Sure, Frank thought. That's why she charged so much for her services. "But Nicola was causing trouble," he guessed.

"He's an ignorant child. He was jealous of Madame's success, and he was trying to convince her to leave here."

"Why would she do that?"

The Professor shifted uncomfortably in his chair. "They are lovers," he admitted. "When Mrs. Gittings discovered Madame, she was supporting him by telling fortunes on street corners. Mrs. Gittings recognized Madame's true talents and brought her here. Madame insisted on bringing Nicola along. She wouldn't come without him, in fact, and so we put him to work. For a while, he wasn't any trouble."

Frank could imagine what happened next. Nicola saw how much money Serafina brought in with her séances and decided they didn't need Mrs. Gittings and the Professor anymore. "So Mrs. Gittings wanted to get rid of him."

The Professor nodded. "They had a terrible fight about it last night."

"Did she throw him out?"

"No," the Professor admitted angrily. "Madame refused to continue her work unless Mrs. Gittings allowed him to stay."

"Sounds like a compromise," Frank observed.

"One that pleased no one," the Professor said bitterly. "So Nicola found a solution of his own."

Someone knocked on the door. Frank muttered a curse and got up to answer it. The cop guarding the front door grinned sheepishly. "Sorry to bother you, but Donatelli's here with a lady. She says she's come for Mrs. Brandt."

"Wait here," Frank told the Professor.

He stepped into the hallway and saw Sarah Brandt standing there. The sight of her brought him a surge of unreasonable joy even though he hated the very thought of having her at a murder scene. She gave him the smile he loved, which only made it worse.

He nodded politely, careful not to say her name. "Your mother's in there," he said, nodding toward the office door, which opened as he spoke. Mrs. Decker stuck her head out.

"Mother," Sarah said.

"Oh, Sarah, I'm so glad you're here," Mrs. Decker said with relief.

Then the door to the parlor opened and Madame Serafina cried, "Mrs. Brandt, oh, please, you've got to help us!"

Before anyone could stop her, she threw herself into Sarah's arms and began to sob.

Sarah looked up at Frank accusingly.

"I haven't even talked to her yet," he defended himself.

"They're going to arrest Nicola," Madame claimed to Sarah. "But he didn't do anything. I swear to you, he's innocent!"

"Who's Nicola?" Sarah and her mother asked in unison.

"Her lover," Frank said.

This shocked Sarah and her mother and made Madame sob more loudly.

They all heard a disturbance upstairs followed by shouting. Nicola was probably trying to get downstairs to find out why his lover was crying. Frank noticed Gino Donatelli standing behind Sarah. "Donatelli, go upstairs and see what you can get out of that Nicola fellow."

Donatelli pushed by them and hurried up the stairs. Frank turned back to Sarah and her mother, who were still trying to comfort Madame Serafina.

"What on earth is going on?" Sarah asked him.

He wanted to tell her it was all none of her business and why didn't she just take her mother home and forget she'd ever been in this house? He wanted to get her as far away from here as possible and erase any memory of Madame Serafina from her mind. He wanted to perform a miracle. Unfortunately, it was far too late even for a miracle.

Instead he sighed with resignation and said, "Why don't you take Madame Serafina back into the parlor and get her calmed down?"

6

SARAH COULD SEE HOW MUCH MALLOY WANTED HER OUT of there. He hated involving her in murder investigations. How many times had they both vowed she'd never be involved again? She almost wished she could oblige him this time, but with the poor girl sobbing in her arms, she couldn't possibly walk out, not even if it meant protecting her mother from scandal. In point of fact, her mother didn't look like she was all too eager to leave either.

"There, now," Mrs. Decker was saying soothingly. "Crying isn't going to help anything. Why don't you come back inside here with us."

"You won't leave me alone?" Madame said, looking more like the young girl that she was than the sophisticated spiritualist she'd pretended to be.

"Absolutely not," Sarah assured her, pretending not to notice the face Malloy made when she said it. She turned the girl and walked her back into the parlor, her mother close behind. When the doors were safely shut behind them, Sarah seated the girl on one of the sofas and sat down beside her. "Can I get you something? Some tea?"

"No, no," Madame said quickly. "I . . . What will they do with Nicola?"

"Who's this Nicola?" Mrs. Decker asked, taking a seat in the chair beside the sofa.

"He is my *fidanzato*," she said. "We are to be married. I am not sure of the word . . ."

"Fiancé?" Sarah supplied.

"Yes," she said. Her remarkable eyes shone with unshed tears.

"But why would he want to kill Mrs. Gittings?" Sarah asked.

"He would not," Madame assured her. "He would not want to kill anyone, but the police will accuse him, and because he is poor, no one will believe him, and he will hang—" Her voice caught on another sob.

"Slow down!" Sarah cried. "You're getting way ahead of yourself. I promise you, Detective Malloy won't arrest him if he's innocent."

"How can you know? He is the police!" Madame reminded her tragically.

She was right, of course. The New York Police were notorious for arresting whoever might be handy, with no regard for what the truth might be. Unless someone paid them a "reward" to find the real culprit, anyone might be charged and convicted of a crime. This Nicola sounded like someone who could easily fall into that category. "Mr. Malloy is a friend of mine," Sarah said. "That's why my mother insisted that he be called in to investigate."

"You know a policeman?" Madame asked, staring at Sarah

and her mother in amazement. People like Mrs. Decker did not know policemen.

"Yes, we do," Mrs. Decker confirmed. "Mr. Malloy will make sure that the real killer is found and punished."

Sarah hoped he would be able to do this. Right now, she knew too little of what had transpired here to be sure. "Can you tell me what happened? The policeman who came to get me didn't know very much except that Mrs. Gittings had been stabbed."

Madame straightened, looking back at Sarah with some apprehension. "I do not know what happened," she said rather stiffly. "I was . . . Yellow Feather was there. I was in a trance. The first thing I knew was Mrs. Burke was screaming that Mrs. Gittings had fainted."

Sarah wanted to ask her a question, but her mother jumped in before she could.

"It was horrible, Sarah. Yellow Feather was trying to contact Maggie, but there were a lot of spirits there today, and they were all talking at once. He couldn't hear what she was saying. He started shouting, trying to quiet them down, and then everyone else starting talking at once."

"The spirits?" Sarah asked in confusion.

"No, of course not. Everyone in the room. They all wanted to ask questions, so they started shouting, trying to make themselves heard. They were extremely rude," she added, a bit outraged. "I couldn't understand a thing."

"When was Mrs. Gittings stabbed?" Sarah asked. She glanced at Madame Serafina, but she was studying her hands where they were folded in her lap.

Her mother had to think about it. "That's just it, we don't know exactly when she was stabbed. She didn't scream or anything, so far as I heard, which now seems very strange. Wouldn't you scream or at least cry out if someone stabbed you? The first hint we had that something was wrong was when Kathy . . . Mrs. Burke, she started screaming."

"Did she see Mrs. Gittings get stabbed?"

"Oh, no," her mother assured her. "None of us did. The room was dark, just the way it was at the séance you attended, dear."

Sarah nodded, remembering how she hadn't been able to see a thing in the pitch-dark room. "Were you holding hands?"

"Yes, just the way we did that other time. Everyone was holding someone else's hands or, rather, their wrists. So of course we would have known if anyone at the table had let go to . . . Well, you know. Then Kathy . . . Mrs. Burke started to scream that Mrs. Gittings had fainted. That's what she thought, of course."

"Why did she think that?"

"Because she fell out of her chair, and naturally, she wouldn't assume the woman had died, at least not at first. Mrs. Burke said she fell against her. She was quite hysterical when she realized the woman was actually dead."

"I'm sure she was," Sarah said. "When did *you* realize that?"

"As soon as someone opened the door, and we got a good look at her. The knife . . . Well, we all saw it sticking out of her back." Suddenly, her mother looked a bit pale.

Sarah reached over and took her hand. "I'm so sorry you had to go through this."

"Not your fault," her mother reminded her sheepishly. "You made me promise not to come back here, didn't you."

"I'll say I told you so later," she promised in return and turned back to Madame Serafina. "Could anyone else have gotten into the room?"

"Oh, no," Mrs. Decker answered for her. "Remember, we

would have seen if someone had opened the door. I'm sure no one else could have come in."

Sarah nodded, recalling quite clearly. That meant someone at the table must have killed the woman, although that didn't really seem possible. Fortunately, figuring out how it had happened was Malloy's job. She might be able to help him along, though. "Do you have any idea why someone would *want* to kill Mrs. Gittings?" she asked the girl.

Madame Serafina looked up, her expression guarded. "No, none at all."

"What do you know about her?" Sarah asked. "Does she have any family? I suppose someone should send for them, if they haven't already."

"No, she has no family," Madame said quickly.

"That must be why she spent so much time here," Mrs. Decker said. "Mrs. Burke said she attended all the séances."

But Sarah was still looking at the girl. She was hiding something. "Madame," she said kindly. "What do you know about her? You have to tell us everything so we can help you," she added, not sure if it was true but knowing it would work.

"Mrs. Gittings is . . ." The girl looked uncertainly at Mrs. Decker, then back at Sarah again. Her dark eyes looked even darker. "This is her house. She . . . finds people to come here, and she takes the money."

"Are you saying that she's your manager?" Sarah asked in surprise.

"Yes, that is it. She is my manager," she said, grateful for the suggestion. "She takes care of everything for me so I do not have to worry." This sounded like something Mrs. Gittings would have told her.

Sarah looked at her mother, who gave her a small shake of the head to indicate she'd had no idea. Sarah wondered briefly if Malloy knew this yet. "So you live here with her and . . . and who else?"

"Nicola," she admitted reluctantly. "And the Professor."

"How did you get involved with her in the first place?" Sarah asked, excusing her nosiness with the certainty that any information she could get about Mrs. Gittings might help identify her killer.

"She found me," the girl said, obviously choosing her words carefully. "I was telling fortunes. I told her fortune one day, and she said I had a gift. She said I was wasting my talent, and she could help me. She said I could be rich."

"So she brought you here?" Sarah guessed.

"Yes. She helped me to . . . to contact the spirits. Then she found people to come." The girl was starting to look uneasy again.

Sarah had a million questions about how Mrs. Gittings had helped her to contact the spirits. "How did she—?"

"Please," Madame interrupted anxiously. "What will happen with Nicola? He did not do anything wrong. You cannot let them take him to jail!"

"Nobody's going to take him to jail," Mrs. Decker promised rashly.

"That policeman hit him!" the girl said, tears pooling in her eyes again.

"Which policeman?" Sarah asked. "Not Mr. Malloy!"

"No, no, one in uniform," the girl said, the tears spilling down her cheeks. "Please, do not let anything happen to him!"

"If he's innocent, nothing will happen to him," Sarah promised even more rashly. "But the only way to prove he's innocent is to figure out who really did it. Do you have any idea at all?"

"None!" the girl insisted. "Please, can you find out what they are doing to Nicola? Can you talk to your friend Mr. Malloy and ask him?"

Sarah gave her a reassuring smile. "I'll see what I can do."

FRANK WENT BACK TO FIND THE PROFESSOR SITTING WITH his head bowed, rubbing his forehead. When he looked up, his face was gray with strain.

He took his chair opposite the Professor again. "Who was this Mrs. Gittings to you?"

He stiffened. "I worked for her."

"What else? Don't lie to me," Frank warned. "I'll just get annoyed, and you won't like what happens after that."

The Professor had been around long enough to know how the police behaved when they got annoyed. "We were partners," he said, his face rigid with reluctance.

"You split the profits of this little scam?"

"It's not a scam," he protested indignantly. "Madame Serafina is a legitimate spiritualist."

"Yeah, that's like being a legitimate fake," Frank said. "So you picked this girl up off the street and taught her the tricks of the trade—"

"There are no tricks! You can scoff if you like, but ask any of her clients. They'll tell you."

"I'm sure they will. So you think this Nicola killed Mrs. Gittings because she wanted to get rid of him."

"That's right," Rogers said, pulling himself up straight in the chair again.

"I just have one problem," Frank said. "He wasn't in the room when the séance started, and everybody said that nobody could get in without them knowing it. So how did he do it?"

"I told you, he was hiding."

"Where was he hiding?"

"In the cabinet," Rogers said, as if it should have been obvious.

Now Frank felt stupid. He'd seen that cabinet himself and wondered about it. O'Toole had told him it was empty, so he must have checked it. But Nicola could have gotten out when nobody was looking, sometime after everybody ran out of the room and before the police came. But where had he been hiding in the meantime? He'd have to question the boy next, he decided with a sigh.

This time when someone knocked on the door, he was glad for the interruption.

"Doc Haynes wants to see you," the cop guarding the hallway reported.

Frank crossed the hall to find the medical examiner sitting in one of the chairs at the séance table.

"What exactly was going on in here?" Haynes asked. "O'Toole's been telling me some cock-and-bull story about spirits."

"That girl in the front room, she's some kind of spiritualist," Frank confirmed. "She can talk to your dead mother and find out where she hid the family jewels."

"My family didn't have any jewels," Haynes said with amusement.

"Too bad. But that's what was going on. People pay this girl money so they can sit around a table in the dark and talk to their dead relatives."

"Why would they want to do that?' Haynes asked. "I'm glad most of my relatives are dead so I *don't* have to talk to them."

"I don't understand it either, but that's what was going on."

Haynes looked around. "If they were all sitting around the table, why didn't they see who stabbed her?"

"It was dark. Pitch dark," Frank added. "And they were all holding hands, so nobody could do anything without the people next to them knowing."

Haynes gave this some thought. "Unless one of the people sitting next to her did it. She'd notice one of them let go of her hand, but before she could say anything, she was dead."

"Did it happen that fast?" Frank asked in surprise.

"I'll know more when I do the autopsy, but I'm pretty sure that's a stiletto." He nodded toward the body on the floor. "They go in like a knife into butter, if you're lucky and don't hit a rib, and this fellow was lucky. I'm guessing the knife went right into her heart. She might've felt a pain, but she probably thought it was indigestion or something. She wasn't alive long enough to figure out she'd been stabbed."

"So she wouldn't have cried out?"

Haynes shook his head. "I doubt it. If you see somebody coming at you with a knife and see it go in, you'd scream bloody murder. Not because it hurt so much as because you're scared and you know something bad is happening. Sitting in the dark like that, I'm guessing the last thing she expected was to get stabbed to death while she was talking to her dead relatives."

"You'd think one of them would've warned her," Frank said, glancing down at the body, which had now been covered with a sheet.

"My orderlies will be here in a few minutes to take her away. I'll let you know if I find anything else in autopsy."

"Thanks, Doc."

Frank remembered the cabinet. He walked over and opened the double doors. He wasn't sure what he had expected, but what he saw was an empty cabinet, just like O'Toole had said.

"You finished in here?" O'Toole asked from the doorway.

"I'm finished," Doc Haynes said, getting up wearily.

Frank turned to look at the other detective. "You checked this cabinet when you got here to make sure it was empty?"

"Yeah, like I told you," O'Toole said with some irritation. "We searched this place, top to bottom. I'm telling you, the wop kid wasn't here."

"That Professor fellow says he was hiding in the cabinet during the séance, and he must've sneaked out and stabbed the woman."

"I figured it was something like that," O'Toole said. "But where did he go after that, I'd like to know."

"So would I," Frank said. "Guess I could ask him." He closed the cabinet.

"Mr. Malloy?"

Frank nearly jumped at the sound of Sarah's voice, but he managed to keep his composure. He turned to see her standing behind O'Toole in the doorway.

"I'm sorry to interrupt, but may I speak with you a moment?" she asked.

O'Toole was looking at her like he'd never seen a female before. Frank somehow managed not to punch him, but he did have to use a little force to get him out of the doorway. Frank paused in the hallway, trying to remember which room might be empty. Mrs. Decker wasn't in the office anymore. He pointed toward the door and followed Sarah inside.

He closed the door behind them and turned to face her. For a moment, just one moment, he thought of all they'd been through together and how she was unlike any other woman he'd ever known. He owed her more than he could ever repay, for what she had done for his son and for helping him solve cases he could never have hoped to solve without the knowledge she had of the rich and the world they lived in. Once he'd planned to repay her by finding the man who had killed her husband and bringing him to justice. Now that he'd done so, he knew nothing could ever repay what he owed her, just as nothing would ever bridge the gap that separated an Irish Catholic policeman and the daughter of one of the oldest families in New York.

Before he could surrender to the despair that thought caused him, she said, "I'm sorry to interrupt, but Madame Serafina is worried about that boy, Nicola."

"She should be," Frank said, forcing himself to forget what he could not change and concentrate on the case at hand. "It looks like he's the killer."

"Oh, no," she protested. "What proof do you have?"

"The Professor said he was hiding in that big cabinet in the séance room and sneaked out during the séance to stab her."

"Madame Serafina is sure he didn't do it," she said with a little frown that made him want to grind his teeth. She frowned like that when she was setting her mind to something.

"Of course she is," Frank pointed out reasonably. "They're lovers. Even if she *knew* he did it, she'd be defending him."

"Are you sure he was in the cabinet?" she tried.

"Not yet," he had to admit. "I haven't had a chance to question him, but I was going to do that next. Besides," he added quickly, wanting to convince her before she got too involved in all this, "nobody else who was here even knew who Mrs. Gittings was, so why would they want to kill her? Turns out, she's the one who ran this whole show."

"I know. Madame Serafina just told us."

"Why do they call her Madame Serafina?" Frank asked, strangely annoyed to hear her saying the odd name over and over.

"I have no idea. She's not even married. It's probably something they made up to make her sound more impressive."

"That makes sense," he agreed. "Anyway, this Mrs. Gittings ran everything and showed up at every séance, probably to keep an eye on Serafina. Everybody else thought she was just another . . . uh, client," he said, catching himself. He was going to say sucker, but he'd remembered just in time that Sarah's mother was among them. "So none of them had any reason to kill her."

"What reason did Nicola have?"

"From what they said, he was trying to convince the girl to leave here and go off with him. Maybe he was tired of this Gittings woman taking all the money and figured they could do just as well on their own. Whatever it was, they had a big fight about it yesterday."

"If Serafina was going to run away with him, why would he have killed Mrs. Gittings?"

"She wasn't. She'd promised to stay if Nicola could stay, too, but maybe Nicola wasn't happy about that."

She frowned again, but this time she was just disappointed. "I can see why you'd suspect him. But what about the Professor? He knew her. Couldn't he have been the killer?"

"He said he was in the kitchen during the séance. Apparently, he doesn't go into the room with them, and nobody saw him there. Besides, he was partners with the Gittings woman."

Her face lighted up. "Maybe he was tired of sharing the profits with her," she said. "That would be a reason to kill her."

"If you can figure out how he got into the room, I'll be happy to consider it," Frank told her dryly.

She sighed. "So it looks like Nicola and Serafina are the only ones with a good reason to want her dead, then."

"Yes, it does," he told her with relief. He couldn't believe she'd accepted it so easily. "So why don't you take your mother home and let me sort this out."

She gave him an apologetic smile that was just as beautiful as the regular smiles she gave him. "I know you want us out of here, but we can't leave Serafina. And if you arrest Nicola, she's going to be hysterical. You'll be happy we're here if that happens."

"Nothing could make me happy you're here," he informed her, making her smile again. She was making him forget why *he* was here, though. He needed to get away from her and back to work.

"We'll wait with Serafina until you decide if you're going to arrest Nicola or not," she said. "And maybe I'll be able to find out something helpful from her."

Defeated, Frank opened the door and motioned for her to proceed him out of the room. "Just don't think you're going to get involved in this," he told her in a whisper as she passed.

"I wouldn't dream of it," she assured him without the slightest hint of sincerity.

Frank gritted his teeth to keep from saying anything else. He waited until she was safely back in the parlor again. Then he went upstairs to find Nicola.

He found him in one of the bedrooms with Donatelli. Nicola was sitting on the neatly made bed, and Donatelli was perched on a straight-backed chair, blocking the door.

"What have you found out?" Frank asked Donatelli.

"His name is Nicola DiLoreto. He's known Serafina Straface since they were kids," he reported, not taking his eyes from the prisoner, who stared back with defiance. "They met on the ship coming over from Italy, and their families settled in the same neighborhood. Neither one has any family left, to speak of, so they looked after each other. He worked odd jobs, and she told people's fortunes on street corners for a few cents until this Mrs. Gittings came along. She's the dead woman, isn't she?"

"That's right." Frank was looking at the prisoner, too. A bruise was darkening on his cheek where somebody had socked him.

"The Gittings woman said she could set Serafina up in a first-class place, and people would pay lots of money to see her."

"And that's just what she did, isn't it, Nicola?" Frank said conversationally. "So what was the problem?"

"We have no problems," Nicola said. "Everything is fine."

At Frank's nod, Donatelli got up and let Frank have the chair. He moved it closer to the bed where Nicola was sitting, turned it around, and straddled it, resting his forearms on the back of it as he glowered at the boy.

"That's not what the Professor says," Frank told him.

"He is lying!" Nicola cried.

"Why would he lie?"

"Because he hates me."

"Did you give him any reason to hate you?"

"No!"

"How about threatening to take Serafina away?"

"That is not true," he claimed. "I would never do that."

"Why not?" Frank asked curiously. "Now that you know how it works, you two could set up on your own. You didn't need Mrs. Gittings and the Professor anymore."

"We could never get a house like this," Nicola pointed out. "You need a nice place if you want to get rich people to come."

Frank glanced around the bedroom. The bed Nicola sat on had a cheap, iron frame. The only other furnishings were a washstand and a clothespress that looked like somebody had salvaged from the dump.

Seeing his expression, Nicola said, "They never come up here, the people who come. We kept the downstairs nice for them, though."

Frank nodded. Why waste money on what the customers would never see? "Where were you during the séance, Nicola?"

The boy went rigid and his expression grew wary. "I was upstairs," he tried. "Mrs. Gittings, she didn't like the customers to see me."

That made sense. She could pass Serafina off as a gypsy or something exotic, but people wouldn't expect to see an Italian boy in a nice neighborhood like this. "I thought you were hiding someplace," Frank said.

"I was hiding up here."

"Not downstairs?"

"No, why would I do that?" He had started to fidget.

"I don't know. Maybe you need to be in the séance room for some reason."

"I was not in there," he insisted. "Ask anybody. They will tell you I was not in there."

"They wouldn't have seen you," Frank said. "Because you were in that big cabinet."

His eyes widened in alarm. "No, I was not!"

"I think you were," Frank said mildly, remembering the music that almost everyone in the séance room had said they'd heard. "I think you were in there to help make the noises during the sitting."

"I did not make any noises!"

Frank smiled slightly. An innocent man would have said, "What noises?"

"Somebody made the noises," Frank said.

"The spirits make them," Nicola said. "They sing and they play music."

"How do you know if you weren't there?"

"Serafina told me." He seemed proud of that answer.

"You're in love with Serafina, aren't you?"

"We are going to get married," he said, even prouder of this answer.

"When?"

That stopped him. "When . . . when we have saved up enough money."

"Didn't Serafina make a lot of money doing the séances?"

"Yes, but . . . Mrs. Gittings was holding it for her."

Ah, another reason for Nicola to want to get rid of the woman. "And she wouldn't give it to Serafina if the two of you left here," Frank guessed.

"We did not want to leave," Nicola said, not very convincingly.

"I think you did," Frank said. "I think you wanted to run away with Serafina so you could run your own operation, but Mrs. Gittings wouldn't give you the money if you left, so Serafina convinced you to stay."

"No," Nicola insisted.

"And when you realized that Mrs. Gittings wasn't ever going to give you the money, you knew there was only one way to get it."

"No, that is not true!"

"So you hid in the cabinet, just like you did every time—"

"No, it is not true, I tell you!"

"And when things got really noisy . . . Maybe Serafina made sure things got really noisy—"

"She did not have anything to do with it!"

"And when things got really noisy, you climbed out of the cabinet and—"

"No, I did not!"

"—and you found Mrs. Gittings—"

"No, I swear!"

"—and you stuck your knife between her ribs—"

"Stop it!"

"—and then you climbed back in the cabinet—"

"No, I tell you!"

"—and waited until everybody figured out what happened and ran out of the room—"

"No!"

"—and then you climbed out of the cabinet again—"

"I never!"

"—and hid someplace until you saw your chance to sneak out of the house and get away."

"No, no, I did not! It was not like that at all!"

"How was it then?" Frank asked with great interest.

The boy's dark eyes were large with terror, but he just shook his head. "I did not kill her."

"You know what she was stabbed with?" Frank asked.

Nicola shook his head again, probably not trusting his voice.

"A stiletto."

Nicola swallowed loudly.

"That's an Italian knife, isn't it?" Frank asked.

"I . . . I do not know," the boy claimed.

"Yes, you do. You knew it would be quick and quiet. You knew just where to stick it, too, so she'd die without making a sound."

He was shaking his head, but he was terrified now. He was well and truly caught.

"I can't blame you, Nicola. She was probably a mean old bitch who deserved to die, but it's still against the law to kill her, so I've got to take you in."

"I did not kill her! Please, you must believe me!"

"You'll get your chance to tell it in court," Frank said, pushing himself up out of the chair. He looked at Donatelli. "Take him downstairs and send for a wagon."

"No, please, I did not do it!" Nicola was protesting as Donatelli, grim-faced, grabbed the boy by the arm and dragged him to his feet. He started babbling something in Italian to Donatelli, who remained unmoved.

Frank waited in the hall while Donatelli dragged him out of the bedroom and followed as they stumbled down the stairway together. Nicola was still protesting in Italian, obviously having decided Donatelli was the only one who might believe him.

As they reached the bottom of the stairs, Frank saw the parlor door open and Madame Serafina appeared, looking as wild-eyed as her lover. Sarah and her mother were right behind her.

"What is happening?" Serafina demanded. "Where are you taking him?"

Donatelli said something to her that Frank didn't hear, and she started screaming.

"No! You cannot take him! He did not do anything!"

The Professor had come out of the dining room, and he stood there, stone-faced, watching the scene unfold.

Donatelli was saying something to the girl, and Frank realized he was speaking Italian, and she was still screaming. She'd grabbed hold of Nicola, throwing her arms around his neck in an attempt to rescue him from Donatelli. One of the other cops hurried over to pry her off.

Meanwhile, Sarah Brandt had escaped from the parlor and ran to where Frank stood at the bottom of the steps. "You said you weren't going to arrest him!" she cried.

"No, I didn't," he said wearily. "He killed her."

"He wasn't even there!" she tried.

"He was hiding in that cabinet. He sneaked out in the confusion and stabbed her, then he got back in before the lights came on again. He's the only one who was in the room who even knew her besides Serafina, and he's the only one who had a reason to want her dead."

The cop had pried Serafina's arms from Nicola's neck and was trying to drag her away from him when she heard Frank's last words. She ceased struggling instantly and turned to Frank. "No, he is not!" she cried. "He is not the only one who wanted her dead. They all did, *all* of them! Every single one of them wanted her to die!"

7

SERAFINA BROKE FREE OF THE COP WHO WAS HOLDING HER and ran to where Frank and Sarah stood in the hallway. "They *all* wanted her dead, I tell you! She was taking money from all of them!"

Before Frank could make sense of this, the cop who'd released Serafina opened the front door to the orderlies from the coroner's office who had come for the body. Nobody saw exactly what happened next, but in that one instant of distraction, Nicola slipped out of Donatelli's grasp and ran out the front door.

Someone swore and all the uniformed cops, including Donatelli, ran after him, but the orderlies were in the way, and they all got tangled up, and in those precious few seconds while they got untangled, Nicola disappeared, as Frank learned a few minutes later when they returned empty-handed.

"I swear, I don't know how he got loose," Donatelli said for at least the hundredth time. The other cops were sure he'd let the fellow Italian go. They were all gathered in the office, glaring at him and hoping he'd get all the blame.

O'Toole snorted in disgust, but Frank said, "I know you didn't." Donatelli would have been the last one to let him go, just because if he did, everyone would suspect him of doing it on purpose. "Go down to Little Italy and see what you can find out about him. He probably has friends there who would hide him. Drop some hints about a reward and see if they'll give him up."

Donatelli nodded and left, determined to find the boy if he had to search every tenement in New York City, Frank knew.

He looked at O'Toole, who plainly thought Frank had made a botch of this whole thing. "Have your men search the neighborhood again. Maybe somebody saw where he went," Frank told the other detective.

"Now that your suspect is gone, do you need anybody to stay here to help?" O'Toole asked, sarcasm thick in his voice.

"Leave somebody on the front door in case the press show up," Frank said sharply enough to remind O'Toole who was in charge. "But you can go."

O'Toole sniffed derisively and left, barking orders to his men out in the hallway. After a few minutes, the front door opened and closed, and the house fell eerily silent. Frank rose wearily and made his way across the hall to the parlor, where Sarah and her mother still waited with Madame Serafina.

When he stepped through the door, the girl rose from where she'd been sitting on the sofa between Sarah and her mother. "Did they find him?" she asked anxiously.

"Not yet," Frank said, giving nothing away. "Do you have any idea where he'd go?"

Her expression told him clearly she had no intention of saying so, if she did. "He did not kill her," she said instead.

"Then who did?" Frank challenged.

"I told you, all of them," she insisted.

"All of them?" Frank echoed. "You mean all the people at the séance?"

She lifted her chin in defiance. "Yes."

Frank glanced meaningfully at Mrs. Decker.

"Not Mrs. Decker," she amended quickly. "She was new, and Mrs. Gittings had not started trying to get money from her yet."

"Mrs. Brandt," Frank said. "You and Mrs. Decker should leave. The press will be getting wind of this any minute now, and when they do . . . Well, you know what will happen."

Sarah knew only too well.

Madame Serafina interrupted her. "Mother," she began, but "Please, do not go," Serafina begged Sarah. She seemed genuinely frightened.

"Mr. Malloy won't hurt you, child," Mrs. Decker assured her.

"He has to arrest someone for this," Serafina pointed out, "and Nicola is gone. Please, stay with me!"

Sarah shrugged helplessly, and Frank sighed in defeat. He turned one of the armchairs to face the sofa and sat down, wishing he could put his feet up. "All right, tell me why you think these other people wanted to kill Mrs. Gittings."

The girl sat back down, her expression wary. She was a pretty little thing, he noticed, and those eyes, they could look right through you. She was trying to look through him right now. He gave her no encouragement.

"Mrs. Gittings charged a lot of money for the séances, but she said . . ." She glanced at Mrs. Decker uneasily and then went on. "She said that was just the beginning. She said these people had so much money that they would not miss a little bit more, so she figured out ways to get more."

"To raise money so she could keep coming to the séances," Frank guessed.

"Yes, and Mrs. Gittings would arrange private sittings for her, too, when she could pay for them. But she was getting frightened, Mrs. Burke, I mean. She was afraid her husba[nd] would find out what she was doing. He would have been v... angry."

"He most certainly would," Mrs. Decker co[n...] grimly.

"Mrs. Burke had an argument with Mrs. Gi[...] week," Serafina said. "She thought Mrs. Gittings [...] her too much for the sittings, and she said she [...] jewelry to sell."

"Why didn't she just stop coming?" F[...] reasonably, or so he thought.

"She could not," Serafina told him. "[...] see. I only tell them just enough so [...] again to hear the rest."

"And the next time, you tell the[...] little more," Frank guessed.

"Yes, that is it," she said, rel[...] turned to Mrs. Decker. "I a[...] made me do."

Mrs. Decker looked [...] didn't seem to notice.

"I guess Mrs. Gitt[...] Burke," Frank said, [...]

"Oh, no. In fact [...]

"I'm sure she [...] other woman's j[...]

"I had no [...] Frank assur[...]

"So what a[...]

"How did she do that?" Frank asked with interest. He...
known the séance was more to it than just taking money to let p...
ined there was a confidence game, but he hadn't im...
talk to their dead relatives.
"She would do different things about them and then figu...
would find out things about them and then figu...
"She would find out things... money."
best way to get their money."
"Was she getting money from all the othe...
were here today?" Sarah asked.
Frank gave her a glare designed to sile...
didn't even notice.
"Yes, she had a plan for each of them...
"What was she doing?" Frank asked...
Plainly, Serafina hated to reveal t...
down to where her hands were twi...
"It's all right," Mrs. Decker s...
her. "It's not your fault."
Frank wasn't so sure abou...
reason to discourage the gi...
doing to Mrs. Burke did not...
"Mrs. Burke?"
"Mrs. Burke," Serafina a...
tings hoped." Serafina a...
from her husband a...
her going to séanc...
money for them...
"But she wa...
was she payin...
"She was...
red reluct...
Sarah...
knew somethin...
but Frank gave her a...
to interrupt the girl.

"Albert, Mr. Cunningham, he was in love with me," she admitted a little reluctantly.

Frank had seen that clearly. "Was she charging him for that?" he asked sarcastically.

She stiffened. "I am not for sale, Mr. Malloy."

"I'm sure Mr. Malloy didn't mean that," Sarah said, giving him a black look.

"No, I didn't," Frank agreed. "I mean, was she charging him more to come back because she knew he was in love with you?"

"No, she . . . He had inherited a lot of money when his father died last year, but he didn't know much about business. Mrs. Gittings and the Professor arranged for him to invest some of it with a friend of theirs."

This was getting more interesting now. "Invest? What do you mean by that?"

Serafina's lovely mouth thinned down with disgust. "I told him . . . I mean, Yellow Feather told him about some investments he should make. He would do anything his father told him to do, so I told him that his father wanted him to make these investments."

"But this friend was a fake, wasn't her?" Frank guessed.

"I do not know what they did," Serafina claimed. "All I know is that Mr. Cunningham had lost a lot of money, and Mrs. Gittings said that Yellow Feather had to tell him to invest even more."

Frank could see Sarah's expression out of the corner of his eye. She looked as if she was about to explode. She knew things Frank needed to know, but at least she understood the importance of staying quiet at this moment. "Do you think he'd figured out that Mrs. Gittings was cheating him?"

"I do not know, but he was getting very frightened, too. Mrs. Gittings had tried to talk to him, to convince him ev-

erything would be all right, but he was angry with her, I know."

"That leaves Mr. Sharpe," Frank recalled. "Is he in love with you, too?"

Serafina folded her hands primly. "You will have to ask him about that," she said.

"Why was he angry with Mrs. Gittings, then?"

"Because he . . . he wanted to be my sponsor."

"What does that mean?" Frank asked, thinking he knew but not wanting to make a mistake about it.

"He wanted to buy me a house and support me so I did not have to see other clients. He wanted me all to himself, you see."

"To be his mistress?" Sarah said before Frank could figure out how to ask it.

"Oh, no," Serafina assured her. "He just . . . He believes so strongly, you see. He thought it was wrong that I had to charge people money. He said he would take care of me so I could use my gifts to . . . to help people."

Frank thought that sounded a little fishy, but he let it pass, for now. "I don't suppose Mrs. Gittings liked that idea much."

"Oh, no," the girl said. "But you see, he did not know she was already my sponsor, not at first. He came to me and made me this offer, and I had to tell him that . . . Well, that she would never allow it."

"So he knew Mrs. Gittings was never going to let you go," Frank said.

"Yes," she agreed eagerly. "So you see, all of them had a reason to kill her."

Of course, Frank just had her word for it, and he was pretty sure none of these very rich, powerful people would confirm any of this, especially if it implicated them in a murder. He risked a glance at Sarah, and he could see she also understood the situation perfectly. Justice wasn't blind where rich people were concerned. She looked out for them very carefully and overlooked much more.

"But dear," Mrs. Decker was saying, "none of them could have killed Mrs. Gittings. We were all holding each other by the wrist, remember? Someone would have known if one of us let go to . . . Well, to do murder."

Serafina's lovely face twisted in anguish. "I . . . Yes, but . . . There are ways . . ."

"What ways?" Frank asked with interest when she hesitated.

But she closed her mouth and shook her head in silent refusal.

"The Professor said Nicola was hiding in the cabinet during the séance," Frank said, surprising her. "What was he doing there?"

The girl licked her lips, plainly trying to figure out whether to tell the truth or not. "He . . . He helps me."

"How does he help?" Frank asked.

She hated this. "He makes sounds sometimes."

"What kinds of sounds?" Frank asked.

"Just . . . Today he was playing a fiddle, just scraping the bow to make strange sounds."

"That's what I heard," Mrs. Decker remembered. "I couldn't for the life of me figure out what was making that sound."

"And the noise comes from inside the cabinet," Sarah said, "which is why they sound so strange and far away."

Serafina was looking at her, twisting her hands again. She hated betraying her secrets. She nodded.

"Oh, dear!" Mrs. Decker said suddenly.

Everyone looked at her, but she was looking at Frank, her expression awestruck. "Don't you see, Mr. Malloy? This boy

Nicola, if he was playing a violin . . . I heard that sound the whole time we were talking to Yellow Feather."

Frank frowned, not seeing at all.

She leaned forward in her eagerness to make him understand. "He was in the cabinet, playing the music, the whole time . . . *the whole time Mrs. Gittings was being murdered.* If he was playing the music, he couldn't possibly have killed her!"

THE CORONER'S MEN HAD LONG SINCE REMOVED MRS. GITtings's body, so Sarah felt no hesitation to enter the séance room. She looked around, trying to picture the scene when Mrs. Gittings had been killed.

"All right, what is it you need to tell me?" Malloy asked, closing the door behind him.

"She's telling the truth," Sarah said. "Madame Serafina, I mean. I'm sure Mrs. Gittings must have been doing all those things she said."

"How do you know?" He frowned suspiciously, the way he always did. She supposed he had good reason to be suspicious most of the time, but certainly not of her.

"Because of what happened at the séance I attended, the things Yellow Feather said to them."

Malloy crossed his arms over his broad chest in silent challenge. "What did he say?"

"He said . . . I know it sounds odd, but it was so easy to believe someone else was saying it and not Serafina. Her voice changed completely when Yellow Feather was supposed to be talking. I wonder how she does that."

"You can ask her later," he said impatiently. "What did this voice say?"

"Let me see if I can remember exactly," she said, closing her eyes so she could imagine herself back in time on that day. "Mother could probably remember, too. First of all, Mrs. Burke. Mrs. Burke's sister and her mother—their spirits, that is—were telling her something about a diamond brooch."

"Jewelry," Malloy remembered. "Did they tell her to sell it?"

"Not right out," Sarah said. "It didn't make any sense to me then, of course. I had no idea why Mrs. Burke seemed so upset when Yellow Feather mentioned this brooch that her mother had given her. She said it had been in the family forever, but her mother told her something about it was all right."

"What would have been all right?"

"I'm just guessing, of course, but it seems likely that she was telling Mrs. Burke it was all right to sell this family heirloom. If her mother had given it to her, she probably didn't want to sell it, so Mrs. Gittings would have told Serafina to encourage her to do it."

"How did she even know about it?" Malloy asked skeptically.

That was a good question. "I have no idea. Perhaps we can ask Serafina."

He gave her one of those looks that made her feel hopelessly naïve.

"Serafina wants to protect Nicola," she reminded him. "And she doesn't have to protect Mrs. Gittings anymore."

He shrugged. "What about the others? Did she say anything to them?"

Sarah closed her eyes again. "Cunningham," she recalled, opening her eyes to find Malloy staring at her with unsettling intensity. "He was very anxious to contact his father."

"Did he?"

"No," Sarah remembered, "not that day, although he asked for him several times. It was almost as if . . ."

"As if what?" he prodded.

"As if she was tormenting him. That must be what Serafina meant when she says she only tells them a little each time so they'll keep coming back."

"And if Cunningham didn't hear anything at all, he'd *have* to come back," Malloy guessed.

"That seems cruel," Sarah mused.

"The whole thing is cruel," Malloy reminded her. "She can't talk to the dead any more than I can."

He was right, of course, but she wasn't going to say so. "But Cunningham did keep asking questions. Something about needing his father's advice. He was afraid his father would be angry, although he said that he'd done exactly what his father had told him, and it hadn't worked out."

"That could have been the investments Serafina was talking about."

"Yes, Yellow Feather probably told him his father wanted him to make these investments, and when he lost money, he'd be afraid his father would be angry, and of course then he'd need more advice."

Malloy nodded. At least he wasn't looking down his nose anymore. "What about Sharpe?"

"He was speaking to his wife," Sarah said, and then she remembered something else that made the hair on the back of her neck stand up.

"What is it?" Malloy demanded, seeing her reaction.

"I just remembered, Yellow Feather said someone—one of the spirits—had a rose. Sharpe said that was his wife, that he'd always given her roses for their anniversary."

"What's so surprising about that?"

Sarah felt a chill at the memory. "I could smell roses!"

"It was your imagination," he scoffed.

"No, no it wasn't. I could really smell them. It was faint at first, but then, I was almost sick from the scent, it was so strong. Mother smelled it, too."

"Another one of Nicola's tricks, probably," Malloy said.

Sarah looked around, trying to figure it out. "Did Serafina say Nicola was in the cabinet?" she asked, walking over to it.

"The Professor said it."

"Where *is* the Professor?" she asked, reaching for the knobs on the cabinet doors.

"Still in the dining room where I sent him after Nicola escaped, I guess," he said.

Sarah pulled the cabinet open. She'd half expected to find a violin lying there, but the cabinet was completely empty. "It's big enough for someone Nicola's size to sit in," she noted.

"But wouldn't somebody open it, just to make sure nobody was inside?" Malloy asked.

"Nobody did the day I was here, but I suppose that's always a possibility. If they saw Nicola in there, the whole scheme would collapse." Sarah turned to see Malloy pulling open the door to the hallway. "Where are you going?" she asked, but he was gone.

Sarah hurried after him. He pushed open the door at the end of the hallway and disappeared inside. She followed, finding herself in the kitchen, but Malloy was looking at one of the walls. A black curtain hung down near the corner, and he pushed it back to reveal a doorway, and ducked inside. She was right behind him.

"What's this?" she asked, looking around. They'd entered a long, narrow space crowded with all sorts of curious objects. She saw some crates filled with the leftovers of someone's life. A gramophone sat on a battered stand of some sort. Oddly, and looking completely out of place, a small safe sat at the far end of the room.

"This is a false wall," he said, pointing. "It's the back side of the séance room, where the cabinet is."

Sarah could see that now. Why would they have built a false wall? Then she noticed the window on the other side of the narrow space and realized they had probably wanted to ensure that no light from a window would spoil the total darkness needed for the séance.

Malloy reached down and picked up a violin, holding it up for her inspection.

"Is that Nicola's fiddle?" she asked.

"I'm going to guess that it is," he said.

"How did it get in here?"

"He probably brought it with him when he sneaked out of the séance room to hide."

"Is this where they found him?" she asked.

"No, he . . ." Malloy stopped and looked around again.

"What's the matter?"

Malloy frowned. "They didn't find him at all," he said, obviously thinking out loud. "O'Toole said they searched the whole house, but they didn't find him."

"Maybe they didn't find this space."

"No, they found it. O'Toole told me about it."

"And Nicola wasn't here?"

"Not when they searched it," he said, still thinking, puzzling it out.

"Then where *did* they find him?"

"Donatelli caught him sneaking out the back door," he said. "I'd sent for him because he was the only one I could trust to get you here without the press finding out about your mother. Luckily, he came in the back, and when he got here, Nicola was going out the back door."

"But where could he have hidden all that time?" she asked.

Malloy didn't answer. He was still looking at the wall. He set the violin down and started running his hands over the wall.

"What are you doing?" she asked, but of course he didn't answer. He'd found what he was looking for, and suddenly, a small section of the wall swung silently toward him.

Sarah cried out in surprise. "What on earth?"

"Look at this," Malloy said in triumph.

Sarah peered into the opening to see the interior of the cabinet. The inside of the section of wall was lined with the same wood as the cabinet, so when the makeshift door was closed, the opening would be invisible. "For heaven's sake!"

"He probably didn't get into the cabinet until the séance started. That way if somebody looked inside, they'd know it was empty."

"Then he could slip in and nobody would be the wiser," Sarah said, looking around at the crates with new eyes. "What do you suppose he used these things for?" She pulled a hollowed-out block of wood from the top of one crate and examined it curiously.

Malloy took it from her and rapped it with his knuckle, making a sound like the clopping of a horse's hooves. Her eyes widened in surprise. "Good heavens!"

Malloy glanced around. "I'm sure he could make just about any sound Serafina might need with this stuff."

"And the gramophone," Sarah said. "What would he use that for?"

Malloy reached down and picked up a wooden box filled with dozens of cardboard tubes about four inches long and two inches in diameter. Sarah saw that they held records, the hard wax phonographic cylinders that played music on the gramophone. Each tube had something handwritten on top of it, descriptions like "woman scream," "sewing machine," "cow mooing," and "birds."

Then she saw one that made her gasp. It said, "baby crying."

"What?" Malloy asked, looking at the boxes and trying to figure out what had shocked her about them.

"This." She pulled the small tube out and showed him what it said. "During the séance I attended, we heard a baby crying. We thought . . . that is, it was supposed to be my sister Maggie's baby."

"Good God," Malloy said grimly.

"Madame Serafina could certainly come up with any sound she might require with these things," Sarah said bitterly.

"With Nicola's help," Malloy added. He set the box down and began to study the opening into the cabinet again. "After Mrs. Gittings was killed, Nicola must've come through the opening into this area and hidden in here until they'd checked the cabinet. Then he would have gotten back into the cabinet until they searched in here. That's why O'Toole's men didn't find him. When he thought it was finally safe, he tried to sneak out of the house. He would've gotten away, too, if Donatelli hadn't come along when he did."

"But that still doesn't explain how he could've been playing the violin and stabbing Mrs. Gittings at the same time," Sarah pointed out.

"Maybe one of these records is a violin playing," Malloy said. "Or maybe the Professor has another explanation. He's pretty sure the boy is guilty."

"Maybe he's just trying to cast suspicion away from himself," she said.

"I already thought of that, but unless he was back here

with Nicola, he couldn't have gotten into the room without somebody seeing him."

"And if he'd been in the cabinet with Nicola, I'm sure Nicola would have mentioned it," she added.

Malloy pushed the door shut. It latched with a barely audible click. "Clever," he remarked.

"This looks very bad for Nicola, doesn't it?" Sarah said.

"Yes, it does," he admitted. "All the people at the séance were holding each other's wrists the whole time, and I don't see how anybody else could've gotten into the room. And him running away makes it look worse."

"Not necessarily," Sarah disagreed. "He knew he was going to get blamed, guilty or not, so what other choice did he have?"

Malloy wouldn't want to admit she was right, so he just shrugged. "I need to talk to the Professor again."

"And then what will you do?"

"Keep looking for Nicola, although he's not going to be easy to find."

"What about Serafina?"

Malloy frowned. "What about her?"

"If you leave her here, she's going to disappear, too, along with any chance you have of finding Nicola."

"I know," he said, surprising her. "I'll have to lock her up."

"No!" Sarah exclaimed in horror. "I didn't mean—"

"What other choice do I have?" he asked her impatiently. "If the two of them meet up, we'll never see either of them again, and a killer will go free."

Sarah wanted to argue, but she didn't have a moral leg to stand on. When she'd first met Malloy, he probably would have let Nicola go and never thought a thing of it, because this was not the kind of crime the police would normally investigate. Nobody really cared that Mrs. Gittings was dead, except perhaps her partner in crime, and certainly, no one would offer a reward for finding her killer. Only a public outcry or a handsome reward could motivate most police detectives to investigate at all. Malloy had changed in the year since she had met him, however, and now he wanted to see justice done. She couldn't discourage him in that. "Do you *have* to lock her up?"

"I have to know she's not going to meet up with Nicola someplace and leave town."

Sarah nodded her understanding while her mind raced, searching for another option. "I'll go wait with her while you talk to the Professor."

FRANK FOUND THE PROFESSOR WAITING PATIENTLY IN THE barren dining room. He rose from where he'd been sitting in one of the chairs and looked at Frank expectantly.

"Did you help Nicola with the séances?" Frank asked.

The Professor blinked in surprise, but he recovered quickly. "I don't know what you mean."

"Yes, you do," Frank said, not in the mood for games. "I found the door into the cabinet and all the things he used to make noises. Serafina said he was playing the fiddle today during the séance. Did you usually go back there to help him?"

"No," he said, his cheeks flushed with anger that Serafina had betrayed their secrets. "There's too much danger a second person will bump into something or make noise. Nicola worked alone."

"Do you have any idea where he'd go to hide out?"

"None at all," the Professor said, still stiff with suppressed anger. "Believe me, if I did, I would tell you. He may have some Italian friends who would protect him, but I'm sure they'd want to be paid for their trouble."

"Did he have any money to pay them with?"

"Mrs. Gittings was too clever to give either of them money. They would be gone in an instant."

"Along with your livelihood," Frank remarked, earning another scowl from the Professor.

"I will notify you immediately if he returns here," he said, ignoring Frank's provocation.

"Do you think he will?"

"He won't go far without Serafina."

"Ah, yes, young love," Frank said sarcastically.

The Professor sniffed in derision. "Love or not, she's his livelihood, too."

Another good reason to lock Serafina up, Frank thought. "I'm taking Serafina in."

"What do you mean?" the Professor asked in alarm.

"I mean I'm going to lock her up until we find Nicola, so they don't both disappear."

"But what about her other clients?" he protested. "They're already scheduled to come. They'll be expecting her to be here for a sitting."

"Then you can tell them how lucky they were not to be here when Mrs. Gittings got stabbed," Frank said.

He left the Professor sputtering more protests and walked down the hall to the parlor, where the three women were still waiting. He pushed open the door and found them huddled together on the sofa, Serafina in the middle while Sarah and her mother tried to comfort her while she wept. Damn, Sarah must have already told her she was going to jail.

They all looked up, and Sarah rose to her feet, that determined look on her lovely face that always meant she was going to do something to make him angry.

"We've worked everything out, Mr. Malloy," she told him. "Serafina is going to come and stay with me until you find Nicola."

8

SARAH BRACED HERSELF FOR MALLOY'S RESPONSE, BUT SHE wasn't going to back down. She didn't like the idea of an innocent girl like Serafina going to The Tombs, which was what they called the city jail because a creative architect had designed it to look like an Egyptian tomb. Heaven only knew what might happen to her there among the prostitutes and hardened criminals she would encounter.

Malloy said, "Can I speak to you in private, Mrs. Brandt?" He didn't look angry exactly, but then he wouldn't want her mother or Serafina to see that he was angry with her.

"Certainly," she said and preceded him across the hall into the office again. The instant the door was closed behind them and before he could explode, she launched into her justification. "I can't allow you to lock a girl like that up in the Tombs. You know what that place is like, and besides, if she's locked up, she won't have any chance at all to contact Nicola, so how can you hope to find him?"

"Do you know what you're getting into?" he asked, still scowling at her.

"What do you mean?"

"I mean, Nicola might very well be the killer. Do you want to take a chance of him coming to your house?"

"Nicola isn't the killer. Serafina swears he was playing the violin, and my mother heard him. Besides, even if he's guilty, he'd have no reason to harm any of us," she insisted, "especially if we're protecting Serafina."

"He would if he thought you were trying to get him caught."

"We're not going to get him caught. How could we? And why would he come to my house at all? He just has to stay away, and he'll be safe," she pointed out reasonably.

"All right."

Sarah gaped at him. She'd never known him to be so obliging. *"All right?"* she echoed uncertainly.

"Yes, it makes perfect sense to take Serafina to your house. She probably knows where Nicola is hiding, and maybe you can get it out of her. Or if Nicola really is innocent, maybe you can find out something from Serafina that will help figure out who the real killer is."

Sarah couldn't think of a thing to say.

Malloy studied her for a moment and his mouth quirked in what might have been a smile. "Was that all it took?"

"What?" she asked, completely bewildered.

"To shut you up," he clarified with a definite grin this time. "All it took was agreeing with you."

She glared at him. "If you'd ever tried agreeing with me before, you'd have known that," she snapped.

"I had to wait until you were right about something," he

replied, then hurried to open the door before she could smack him, which she dearly wanted to do. "Get Serafina out of here."

Sarah made a rude noise. "I'll take her upstairs to pack some things," she said, breezing by him out the door and into the hall. Being right should feel better than this, she decided. But at least she'd gotten her way about Serafina.

Serafina and Mrs. Decker looked up expectantly when Sarah went back into the parlor. "He said you could come home with me," she reported.

"Thank heaven," Mrs. Decker said, and Serafina breathed something in Italian that might have been a prayer.

"I'll take you upstairs so you can pack some clothes," Sarah said. "Then my mother's carriage can take us to my house."

"Thank you, Mrs. Brandt," Serafina said, her eyes still wet with tears. "I could not bear the thought of going to jail."

Sarah smiled reassuringly and led her out into the hall and up the stairs. The one police officer who had been left to guard the door watched them curiously but made no move to follow.

Upstairs, Serafina entered one of the bedrooms. She pulled a battered carpetbag out from under the bed and set it on the coverlet. She pulled it open and checked inside, then quickly closed it again. Then she looked up and managed a smile. "This won't take long," she promised, and went to the chest of drawers. She pulled out some undergarments and quickly bundled them up and stuffed them into the bag. She only had two dresses hanging in the clothespress, and she quickly packed them as well, along with a pair of house slippers and a nightdress. The few toiletries on the washstand went in last, and then she buckled the bag securely. "I am ready."

As they made their way down the stairs again, they found

the Professor waiting for them at the bottom. "You shouldn't leave," he told her sternly.

"I have no choice," she replied testily. "If I do not go with Mrs. Brandt, they will put me in jail."

The Professor frowned at her. "What about your other clients? Will you come back to see them?"

"I . . . I do not know," she said, glancing uncertainly at Sarah.

"When they read about Mrs. Gittings in the newspapers, I doubt they'll even show up," Malloy said, coming back in the front door. "Mrs. Decker's carriage is out front. I still don't see any reporters, so you should be able to get away without anybody seeing you."

Mrs. Decker stepped into the hallway from the parlor. "Come, my dear," she said to Serafina. "Everything will be all right, you'll see."

Sarah doubted this very much, but she didn't want to upset Serafina. The girl went to Mrs. Decker and the two started toward the front door, which the cop was holding for them.

Malloy touched Sarah's arm as she passed. "Tell Maeve to find out as much as she can about her," he said softly, so that only she could hear.

Sarah's eyes widened in surprise. "So that's why you wanted to send her to my house!"

He shrugged, feigning innocence. "I'll come by tomorrow to see how you're doing with her."

"Catherine will be very glad to see you," she told him acidly, and followed her mother and Serafina out to the waiting carriage.

The driver was trying to take Serafina's bag, but she was saying, "No, please, I want to keep it with me!"

"It's all right, Peter," Mrs. Decker told him, and he nodded and helped them all into the carriage.

"I can't believe there are no reporters here yet," Sarah said as the carriage pulled out into the street.

"Yes, we've been very lucky," her mother agreed.

"Why would reporters be here?" Serafina asked.

"Because they like to write about sensational murders," Sarah explained. "Lots of people will buy their newspapers to read about them."

"Why is Mrs. Gittings's murder sensational?" Serafina wanted to know.

"Because rich people are involved," Sarah said.

"Don't be vulgar, dear," her mother chided.

Now Serafina was even more confused. "Why is that vulgar?"

"Because rich people don't like to talk about how much money they have," Sarah said, with a sly glance at her mother.

"Why not?"

"Because it's not important," Mrs. Decker said in an obvious attempt to change the subject. "You'll be very comfortable at Mrs. Brandt's house, I think."

"I am very grateful to you," Serafina said to Sarah. "Maybe I can be some company for you, since you live alone."

"I don't live alone," Sarah said with a small smile.

Serafina frowned. "But you are a widow, are you not?"

"How did you know that, my dear?" Mrs. Decker asked in surprise.

"I can feel it," the girl said, perfectly serious. "And you have no children. I feel that, too."

Sarah smiled again at the girl's attempts to prove her supernatural powers. "I have a daughter."

Serafina wasn't convinced. "She was not born to you, I think," she argued.

"No," Sarah had to admit. "I recently adopted her. And her nursemaid lives with us, too."

Serafina nodded, as if she'd known all along. "That is why I could not see her."

Sarah wasn't quite sure what to say to this, so she changed the subject again. "Do you have any idea where Nicola would have gone?"

"No," she said. "We have no family, no one he could trust."

"No friends?" Mrs. Decker asked.

"No one he could *trust*," Serafina repeated. "When the police are looking for you, you must be very careful."

Sarah was sure that was true. "Mr. Malloy found the opening into the back of the cabinet," she tried.

Serafina's eyes widened, but she didn't say anything.

"What are you talking about, dear?" her mother asked.

"The wall in the séance room, the one where that big cabinet sits, is a false wall. There's a space behind it, and there's an opening in the back of the cabinet, so someone can go in and out."

Mrs. Decker gasped in surprise. "Is that true?" she asked Serafina.

The girl pressed her lips together, plainly loath to reply. "Mrs. Gittings," she said after a moment, the words strained and reluctant. "She thought we needed to make a bigger show. She did not think that talking to the spirits was enough."

"They have a gramophone back there," Sarah told her mother.

"A gramophone? Whatever for?" Mrs. Decker asked.

"One of the records was of a baby crying," she said, glancing at Serafina to see her reaction.

Mrs. Decker gasped again. "Is that how you made me think you were talking to my daughter?" she demanded of the girl.

Serafina's face looked as if it had turned to stone, but her dark eyes shone with suppressed fury. "I told you, Mrs. Gittings wanted to make a big show. I did not like it. I just wanted to talk with the spirits, but she said no one would come unless we did those other things."

Mrs. Decker sank back against the cushioned seat, not certain what to make of it.

"I will contact your daughter for you, Mrs. Decker," Serafina said quickly, sensing that she was losing the confidence of one of her benefactors. "Now that Mrs. Gittings . . . She will no longer make me tease people so they will come back again and again. I can find out the truth for you. I will not even charge you a fee."

"We'll see," Sarah said before her mother could respond. "It might be better if you just use this time to rest. How did you first learn to . . . to contact the spirits?" she asked to change the subject yet again.

"My mother used to read the cards," she said. "I learned from her. When she died . . . I had to earn my own living. I am a good girl, Mrs. Brandt. I did not want to go to one of those houses where the men visit women."

"Of course not," Sarah said. Girls like Serafina, left alone in the world with no way to survive, too often ended up selling the only thing they had of value—themselves.

"I would sit on a street corner. I had a crate with a cloth over it to spread out the cards. I would tell people's fortunes. I can also read palms. I was . . . very good," she added, lowering her gaze modestly.

"It's a long way from telling fortunes on a street corner to conducting séances on Waverly Place," Sarah observed.

"Mrs. Gittings did that," Serafina said simply. "She came by where I was working one day, and I told her fortune. She said I had a gift. She said I should not be wasting my talents for pennies. She said I could be rich if I would let her help me."

"You must have been very excited," Sarah said.

"Oh, yes," Serafina said, remembering that time. "Nicola, he got work whenever he could, and we looked after each other, but we were always very poor. Sometimes we had no place to sleep. Mrs. Gittings said we would live in a big house and have anything we want."

"And she brought you to that house?"

"Yes. She said she owned it, but I found out later she is only renting it. She did not even buy furniture for the rooms we did not use. She said there was no need, because we would be moving to a bigger house soon. We just needed a few more clients."

"And did you get rich?" Mrs. Decker asked, having recovered from her shock about the gramophone.

Serafina looked at her with sad eyes. "She kept all the money for herself. She said she was saving it for our future. She said it was business, that we would need a bigger house, nearer to where rich people lived, and when we got that, we would have many more clients and make much more money and get truly rich."

"I'm afraid that gives you and Nicola a very good reason to want Mrs. Gittings dead," Sarah said.

Serafina looked up at her in surprise. "But without her, we would have nothing. We could not afford to rent a house ourselves, and we could not support ourselves if we went back to the streets."

"Mr. Sharpe would have given you a house," Sarah recalled, and suddenly realized she hadn't finished telling Malloy what she knew about Sharpe. She'd gotten distracted by the cabinet when she was telling him about Sharpe's experiences with the spirits.

"Mr. Cunningham probably would have, too," Mrs. Decker added.

But Serafina was shaking her head. "Neither of them

would have allowed Nicola to come with me. Men are too . . . too jealous, and I could not go without him. And if I did want to go with one of them, I did not have to kill Mrs. Gittings. I could just leave her," she added reasonably.

Sarah had to admit she was making a good case. "Did Nicola get along with Mrs. Gittings?"

She lowered her gaze again. "He was angry that she would not give us our part of the money, but he did not kill her," she added quickly. "She had the money locked in a safe, and if she was dead, we could never get it out."

"What about that Professor fellow?" Sarah asked. "How does he fit into all of this?"

"He is Mrs. Gittings's lover," Serafina said baldly.

"He is?" Mrs. Decker exclaimed in surprise. "How very curious."

Serafina seemed surprised at her surprise. "They have known each other for a long time."

"How did they make a living before they met you?" Sarah asked.

"I do not know," Serafina claimed. "But I do not think they are honest people."

Sarah couldn't help thinking that's how Malloy would have described Serafina and Nicola, too.

"If Nicola didn't do it, who do you think did kill Mrs. Gittings?" Sarah asked.

"I do not know, but it must be one of the clients in the room."

"But we were all holding each other's hands," Mrs. Decker reminded her.

"If someone let go of Mrs. Gittings's hand, she cannot tell us now, can she?" Serafina said grimly.

Sarah looked at the girl in surprise. Neither she nor Malloy had thought of this. "Who was sitting beside her?"

Serafina pressed her lips together, but Mrs. Decker said, "Mrs. Burke and Mr. Sharpe."

Both of them had reason to wish Mrs. Gittings out of the way, at least, but did they have enough reason to kill her? And even if they did, would they have actually done it?

"Mr. Cunningham was sitting too far away," Mrs. Decker was saying, "and I was holding his wrist, so I know he never moved from his chair."

"And of course you didn't kill her, Mother, so you're a reliable witness."

Mrs. Decker blanched. "Don't even think that! I couldn't possibly be a witness to anything. Your father would never allow it."

"I only meant as far as determining who was where when Mrs. Gittings was killed," Sarah clarified.

"No one will be a witness," Serafina said in despair, her wondrous eyes filling with tears. "They will all say they were not there at all and that Nicola killed her. No one will help us!"

"Don't worry," Sarah said, taking her hand. "Mr. Malloy will find out the truth."

But the tears began to stream down Serafina's face. She knew Sarah was lying to be kind.

After what seemed like hours, they finally arrived at Sarah's house. The driver helped them down, but once again, Serafina refused to allow him to carry her bag. She clutched it tightly as they climbed Sarah's front steps.

By the time Sarah had unlocked the door and pushed it open, Catherine was already racing down the stairs to greet her. She stopped short when she saw Serafina and stared at the stranger.

"Catherine," Sarah said, "I've brought a guest home. This

is Miss Serafina Straface. She is going to stay with us for a few days."

Catherine gave a polite little bob and murmured something that sounded like, "Pleased to meet you," although Sarah couldn't have sworn to it. She was still staring with more than polite curiosity at their guest. That was when Sarah realized that Serafina was still wearing the flowing black gown she wore for the séance. She looked like a character in a play who had wandered out of the theater and gotten lost.

Maeve was coming down the stairs at a much more digni-fied pace, and she also stopped to stare curiously at the stranger. Sarah introduced the two girls and watched as they eyed each other suspiciously. She could hardly wait to hear what Maeve thought of the spiritualist.

Sarah turned to her mother, who was hovering anxiously behind them. "You should go on home now, Mother. I'm sure you're exhausted."

"No!" Catherine protested, and hurried to greet Sarah's mother, ducking around the now-forgotten guest.

Mrs. Decker leaned down to give Catherine a kiss. "I can't stay today, my darling, but I'll come for a visit tomorrow, I promise."

Catherine pretended to pout, and Mrs. Decker promised a gift when she returned, and thus her departure was success-fully negotiated.

"Are you sure you'll be all right?" she asked Sarah before she left.

"Oh, yes, and if we need anything, we'll let you know. Go on now. You'll want to be home when Father gets there."

Reluctantly, Mrs. Decker took her leave.

When the door had closed behind her, Maeve eyed Sera-fina up and down and said, "You're the spiritualist."

"What's a spirit-ist?" Catherine asked, struggling with the unfamiliar word.

"Someone who tells people stories," Maeve said before Sarah could think of a suitable answer.

"I like stories," Catherine said brightly. "Will you tell me one?"

"Maybe later," Sarah said, shooting Maeve a warning look. "Serafina is very tired, and she needs a quiet place to rest. I thought she could share your room, Maeve. Would that be all right?"

"Oh, yes," Maeve agreed quickly, almost as if she already understood her role in the drama Sarah had set up. "I'll take you upstairs and show you where to put your things. Let me take that for you," she added, reaching for the bag.

"No!" Serafina said, surprising them all with her vehemence. She caught herself instantly. "I mean, that is kind of you, but I can manage. I would like to lie down for a little while, if I could. My head hurts so . . ."

"Would you like something to eat first?" Sarah asked.

"No, no, I could not eat at all," the girl assured her. "I just need to rest."

"Come on upstairs, then," Maeve said, taking the other girl's arm and gently leading her to the stairway.

"Is Mrs. Ellsworth here?" Sarah asked as the girls started up.

"No," Maeve reported over her shoulder with a sly grin, "but I'm sure she'll be here very soon."

Mrs. Ellsworth would have noted the arrival of Mrs. Decker's carriage and seen Serafina alighting. Wild horses couldn't keep her from coming over to investigate.

Catherine started up the stairs after the other girls, but Sarah called her back. "Come and help me in the kitchen, sweetheart, and tell me what you and Maeve have been doing all day."

Sarah, realizing she was famished, had made herself a sandwich and found some cookies for Catherine by the time Maeve returned.

"She's already asleep or at least pretending to be," Maeve reported, taking a seat opposite Sarah at the kitchen table. "Who was it who . . . ? She glanced at Catherine, who was listening avidly to every word. "Who got sick?"

"Mrs. Gittings," Sarah said. "She was Serafina's . . . I'm not sure what the correct term would be, but she was in charge of the whole thing. It was her house and she was the one who set up the séances."

"I figured she must've had somebody helping her. She's young to be so successful, with so many rich clients and all."

"Mrs. Gittings found her telling fortunes on street corners."

"Did she read palms or cards?" Maeve asked with interest. Plainly, she had more than a passing knowledge of such things.

"Both, she told me. She also said she was very good at it."

Maeve grinned. "I'm sure she was. So why is she here?"

Sarah looked at Catherine, who was eating a cookie and still listening intently to every word. "Mr. Malloy agreed with me that she would be better off here. Her fiancé, a fellow named Nicola, he's . . . Well, he seems to have wandered off, and Mr. Malloy thought it would be a good idea to keep an eye on her until he turns up again."

"Will he turn up here, do you think?"

"I doubt it. He won't know Serafina is here," Sarah said, "and he won't want to show his face anyplace where he might be recognized."

"Why won't he want to show his face?" Catherine asked, her eyes wide with interest.

Sarah gave her a reassuring smile. "Because he's hiding, the way you and Maeve play hide and seek sometimes. He doesn't want anyone to find him."

"So he's the one?" Maeve asked cryptically.

"Serafina swears he isn't," Sarah replied just as cryptically. "But Mr. Malloy suspects him."

Maeve nodded wisely.

"Is Mr. Malloy coming to visit, too?" Catherine asked.

"As a matter of fact, he is," Sarah said. "But not until to-morrow. You'll have lots of company tomorrow."

Catherine clapped her hands, sending cookie crumbs flying, which made her giggle in delight.

Maeve would have asked another question, but just then, Mrs. Ellsworth knocked on the back door. Catherine let her in, and they spent a few minutes in greetings.

"I had some bread in the oven and had to wait until it was done before I could come over," she explained, her well-lined face alight with curiosity. Sarah could imagine how impatient she must have been to get over here and find out what had happened. She was looking around, obviously expecting to see the strange woman who had arrived with Sarah in her mother's carriage.

"Come along, Catherine," Maeve said, taking the child by the hand. "Mrs. Ellsworth and your mama want to talk. But we have to be very quiet upstairs, so we don't wake our guest."

"Why is she sleeping in the daytime?" Catherine asked as they disappeared into the next room.

When the girls were gone, Mrs. Ellsworth, who had taken a seat at the kitchen table, asked, "Who on earth was that woman you brought home?"

"That was Madame Serafina."

"The spiritualist?" Mrs. Ellsworth asked in amazement. "What is she doing here?"

"A woman was murdered at her séance today."

"Is that where you were today? When I stopped by earlier, Maeve just said you'd been called out, so naturally, I thought you were at a delivery."

"That *is* where I went when they sent for me, but I wasn't there when it happened," Sarah explained. "My mother was, though."

"I thought she was finished with all of that!"

"So did I." Sarah sighed. "She went back today, however, and one of the people at the séance was murdered. Naturally, my mother wanted to keep her name out of it if she could, so she sent for Mr. Malloy."

"How very sensible of her. And he naturally sent for you. Please, tell me everything that happened," she pleaded.

Sarah did so, answering Mrs. Ellsworth's many questions as she went along.

"Oh, my," Mrs. Ellsworth exclaimed when Sarah was finished. "I can't believe Mr. Malloy agreed to allow Madame Serafina to come here. Isn't he worried that the killer will show up?"

"We aren't sure that Nicola really is the killer," Sarah reminded her. "Serafina swears he isn't."

"Of course she does, but what if he is and what if he shows up on your doorstep?"

"There's no reason why he should," Sarah said. "And even if he does, there's no reason for him to harm any of us."

"I certainly hope you're right. But how long do you intend to keep the girl here? They might well never locate this Nicola fellow. What will you do then?"

"I guess we'll decide when the time comes. Meanwhile,

we're going to see if we can find out what Serafina really knows about the murder and if there's anything else she hasn't told us yet."

"Oh, how very clever of you!"

"Yes, it is," a voice behind Sarah said. She turned to see Serafina standing there.

"Oh," Sarah exclaimed, wondering how much the girl had overheard and trying to recall what she had been saying. Nothing too insulting to her guest, she hoped. "How are you feeling?"

"I am hungry now," Serafina admitted, eyeing Mrs. Ellsworth suspiciously.

"Sit down and I'll fix you something to eat." Sarah introduced the two women, then started making a sandwich for Serafina and boiling water for tea.

Serafina sat down across from Mrs. Ellsworth, who was studying her with an intensity that was almost rude.

"Do you believe in the spirit world, Mrs. Ellsworth?" Serafina asked in a voice Sarah recognized as that of the professional spiritualist she had met that first day and not the frightened young woman she had brought home with her this afternoon. Her nap had restored her self-confidence.

"Oh, yes," Mrs. Ellsworth assured her. "If you mean do I believe in heaven and hell, that is."

The girl reached across the table and laid her hand over Mrs. Ellsworth's and closed her eyes for a long moment. Mrs. Ellsworth watched her in silent fascination. "I see a father figure. You have been thinking about him."

"That must be my late husband," Mrs. Ellsworth said in surprise. "I was just thinking about him the other day."

"I sense that you have a question, something you would like to have answered."

Sarah's instinct was to interrupt, but held her tongue, curious to see what would happen.

"I do!" Mrs. Ellsworth exclaimed. "I was telling Mrs. Brandt about it not too long ago. I was wondering where he had put his pocket watch. I never found it after he died."

"Yes, that is what I am seeing. A gold pocket watch. It was very important to him."

"Yes, his father gave it to him. He was very ill before he died, and he started hiding things. I found most of the things, but not the watch."

"You are right, he did hide it." She closed her eyes again. "I see a dark place, small and dark. And the letter B."

"The letter B?" Mrs. Ellsworth echoed uncertainly.

Serafina opened her eyes again. "Yes, something starts with the letter B. He wanted to keep the watch safe."

"Oh, yes, he always said it should go to our son, Nelson," Mrs. Ellsworth said. "That's why I was so upset when I couldn't find it."

"He did not want it to be lost, so he hid it very well. You will find it soon."

"Really?" Mrs. Ellsworth said.

Sarah set the plate down in front of Serafina with a deliberate clunk. "Let's let Serafina eat now," she suggested.

"Thank you," Serafina said with sincere gratitude and began to devour the sandwich Sarah had made her.

"Did you hear that, Mrs. Brandt?" Mrs. Ellsworth asked. "She told me where to look for my husband's watch."

"Yes, I heard," Sarah said, watching Serafina for any change of expression, but she saw none. "Where do you think it could be?"

"The letter B," Mrs. Ellsworth mused. "That could be the bedroom, of course. Or perhaps the bureau."

Sarah could think of dozens of words starting with B that could provide hiding places for a watch. She'd point that out to Mrs. Ellsworth later, however.

"How do you do that?" Mrs. Ellsworth was asking her. "How do you know things about people, I mean?"

"It is a gift," Serafina replied simply. "I cannot help it."

"I found a penny this morning when I was on my way to the market," Mrs. Ellsworth told Sarah. "That's good luck, you know. I picked it up, of course. You must pick it up or it won't be good luck. I just knew something good was going to happen today."

Sarah didn't mention that Mrs. Ellsworth hadn't actually found the missing watch yet.

When Serafina had finished the sandwich, she looked up to where Sarah stood pouring tea for all of them. "I know you think I am protecting Nicola, but he did not do this thing. It was one of the others. I know it was. You have to help me find out which one."

"But my dear," Mrs. Ellsworth said without a trace of irony, "can't you just ask the spirits to tell you?"

"Did everyone always sit in the same place at the table?" Sarah asked.

"No," Serafina said. "I tell them where to sit each time, and she is right, he could not see Mrs. Gittings in the dark."

But Sarah was pretty sure it would be easy enough to memorize the layout of the room, and if Serafina told people where to sit . . . Well, finding Mrs. Gittings would certainly be possible. That's what Malloy would say, anyway.

The sound of running feet distracted them, and Catherine raced into the room to remind them it was time to coo~~k sup~~per. Maeve took charge of the kitchen, and all conve~~rsation~~ about murder ceased in deference to Catherine's tende~~r~~

THE NEXT MORNING, FRANK HAD JUST ARRIVED AT
Headquarters when he got an urgent message from ~~Professor~~
Rogers, asking him to return to the house. Frank ~~thought~~
Nicola wouldn't have shown his face there again, w~~hich was~~
the only reason he could imagine that the Profess~~or would~~
call him back, but he made the trip down to Wav~~erly Place~~
just in case.

The Professor answered Frank's knock and ush~~ered him~~
inside after looking around to see if anyone was l~~ooking~~
on the street.

"The newspapermen were here for hours last ~~night," the~~
Professor informed him as if he thought it was Fr~~ank's fault.~~

"Did you tell them anything?"

"No, but the neighbors . . . I saw them ans~~wering their~~
questions."

"The story was in the evening editions," Fra~~nk said,~~
"but they don't have much of it right. If they do~~n't find out~~
of who the clients were, they'll lose interest."

9

SARAH HAD TO SWALLOW THE BARK OF LAUGHTER THAT
rose up in her throat. If she laughed, Serafina would never
trust her again. But Serafina wasn't looking at Sarah at all.
She was speaking to Mrs. Ellsworth.

"I have tried to ask them," she said solemnly, "but they
will not speak to me about this."

"Whyever not?" Mrs. Ellsworth asked, outrage~~d on her~~
new friend's behalf.

"She is?" Serafina exclaimed as Sarah winced

"Oh, yes, she's helped Detective Sergeant

dozens of cases."

"Not dozens," Sarah protested, although som...

seem like it. "Just a . . . a few."

"Then you *can* help me," Serafina said wi...

spirits have not deserted me at all. They have...

Sarah took a seat at the table and passed th...

her guests so they could sweeten their tea. "Yo...

me before I can help you," she said. "You have...

thing you know about everyone involved. If ...

at all of saving Nicola, we must find the real...

"Mrs. Brandt said your Nicola was pla...

through the séance, so he couldn't be the...

worth said.

"That is right, he was."

"How do we know it wasn't just one o...

records?" Sarah challenged.

"Because we do not have the violin on...

replied. "We do not know what the spirit...

must listen and play music to suit what I...

back to the house so you can see we have no...

promise, you will see this is true."

"He could have been walking around the room in the dark, though, and stabbed Mrs. Gittings while he was playing," Sarah tried.

"He never comes out of the cabinet," Serafina insisted.

"That would be very difficult to prove," Sarah argued.

"But playing a violin takes two hands," Mrs. Ellsworth pointed out. "How could he hold a knife? And if the room was dark enough that they couldn't see him, how could he see where Mrs. Gittings was to stab her?"

The Professor sniffed in disdain.

"Is that why you sent for me?" Frank asked in annoyance. "To complain about the newspapermen?"

"No, I want to report a robbery."

"A robbery? What was stolen?"

"Several thousand dollars," the Professor reported. Plainly, he was furious and controlling it with great difficulty.

Frank studied him for a long moment. "Is this the money that Mrs. Gittings was holding for Serafina and Nicola?"

"It was *all* the money," he said bitterly.

"Where did you keep it?"

"Locked in a safe."

Frank remembered seeing a safe in the narrow space behind the false wall. "When did you find out it was missing?"

"This morning."

Frank was growing increasingly irritated with the Professor's miserly answers. "Show me the safe."

"It's in here," he said, and as Frank expected, he led him to the narrow space behind the false wall.

The morning sun filtered through the curtain, showing the dust motes hanging in the stale air. Frank had noticed the safe in the far end of the space yesterday, but hadn't given it any particular significance. Now the door hung open, and the safe was clearly empty.

"Is this how you found it?"

"No, it was locked."

It had been closed when Frank saw it yesterday. "Why did you open it?"

"I . . . I thought I might need some money."

Frank wondered idly if the Professor had decided to take the money and disappear himself, before Serafina could lay claim to it. "Who had the combination?"

"Just Mrs. Gittings and myself," he said.

"Maybe she put the money someplace else," Frank suggested, thinking she might have put it someplace the Professor couldn't find it.

"No, it was all there yesterday, right before the séance," he said. "I collected the fees from everyone and put them into the safe while Madame was greeting the guests, just like I always do, and everything was fine then."

"Are you sure you locked it?"

"Of course," the Professor snapped, losing his battle to control his anger. "Don't you see what happened? That little rat stole it!"

"What little rat? You mean DiLoreto?"

"Of course I mean DiLoreto. Who else could have done it?"

"I thought he didn't know the combination," Frank reminded him.

"He's a sneaky little bastard," the Professor said through gritted teeth. "Who knows what he knew? Maybe he knows how to crack safes."

Frank doubted the boy would have been working for a phony spiritualist if he knew how to crack safes, but he decided not to mention that to the Professor. He was already upset enough. "If DiLoreto stole this money . . . How much was it, again?"

"I don't know exactly, but it was over five thousand dollars," the Professor told him, seething at the very thought.

"I saw him right before he ran off," Frank recalled, picturing the boy in his mind with his slim figure dressed in tightly fitting black clothes, which were ideally suited for slipping into and out of cabinets without catching on corners. "He wasn't carrying anything, and he couldn't have had that much money stuffed in his pockets."

"He must have come back for it last night, while I was asleep. He has a key to the house."

"That still doesn't explain how he got into the safe."

"I told you—"

"I know, he's a safe cracker. Or maybe you left it unlocked."

"I didn't leave it unlocked, I tell you."

"Have you searched the rest of the house? Just in case Mrs. Gittings put the money someplace else?" Frank prodded.

"I searched," he said, his face now an alarming shade of purple, "even though she was dead, as you will recall, and couldn't have put it someplace else."

"Who else knew the safe was there?"

"Nobody. Just the four of us. No one else ever came into this room."

"Did Serafina know how to open the safe?"

"No. I told you, we would never have given either of them the combination. If they got the money, they would have run off."

This was all very interesting, but Frank really didn't care what had happened to the money. Except that if Nicola had it, they'd never see him again. He probably would have gone back to Italy by now.

"When we find DiLoreto, we'll ask him about this," Frank told him.

"And what am I supposed to do in the meantime?" the Professor asked furiously.

Frank wanted to suggest he get an honest job, but he said, "That's up to you."

This was not the answer the Professor wanted to hear. "When will Serafina come back? She has clients scheduled today."

"That's up to her. I'll mention it to her when I see her."

"And what are you going to do about this?" he demanded, gesturing angrily toward the open safe.

"I'll file a report, and keep looking for DiLoreto."

The Professor swore a colorful oath that told Frank he wasn't as cultured as he pretended to be.

Frank decided he wouldn't wait to visit Sarah's house. He wanted to find out what Serafina knew about the missing money.

MAEVE OPENED THE DOOR AND GREETED HIM WARMLY, followed by Catherine, who threw herself into his arms.

"I'm getting married," she informed him when he'd picked her up.

"Who's the lucky fellow?" Frank asked in amusement.

Catherine giggled. "I'm getting married," she repeated, holding up one small palm and pointing to a specific spot. "See, right there."

"Madame Serafina was reading our palms this morning," Maeve told him with some amusement of her own.

Frank nodded his understanding. "And are you getting married, too, Maeve?"

"Of course," Maeve assured him with a gleam in her eye the only clue that she wasn't perfectly serious. "All single young ladies are going to get married. Even Mrs. Brandt," she added archly.

Before Frank could react to this amazing piece of information, Sarah Brandt called his name.

"Malloy," she said, coming toward him through the front room. She was smiling the way she always did when she first saw him. Well, almost always. If there was no dead body involved. "You're out early this morning."

"I couldn't wait to see my favorite girl," he said and

watched her eyebrows rise in surprise before turning to Catherine, whom he still held in his arms. "And now she tells me she's getting married."

Catherine laughed in delight.

"Have you found Nicola?"

They all turned to where Serafina stood. She'd followed Sarah out of the kitchen and was standing in the middle of the office, her hands clenched tightly at her waist. She looked very different today. She was wearing an ordinary dress instead of that black flowing thing she'd had on yesterday, and her hair was down and tied with a ribbon. She could have been a schoolgirl.

"No, I haven't," he said. "I thought the Professor might offer a reward, but it seems someone has stolen all of his money."

Sarah and Maeve gasped in surprise, but Serafina's reaction was much milder. She simply lifted her chin, almost defiantly.

"When did this happen?" Sarah asked.

"Sometime between when the séance started yesterday and this morning. The Professor thinks Nicola came back in the night. He has a key to the house."

"He does not know the combination to the safe," Serafina said.

"Do you?" Frank asked curiously.

Her dark eyes blazed. "Of course not. Mrs. Gittings, she would never trust us. She was afraid we would take the money and run away."

"Maeve, why don't you take Catherine over to visit Mrs. Ellsworth?" Sarah suggested.

Catherine made some inarticulate sounds of protest, but Maeve predicted she would receive a treat at Mrs. Ellsworth's and promised to bring her back before Mr. Malloy left again.

After a few minutes, Maeve had her buttoned into a jacket and out the door.

"Come in and have some coffee with us, Malloy," Sarah said.

They all filed into the kitchen, and Sarah poured coffee for them. Malloy usually felt comfortable here in Sarah's kitchen, but Madame Serafina's unease was affecting them all. She sat stiffly in her chair, making no effort to taste the coffee or even to make eye contact.

"Does Nicola know how to break into a safe?" he asked baldly when the silence had stretched for a while.

"What?" Serafina asked. Plainly, this was not what she'd been expecting to be asked.

"Does he know how to break into a safe?" Frank repeated. "Somebody opened the safe, took the money out, and locked it back up again so the Professor wouldn't know it was gone until he went looking for it."

"Nicola does not know anything about safes," Serafina said.

"Then what happened to the money?"

"How should I know?" Serafina snapped. She was angry. Not as angry as the Professor had been, but still angry. "Maybe he hides the money and pretends it is stolen to get Nicola in more trouble."

Frank hadn't considered this possibility, but the Professor had seemed genuinely upset. He'd looked like a man who had been robbed. "What about you?" Frank asked. "Do you know anything about safes?"

She seemed shocked. "No!"

Frank took a sip of his coffee. "If Nicola took the money, he's probably on his way back to Italy by now," he observed mildly.

"He will not leave me," Serafina said with the confidence

only young love can produce. Frank noticed she didn't deny he'd taken the money, though.

He turned to Sarah. "Have you found out anything new?"

"Not really," she said, glancing at Serafina. "But I did remember something I didn't tell you yesterday."

"What's that?" he asked with a frown.

"I was telling you about Mr. Sharpe, about how I smelled roses when he was talking to his wife's spirit," she reminded him. "But before I could tell you everything, you ran out of the room."

Frank nodded. That was when he'd remembered about the space behind the cabinet and gone to look at it himself. "What else do you know about him?"

"Remember Serafina said he wanted to take her away from Mrs. Gittings and set her up in her own house?" she asked, glancing at Serafina again. "In the séance I attended, he was asking his wife for advice about something, and Serafina told him to follow his heart."

"I told him nothing!" she protested. "The spirits tell him. I do not even know what they say!"

Sarah ignored her. Obviously, she had forgotten she had confessed to having Yellow Feather tell the clients what Mrs. Gittings wanted them to hear. "He was thinking about doing something dangerous, and Serafina told him not to be afraid."

"I told him nothing!" Serafina insisted.

"The spirits then," Sarah conceded generously. "Someone told him not to be afraid and to follow his heart."

"What was he thinking about doing that was dangerous?" Frank asked Serafina.

"I do not know," she said sullenly. "You will have to ask him."

Frank rubbed his chin thoughtfully. "Now that's a problem," he said, "because Mr. Sharpe is a rich man with power-ful friends. I can't ask him anything, because if I do, I'll lose my job."

Serafina looked at him in surprise. "But you are the police."

People like Serafina, powerless people with no money, were terrified of the police.

"Mr. Malloy is right," Sarah was saying. "People like Mr. Sharpe and . . . Well, like all the people at the séance, they don't have to be afraid of the police."

"Why not?"

"Because . . ." Sarah was searching for an explanation the girl could understand.

"Because they have enough money to buy their way out of trouble," Frank explained for her.

"Is this true?" she asked Sarah, outraged.

"I'm afraid it is."

"Even if one of them killed Mrs. Gittings?" the girl asked.

"Probably," Frank said. "No one wants to protect Nicola except you, and the others would be happy to see him charged with the murder, guilty or not, because that would mean they wouldn't have to worry about any scandal touching them."

The girl's eyes filled with tears. "Mrs. Brandt, you cannot let him blame Nicola for this! He is innocent!"

Sarah turned to him with that expression he hated, the one that said she wanted him to do something he didn't want to do. "Can you at least question them?"

Frank shook his head. "The boy did it. He's the only one who could have."

"No, that is not true!" Serafina cried.

"All the others were holding hands," he reminded her. "If they moved, somebody would have noticed."

"But what if one of the people on either side of Mrs. Gittings did it?" Sarah said too eagerly. "One of them could have let go of her hand, and before she could say anything, he stabbed her."

"He?" Frank asked.

"Mr. Sharpe was on her left," Sarah said. "He was thinking about doing something dangerous."

Frank glared at her.

"Mrs. Burke was on the other side of her," Serafina added. "Mrs. Gittings would not let her come back to see me again until she brought more money."

"She was selling her jewelry," Sarah reminded him. "And she was afraid her husband would find out."

Frank didn't want to hear any of this. "That's far-fetched," he tried.

"There is another way," Serafina said.

They both looked at her in surprise.

"Another way to what?" Sarah asked.

"To . . . to free your hand," she admitted reluctantly.

"What do you mean?" Frank asked, figuring this was some kind of trick, a desperate attempt to cast suspicion on anybody but DiLoreto.

"Please, put your hands on the table," she said, moving the coffee cups aside as Frank and Sarah each laid their palms on the tabletop.

Serafina reached across with her left hand and took Frank's right wrist. "Please, hold Mrs. Brandt's wrist with your other hand," she instructed him.

Frank took Sarah's right wrist with his left hand, and she in turn clasped Serafina's right wrist with her left hand.

"This is how we hold our hands when the lights are on," Serafina said. "Then I get up and turn out the light and close the door." She pulled her hands free of theirs, as if she were getting up. "When I come back," she continued. "Sometimes I do this."

She kept her right hand off the table, and offered her left wrist to Sarah, who clasped it, and then she clasped Frank's wrist with the same hand.

"In the dark, you will not see this," she said, pointing to the way they were both clasping the same one of her hands. "And I have one hand free to . . ." She raised her hand as if she held an invisible knife and brought it down toward Sarah, who instinctively recoiled.

Frank jerked his own hand away and glared at her. "But nobody would know how to do that except you."

"Mr. Cunningham knows how," she said. "He told me he knew that I sometimes keep one hand free. He was very proud he had figured this out."

"But he was too far away to stab Mrs. Gittings," Frank said.

"If he figured it out, the others could have, too," Sarah said.

Frank frowned at her. "The DiLoreto boy still had the best reason to want her dead," he reminded her. "The Professor said she wanted to get rid of him. They had a fight about it the night before she died."

"But she said he could stay," Serafina argued. "I told her I would leave with him if she sent him away."

The Professor had said the same thing, so that part was true, at least. "But he might have thought if he killed her—"

"No!" Serafina interrupted in frustration. "If he killed her, we would be telling fortunes on the street again."

"Not if Sharpe set you up in a house like he wanted to," Frank reminded her.

"But Nicola could not come with me. And if Mrs. Gittings was dead, we would have nothing."

"Except her money," Frank tried. "With her dead, Nicola could come back and steal the money—"

"No, no!" she cried. "He stole it before she died!"

Frank and Sarah gaped at her as she clapped a hand over her mouth, aghast at what she had just said.

"Nicola stole the money?" Frank asked, using his police detective's tone.

Her eyes widened in terror. "It was really our money," she said. "I had earned it, but she would not give it to us. She would give us nothing!"

"How did he steal it? You said you didn't know the combination to the safe," Sarah said.

"We . . . we made a small hole in the wall so we could watch when she opened the safe," she admitted. "We were waiting until the end of the month, before she paid the rent, so . . ." She gestured vaguely.

"So there'd be more money to steal," Frank offered.

"But it's not the end of the month yet," Sarah pointed out.

"After the fight with Mrs. Gittings, we decided we could not wait," Serafina said.

"Exactly when did he take the money?" Frank asked.

"Yesterday, right after everyone arrived for the séance. The Professor locks the money in the safe, then he comes to the parlor to help me escort people into the séance room. Nicola took the money from the safe when the Professor and Mrs. Gittings were with me and the clients in the parlor and . . . and he hid it."

"Where did he hide it?" Frank asked.

"He . . . In my bedroom," she admitted reluctantly. "In my carpet bag."

"Oh," Sarah said in surprise. Frank glanced at her questioningly. "I noticed that she was very protective of the bag on the trip over here," she explained.

"So you have it here with you?" Frank asked.

"Yes, but it is mine! I earned it!" she cried, her face crumbling.

"Don't worry, I'm not going to take it," Frank assured her. "I just wanted to know where it was. So DiLoreto took the money before the séance even started."

"Yes, that was our plan. Then we were going to wait until they were asleep that night, Mrs. Gittings and the Professor, and we would run away together."

"Where were you going to go?" Sarah asked.

"To another city," Serafina explained, leaning forward in her desperation to make them understand. "With the money, we could rent a house and I could do readings and we would not need Mrs. Gittings anymore. So you see, we did not need to kill her."

"And killing her would just complicate things for them," Sarah pointed out, earning another frown from Frank. "Why would they want to upset the clients or get the police involved? If they killed her, they were bound to get caught."

The timing of the theft of the money was exactly right. The Professor had said it was all there when he put in the fees for the séance. Nicola had no opportunity to hide it after the séance started because he was busy making the background noises, and after the murder, the house was full of cops who would have noticed him carrying a sack of money around. And he couldn't have come back and stolen it later, because Serafina had it with her when she left the house.

"Nicola did not kill her, Mr. Malloy," Serafina said again. "Please, you must believe me."

"Can't you at least question the other people at the séance to see if you can figure out what really happened?" Sarah asked again. "If the boy is innocent, you can't let him hang."

Frank sighed in defeat. "I might be able to talk to each of

them *once*," he admitted grudgingly, "if I say I'm trying to collect more evidence against DiLoreto and if they'll let me in at all. But if they refuse to talk to me, I can't force them. *And . . .*" he continued when Sarah started to look hopeful, "I can't treat them like criminals."

"What does that mean?" Serafina asked Sarah.

"It means he has to be polite and not make them angry," Sarah said.

"Which means they might not tell me the truth," Frank said. "Especially the one who killed her, if one of them did. And unless one of them confesses to killing Mrs. Gittings, I won't be able to arrest any of them even if I'm sure they did it."

"But at least you'll know Nicola is innocent," Sarah said.

"And you will let him go free," Serafina added, her lovely eyes full of hope.

How did Frank let Sarah get him into this? He'd had a perfectly good suspect that nobody would care anything about except this girl whom nobody would care anything about, but now he was going to have to go uptown and bother people who never got bothered by the police because they were too important. And with Roosevelt gone, he had no one to stand up for him if one of these important people got offended and wanted him fired.

He looked up to find Sarah studying him as if trying to read his thoughts. She opened her mouth to say something, but the sound of her doorbell distracted them. Sarah got up to answer it.

While they waited for her, Frank said to Serafina, "The Professor said to tell you that you've got clients scheduled today. He wanted to know if you were coming back to see them."

"He is worried about money," she sniffed derisively.

"He should be," Frank said. "You didn't leave him any."

She didn't look very repentant. "Maybe I should go back," she said after a moment. "Just in case someone comes to see me."

"And in case DiLoreto comes looking for you," Frank suggested.

She looked up in surprise. "I . . . I did not think of that."

"Yes, you did," Frank said. "He'll be wondering where you are."

Frank heard a familiar voice, and he rose as Sarah returned to the kitchen with her mother.

"Mr. Malloy, it's so good to see you," she said in greeting, but her gaze went immediately to Serafina. "How are you, my dear?"

Serafina burst into tears, which immediately won the sympathy of both women, who rushed to comfort her. Frank stood back, watching for any sign that Serafina's outburst was faked to distract Frank from thoughts of DiLoreto. She'd managed real tears, he noted, lending an air of authenticity to her outburst.

"What have you been doing to her?" Mrs. Decker demanded of him.

"Nothing, Mother," Sarah assured her. "We've just been discussing the reasons Nicola couldn't have murdered Mrs. Gittings."

"Not *couldn't*," Frank corrected her. "*Wouldn't*."

All three women gave him black looks.

"Did she at least convince you that he's innocent?" Mrs. Decker asked.

"She convinced me it's possible," Frank admitted.

"The problem," Sarah said quickly, before her mother

could respond, "is that Mr. Malloy will be risking his job if he goes to question the others at the séance who might have had a reason to murder Mrs. Gittings."

"How would he be risking his job?" Mrs. Decker asked.

"Think about it, Mother," Sarah said. "What would Father do if a police detective came to your house to question you about a murder?"

Mrs. Decker only needed a moment to imagine the scene. Felix Decker would have used all of his power and influence to make sure such a thing never happened again. "Oh, dear."

"Exactly."

"But Theodore—" she tried, obviously remembering how their old family friend, Mr. Roosevelt, had always supported Malloy's efforts.

"Theodore has resigned as police commissioner," Sarah said. "He's going to Washington to be assistant secretary of something or other."

"The Navy," Frank supplied helpfully.

"The *Navy*?" Mrs. Decker echoed in astonishment. "What does Theodore know about the Navy?"

"Who is Theodore?" Serafina asked tearfully.

"No one, dear, it doesn't matter," Mrs. Decker said, dismissing the brand-new assistant secretary of the Navy with a wave of her hand. "But if Mr. Malloy can't question these people, how are we to determine what really happened to poor Mrs. Gittings?"

"We were just discussing that when you arrived," Sarah explained. "And I was going to offer my own services. I could call on them and question them myself."

"No, you can't," Frank protested, and he was gratified when Mrs. Decker confirmed it.

"Oh, no, my dear, you couldn't possibly," she said. "I'm sure they would refuse to see you, under the circumstances. But," she added archly, "I'm sure they would all be more than glad to welcome me. We can visit them together."

10

"WHAT?" MALLOY DEMANDED, OUTRAGED.

"Oh, Mother, do you really think that's wise?" Sarah asked, not paying any attention at all to Malloy. She'd known he would give her an argument about getting involved, so she'd already determined to ignore it. She hadn't expected her mother to offer her help, however.

"I'm *sure* it's not wise," Mrs. Decker said, "but I intend to do it anyway. How else can we save that poor young man?"

"Mrs. Decker," Malloy said, trying to sound reasonable instead of furious and failing miserably, "if one of these people killed Mrs. Gittings, you might be in danger yourself."

"Danger? Nonsense! Why would anyone want to harm *me*?"

"Somebody who's killed once won't stop at killing again to protect himself," Malloy argued.

"But I have no intention of letting anyone know I'm investigating the murder," Mrs. Decker pointed out reasonably. "Who would believe such a thing in any case? I'll just be calling on them to find out how they are coping after the tragedy."

"I think that might work," Sarah said to Malloy, who looked like he might be in danger of having apoplexy.

"What do you think your father would say if he found out your mother was investigating a murder?" he asked.

"I'm sure he would have a lot to say *if* he knew," Mrs. Decker said before Sarah could answer. "But I have no intention of telling him, and I'm sure no one else does either."

Malloy was rubbing his head as if it hurt him. Sarah felt a flash of pity for him. He really did not stand a chance of prevailing.

"What can I do to help?" Serafina asked.

"Nothing," Malloy told her sharply.

"You can tell us everything you know about these people," Sarah said, giving him a glare that he returned. "Let's all sit down," she added. "Mother, would you like some coffee?"

When everyone was seated around Sarah's kitchen table with a fresh cup of coffee, Mrs. Decker asked, "Where are the girls?"

"I sent them to Mrs. Ellsworth so we could talk in private," Sarah said.

"That's a relief. I wouldn't want Catherine to overhear us. Now what were we discussing?"

"Serafina is going to tell us what she knows about the other people at the séance." Sarah gave the girl an encouraging smile.

"Where should I start?" she asked uncertainly.

"With Mrs. Burke," Mrs. Decker said. "What you don't know, I'm sure I can supply. I've known her for years."

Serafina took a deep breath as if to fortify herself. "She has been coming to see me since last fall. She wanted to contact her sister."

"Yes, they had a quarrel," Mrs. Decker said. "The sister died before they could make it up. She told me Madame Serafina contacted her sister, and she was able to apologize and be forgiven."

"Yes, and this made her very happy," Serafina reported. "But Mrs. Gittings wanted her to keep coming back, so I had to tell her that her sister had important messages for her. We had a private sitting for her, and her sister told her things about her children."

"Mrs. Burke's children?" Sarah clarified.

"Yes, they are . . . not happy," Serafina hedged.

"Kathy's son is a worthless profligate," Mrs. Decker reported. "His father has had to rescue him time and again, but he never seems to learn his lesson."

"What is a profligate?" Serafina asked.

"A bum," Malloy offered. Sarah was glad to note that he had gone from furious to resigned. "What about her other children?"

Serafina didn't like this one bit. "One daughter is respectable and married, but the other . . ."

"The other is married as well," Mrs. Decker supplied, "but she's far from respectable. She married an older man, and she's taken a series of lovers through the years. Her conduct has been so blatant that some families won't even receive her anymore."

"She wanted someone to tell her what to do for her children," Serafina said. "So I asked the spirits to help her."

"You said her husband wouldn't give her money for the séances anymore," Sarah reminded her.

"No, she said he cut off her allowance," Serafina said.

"Oh, dear," Mrs. Decker said. "He must have been very angry with her to do that."

"I was trying to help her," Serafina said, looking at each of them in turn to judge their reaction. "But Mrs. Gittings kept asking her for more money. She did not care how Mrs. Burke got the money, and she said I should not care either. She said Mrs. Burke is rich, and I should not feel sorry for rich people."

"Who told her to sell her jewelry?" Malloy asked.

Serafina bit her lip. "Mrs. Gittings did at first. I never talked to anyone about money, but . . ."

"But what?" Sarah coaxed.

"But Mrs. Gittings said the spirits must tell her to sell something. I had to do what she said, even though I knew it was wrong," she added desperately.

"Of course you did, dear," Mrs. Decker said, patting the girl's hand.

"Did Mrs. Burke ever threaten Mrs. Gittings?" Malloy asked, ever the policeman.

"You mean threaten to hurt her?" Serafina asked uncertainly.

"Any kind of threat," Malloy replied.

"I did not hear it if she did. Mrs. Gittings would talk to the clients alone when she . . . when she wanted to get them to pay more. She did not want them to think I cared about the money."

"When I was at the séance," Sarah said, "the spirits told Mrs. Burke to sell something her mother had given her. A brooch of some kind, I think. Did she sell it?"

"I do not know," Serafina claimed. "She returned yesterday, but I think . . ." She seemed to catch herself.

"What do you think?" Sarah prodded.

"She was still asking her mother if she should sell it, so I think she did not, at least not yet."

"How was she paying for the séances, then?" Malloy asked.

Serafina stole a guilty glance at Mrs. Decker, then looked down to where her hands were clenched on the tabletop.

"What is it, Serafina?" Sarah prodded. "We can't help you if you don't tell us the whole story."

Serafina swallowed. "Mrs. Gittings told Mrs. Burke that she could come back if she brought someone new."

"Had she brought other people there before?" Sarah asked.

"No, but . . . but Mrs. Gittings said she would charge the new person twice the fee so Mrs. Burke did not have to pay."

Mrs. Decker gasped in outrage. "I can't believe Kathy would do something like that!"

"She was desperate, Mrs. Decker," Serafina said, defending her. "You do not know . . ."

"Well, I'll certainly have something to say to her about it," Mrs. Decker said.

"Do you think she was desperate enough to kill Mrs. Gittings?" Sarah asked.

"She was very angry," Serafina said. "And frightened. And she asked me . . ."

"What did she ask you?" Malloy prodded.

"She asked me if I knew Mrs. Gittings was demanding so much money from her."

"What did you tell her?" Sarah asked.

Serafina bit her lip, as if she were carefully considering her reply. "Mrs. Gittings always said I should never talk about money with the clients, so I told her if not for Mrs. Gittings, I would not even charge her."

"Oh, my," Sarah said softly.

Serafina realized everyone was staring at her. "What is wrong?" she asked in alarm.

"You gave Mrs. Burke a very good reason to get rid of Mrs. Gittings," Malloy said grimly.

The girl looked horrified.

"I don't care what reasons she had or how desperate she was, I just can't imagine Kathy Burke stabbing anyone like that," Mrs. Decker said, defending her old friend.

Sarah knew better than to offer an opinion. Even her limited experience with investigating murders told her that often the most unlikely suspect was the guilty one. "What about Mr. Sharpe?" she asked, remembering that he was sitting on the other side of Mrs. Gittings and would have had an even better opportunity to stick the knife into her back.

"He is a very proud man," Serafina said. "He is used to having people do what he wants."

"What did he want you to do?" Sarah asked.

"Not what you think," the girl hastened to explain.

"I wasn't thinking anything," Sarah lied.

"He has visited many spiritualists," Serafina said. "He never believed in any of them until he came to me."

"How did you convince him when the others didn't?" Malloy asked.

"I do not know," Serafina said, "but many of them are fakes and not even good fakes at that."

Sarah gave Malloy a warning glance. She knew he agreed with her that *all* spiritualists were fakes. She didn't want to offend Serafina just when she was starting to give them useful information, though.

"How long had he been coming to see you?" Mrs. Decker asked.

"About two months," she said. "He wanted to contact his wife. He loved her very much, and he was lonely without her."

"When I was there, he asked his wife about a decision he was making," Sarah reminded all of them. "Do you know what he was trying to decide?"

"No, I told you before. When Yellow Feather is there, I do not know what is happening. But Mr. Sharpe always consulted his wife before he made a decision. That is why he was so glad when I was able to help him contact her. None of the others could do that."

Sarah suddenly realized something important. "If Sharpe had been to a lot of séances, he might know the trick about holding hands," she told Malloy.

"What trick about holding hands?" Mrs. Decker asked.

Sarah demonstrated it for her.

"Good heavens," she exclaimed. "How clever."

"And Sharpe was sitting right next to Mrs. Gittings," Sarah reminded them. "So he really believed you'd contacted his dead wife?"

"Oh, yes, he was very pleased. He said it was not right that I had to sell my talents, though. He thought I should be free to help anyone who came to me."

"And he offered to set you up in a house of your own," Sarah recalled.

"What did he want in return?" Malloy asked suspiciously.

"Nothing," Serafina assured him. "Except . . ."

Malloy brightened, expecting the worst. "Except what?"

"He wanted me to . . . to test my powers," she admitted reluctantly.

"What does that mean?" Sarah asked.

"I am not sure, but Mrs. Gittings would never allow it."

"There are people who make it their business to show up people who are frauds," Malloy said. "They go to a séance and expose the tricks."

"No, that is not what he wanted to do," Serafina explained

quickly. "He wanted to bring in some people who would ask me questions to prove my powers are real."

"Or that they weren't," Malloy offered.

"My powers are real!" Serafina insisted. "Mr. Sharpe said that when they proved me, I would be famous. I was willing, but Mrs. Gittings refused."

"Why not?" Malloy asked, not bothering to hide his skepticism. "If you could prove you were real, a lot more people would pay to see you. Wouldn't Mrs. Gittings like that?"

Serafina turned the full force of her disdain on him. "If I got famous, I could leave her. She knew Mr. Sharpe had already made me an offer. Others would, too."

Unless they proved she had no powers at all, Sarah thought, which was more likely what Mrs. Gittings feared.

"Did Sharpe ask you to leave Mrs. Gittings?" Malloy asked.

"Not at first," Serafina said. "He did not know she was my manager, so he offered to be my sponsor. He said he would pay for everything so I would not have to take money for my readings anymore. I did not know what to say, so I told him I could not accept. He would not stop asking, though, so Mrs. Gittings had to tell him the truth."

"Were you there when she did?" Sarah asked.

"No, but Mr. Sharpe was not pleased. As I said, he is used to getting what he wants, and Mrs. Gittings was not kind to him. I think she was very happy to tell him about her power over me."

"Did he give up then?" Malloy asked.

Serafina's lovely face hardened. "No, he did not. He tried to convince me to leave Mrs. Gittings. I told him I could not, but I could not tell him why, not the real reason, so he would not stop asking me."

"What was the real reason?" Mrs. Decker asked.

Serafina smiled sadly. "I am sure Mr. Sharpe would not allow Nicola to live with me in the house he was paying for."

"He must have wondered what kind of a hold Mrs. Gittings had over you," Sarah mused. "And why it was so strong."

"And maybe he thought if Mrs. Gittings was dead, she'd be free of it," Malloy added.

"I never thought of that," Serafina marveled.

"Mr. Sharpe seemed like such a gentleman," Mrs. Decker observed. "I just can't see him . . . Well, I must admit I can't imagine *anyone* wanting to stick a knife into a woman in the hope of killing her."

Serafina's fine eyes glowed with suppressed fury. "That is because you did not know her."

Sarah saw Malloy looking at Serafina in a completely new way.

"Did you want to kill her?" he asked casually.

"Yes, I did," she admitted guilelessly, "but I was too afraid." She lifted a hand to her throat. "I do not want to hang."

"Murderers don't hang anymore," Malloy said mildly. "They go to the electric chair."

All three women gasped. Sarah could have cheerfully smacked him, but he didn't seem concerned. He was too busy studying Serafina's reaction.

The blood seemed to have drained from her face. "What does this electric chair do?" she asked in a whisper.

"It kills," Sarah snapped, silently warning Malloy not to offer any details. "It's supposed to be more humane than hanging."

"What does that mean?" Serafina asked in alarm.

Sarah searched for a word. "It's kinder," she tried, although she knew she was misleading the poor girl. She had no illusions that the electric chair was any kinder a way to die than hanging.

"But you're still dead," Malloy said.

"Which is why," Mrs. Decker said, jumping in with a re-proving glare for Malloy, "you need to tell us everything you can to help us find the real killer, my dear."

"Yes," Sarah said quickly. "Who's left?"

"Mr. Cunningham," Mrs. Decker said when Serafina seemed still too stunned to respond.

"He was sitting too far away from Mrs. Gittings," Mrs. Decker said. "He was between me and Serafina, completely on the other side of the table."

"Did he ever let go of your hand?" Malloy asked her.

"Actually, I was holding his wrist and no, I didn't . . . Oh, wait."

"What is it, Mother?" Sarah asked when her mother hesitated.

"I just remembered, he did . . . or rather I did, let go, I mean. When Madame Serafina got up to turn out the light. He started coughing. He said excuse me or something, and he withdrew his hand so he could get out a handkerchief."

"Oh, yes, I remember," Serafina said. "He coughed into it."

"Yes, and he was still coughing when you closed the door and the room went dark. I heard you sit down, and he was still coughing, but then he stopped, and he must have put his handkerchief away, and I felt his wrist brush my hand and I took hold of it."

"Did you have one of your hands free that day?" Malloy asked Serafina.

"No, not that day. I . . . I was supposed to, but I knew I would be leaving that night, so I was not afraid of what Mrs. Gittings would say if everything did not go the way she wanted."

"But you said Mr. Cunningham knew the trick of how to keep one hand free," Sarah remembered.

"Yes, he did."

"What good would that do him, though?" Mrs. Decker asked. "Even if he had one hand free, he would have had to reach around me and Mr. Sharpe both to stab Mrs. Gittings. He couldn't possibly have done that."

"So each of you had hold of his hands—or at least of one of them—when Mrs. Gittings was killed," Malloy asked Serafina and Mrs. Decker.

"Yes," they both agreed.

"And since he couldn't have reached her from where he was sitting, and he couldn't have gotten up without one of them knowing it, he couldn't have killed her," Sarah determined.

"Did he have any reason to want to?" Malloy asked Serafina. "You claimed yesterday that they all did, so what was his reason?"

"He . . . he wanted me to . . ." Serafina could not make herself say the words.

"He's in love with her," Mrs. Decker said for her. "Couldn't you see it yesterday?"

"Yes, I could," Malloy confirmed. "Did he want to marry you, Serafina?"

"No, of course not," she snapped angrily. "He could not marry a girl like me. He wanted me for his mistress."

"Did he actually make you that offer?" Mrs. Decker asked in outrage.

"No, but . . . Mrs. Gittings told me. She said he offered her money to let me go, but it was not enough," she added bitterly.

"Who was it he was trying to contact?" Malloy asked, as if he couldn't remember, although Sarah was sure he did.

"His father. He did not know what to do without his father."

"And what did his father tell him to do?" Malloy asked.

"He . . . Mrs. Gittings made me tell him to invest money in a . . . I do not know. Something her friend was doing."

"Some phony investment scheme," Malloy guessed.

"Why would Mr. Cunningham do that?" Sarah asked.

"Because he needed more money," Serafina said, her cheeks crimson with fury. "Mrs. Gittings told him if he offered more money, he could . . . he could have me."

"That's unspeakable!" Mrs. Decker declared.

"But he lost his money, didn't he?" Malloy asked relentlessly.

"Yes, and then I was supposed to tell him to invest more. Mrs. Gittings kept telling him he needed more and more . . ." Her voice broke, and she covered her mouth, fighting tears.

"What a horrible woman," Mrs. Decker said as Sarah put an arm around Serafina. "I'm not sure whoever killed her did such a bad thing."

"Wait a minute," Malloy said. "I thought Cunningham was rich. Why would he need this phony investment scheme to get the money Mrs. Gittings wanted?"

"His *family* is rich," Serafina said. "But he only gets an allowance. He does not inherit his father's fortune until he is twenty-five, in three more years."

"Where did he get the money to invest then?" Malloy asked.

"From his mother. She . . . He is her only child. She is very generous, but she would not give him money for a mistress," Serafina said, spitting out the last word.

"Thank heaven for that, at least," Mrs. Decker murmured.

"How much money did Cunningham lose to Mrs. Gittings's friend?" Malloy asked.

"I do not know."

"If he was going to use the money to get Serafina away from Mrs. Gittings and then he lost it," Sarah said, "he might have been desperate enough to kill her."

"But we were both holding his hands," Mrs. Decker reminded her.

"Serafina," Malloy said, startling her. "If you can keep one hand free when everybody is holding hands around the table, can you keep both hands free?"

"I do not know," she said in surprise. "I have never tried it."

"Let's try it now," he said, offering Mrs. Decker his wrist. They all joined hands again.

"Now Serafina is getting up, and I'm going to start coughing and let go." Malloy and Serafina freed both of their hands. "Then Serafina comes back, but I don't put my hands on the table this time." He pulled his hands back and put them in his lap. "Mrs. Decker, you'd be looking for my hand in the dark."

"And Serafina would be looking for your other hand," Sarah said, understanding how it could work.

Mrs. Decker took Serafina's wrist in her left hand, but then she shook her head. "No, no. I might take her wrist by mistake in the dark, but I would never believe it was yours, Mr. Malloy."

"Could you have mistaken it for Cunningham's, though?" he challenged her. "He's a much thinner man."

"Yes, he is," Serafina said in surprise. "I had not thought of it before."

"Could that have happened, Mother?" Sarah asked.

"I don't know," Mrs. Decker said with a frown, "but it's possible, I suppose."

"Even if he could get free, he'd still have to find Mrs. Gittings in the dark, though," Sarah pointed out.

"And how would he know where to stab her?" Mrs. Decker added. "He would have had to feel around in the dark, and she would have noticed if someone touched her. Surely, she would have cried out in surprise, if nothing else."

"I don't think it would be too hard," Malloy mused. "He didn't have to walk far, and he'd hear people talking, so he could get his bearings that way."

"He could touch the chairs," Serafina offered.

They all looked at her in surprise.

"You touch the backs of the chairs," she repeated. "That is how you know where you are."

"So he could just walk around the table until he came to the third chair, where he knew Mrs. Gittings was sitting," Malloy said. "The chair back would tell him where her body was, so all he had to do was—"

"That's enough," Sarah said quickly. "We understand. But could he have gotten up quietly enough so no one noticed?"

"Everybody was shouting," Malloy reminded them. "Were you paying attention to the people around you, Mrs. Decker?"

"Not at all," she said in surprise. "I would have known if someone let go of my hand, but if Mr. Cunningham had slid his chair back and gotten up, I doubt I would have noticed."

"But shouldn't someone have noticed when Mrs. Gittings got stabbed?" Sarah asked. "Wouldn't she have screamed or something?"

"I asked the medical examiner the same thing, and he said no," Malloy said. "The knife went straight into her heart, and she died quickly."

"But surely she felt some pain when the knife went in," Sarah said.

"She might've felt a pain, but since she wasn't expecting to be stabbed, she probably wouldn't have thought it was anything really bad," Malloy explained. "Everybody has unexpected pains from time to time. They usually just pass, and we forget about them."

"Oh, dear," Mrs. Decker exclaimed. "I think we've proven that any one of the three of them could be the killer."

"And don't forget the Professor," Malloy said.

"But he wasn't even in the room," Sarah reminded him.

Malloy turned to Serafina. "Could he have gotten in without anybody knowing it?"

She frowned. "He could have come in through the cabinet, but Nicola was in there. He would have seen him, and he would have told me."

"Is there any other way to sneak in?"

"No," Serafina said.

Malloy gave her one of his glares.

The girl blinked but held her ground. "I would tell you," she insisted. "I want to help."

"Of course you do, dear," Mrs. Decker soothed her and gave Malloy a reproving glance.

He ignored it. "Supposing he could have gotten into the room somehow, did he have any reason to want Mrs. Gittings dead?"

Serafina considered the question for a long moment. "I do not know."

"You said they were lovers," Sarah reminded her, thinking that was a strange word to use for middle-aged people but unable to think of another. "Did they get along well?"

The girl shook her head. "Mrs. Gittings was mean to him. She said he was stupid."

"Did they argue?" Sarah asked.

"No, no, the Professor, he is very quiet. He would say nothing when she said mean things to him."

"But she trusted him with the money," Malloy remembered. "He knew the combination to the safe. He could have taken it and disappeared."

"No, they were saving for something," Serafina said. "At least . . ." She stopped, remembering.

"What is it?" Sarah prodded.

The girl pursed her lips as she tried to recall. "At first, the Professor and Mrs. Gittings would talk about what they were going to do when they had enough money. They were going to bankroll something, they said. I did not understand what it was, but they would get very excited when they talked about it because they would get very rich. The Professor, he had done it before, but he was just a steerer then and did not earn much money."

"A *what*?" Malloy asked sharply.

"A steerer," Serafina repeated uncertainly. "I think that is the word."

"What else did they say about it?" Malloy asked urgently.

"I do not know," Serafina said in dismay. "I did not pay attention, but it does not matter, because then she changed her mind."

"What do you mean?" Sarah asked.

"She saw they could make a lot of money from the séances. She said . . . she said it was easier and not as dangerous. She said no one would get killed," she remembered suddenly.

"That's what she said?" Malloy asked. "That nobody would get killed?"

"Yes, this other thing, what the Professor wanted to do, that was dangerous, but the séances were not. She said they attracted a better class of people." Serafina glanced at Mrs. Decker apologetically.

"And did the Professor agree with her?" Sarah asked.

"No, no," Serafina said. "He was not happy. They would argue about it at night sometimes, after Nicola and I went to bed."

"Why didn't he just take the money himself?" Malloy asked.

"They did not have enough yet. I think . . ."

"What do you think, dear?" Mrs. Decker asked when Serafina hesitated.

"I think they would never give me my part of the money," she said bitterly. "I think they would have taken it all and left us with nothing."

Sarah thought that, too.

"So the Professor stayed because he didn't have enough money yet to do whatever it was he wanted to do with it," Malloy said, drawing Serafina's attention back. "But Mrs. Gittings had changed her mind and just wanted to keep doing the séances."

"Yes, she asked did he not like living in a nice house and not worrying about the police. She said he was stupid to think about anything else. But he said they could live in a mansion and never have to work again."

Malloy sat back and considered what she had told him.

"Do you know what it was he wanted to do?" Sarah asked him.

"I have a good idea," he replied.

"What do you think it was?"

"They call it the Green Goods Game."

"What is it?" Sarah asked.

"It's a way to trick people out of their money. They send out letters all over the country, offering to sell people counterfeit money."

"Is that legal?" Mrs. Decker asked in amazement.

Malloy's mouth quirked, but he managed not to smile. "Not at all. But lots of people are curious enough to travel to New York to find out more about it. The operators pay all their travel expenses, too, even if they decide not to buy in. So the suckers come to New York and somebody—the one they call the steerer—meets them at the train and takes them to a hotel. Then the steerer takes them to meet the one they call the Old Gentleman, who is someone who looks very respectable. The Old Gentleman shows them a suitcase full of what they think is the counterfeit money, except it's real money."

"Real money? Why would they show them real money?" Sarah asked.

"To convince them it's good quality so they'll buy it."

"How much does counterfeit money cost?" Mrs. Decker asked with interest.

"Ten cents on the dollar. When the sucker is convinced, he pays for the money, and the operators lock it into a suitcase for him. Then the steerer escorts him right back to the train that will take him back home and puts him on it."

"I do not understand," Serafina said. "How does this make any money if they sell real money for less than it is worth?"

"Because when the sucker is distracted, the operators switch suitcases. When the sucker gets home and opens it, it's full of sawdust or blank pieces of paper or bricks or something."

"But don't they go back to New York and complain that they were swindled?" Mrs. Decker asked, outraged.

This time Malloy couldn't help smiling. "What would they say? That they were trying to buy counterfeit money and someone cheated them?"

The women all exclaimed their surprise.

"How clever!" Sarah said. "And you think this is what the Professor wanted to use the money for?"

"Yes, but they'd need at least ten thousand dollars in cash to show the suckers. The operators usually have somebody who gives them the money to show the suckers and takes about half the profits. The steerer and the Old Gentleman and their other helpers each get a share of the other half."

"How much could someone earn doing this?" Sarah asked.

"At least a couple thousand dollars."

"A year?" Mrs. Decker asked.

"No," Malloy told her. "A *day*."

The women gasped. A couple thousand dollars was a good annual wage for a working man.

"No wonder the Professor was trying to convince Mrs. Gittings to do it," Sarah said.

"But Mrs. Gittings was afraid it was too dangerous," Serafina reminded them.

"It is," Malloy said. "Sometimes the suckers get suspicious, or they figure out what's going on, and they pull a gun or the operators do. Sometimes people get shot."

"So that explains what the Professor wanted the money for," Sarah said.

"If I'm right about it, it does," Malloy allowed. "But none of that matters now. What matters is if it gave him a reason to kill her, and I don't think it did, at least not until they had enough to bankroll him for a Green Goods Game."

"But they fight all the time," Serafina insisted.

"Lots of people fight but never kill each other," he told her. "Beside, they didn't have enough money to set up his own game yet. When they did, he might have killed her if she refused to go along with him on their original plan. But that hadn't happened, and he still needed her to keep running the séances."

"Did he?" Sarah asked.

Malloy frowned. "Did he what?"

"Did he need her to run the séances?" She turned to Serafina. "Could you do the séances without her?"

"I don't . . . Yes, we could," she decided. "At first she got clients for me, but after a while, people began to bring their friends and . . . No, we did not need her anymore."

"So the Professor could have killed her to make sure that she wasn't around to mess up his plans," Malloy said.

"Except," Sarah reminded him with a superior grin, "he wasn't even in the room when she was killed."

II

THAT EVENING, LONG AFTER MALLOY AND SARAH'S mother had left and when Catherine had finally gone reluctantly to bed, Sarah and Serafina had to tell Maeve and Mrs. Ellsworth everything they had discussed earlier in the day. Serafina had chosen not to return to the house on Waverly Place that afternoon as the Professor had asked. Even though she had scheduled clients who might have appeared, she simply couldn't stand the thought of going back into the room where Mrs. Gittings had died.

Mrs. Ellsworth asked dozens of questions during Sarah's narrative as the four of them sat around Sarah's kitchen table, but Maeve just listened quietly, her expression unreadable. She was especially attentive when Sarah was describing the Green Goods Game.

When Mrs. Ellsworth finally ran out of questions, Maeve spoke up at last. "What does this Professor look like?"

They all looked at her in surprise.

"He's tall and very dignified," Sarah said. "Like a butler in a fine house. Dark hair with some gray at the temples."

"That is powder," Serafina said.

"What is powder?" Sarah asked, confused.

"The gray in his hair. He thinks he looks more respectable with gray in his hair."

"How odd," Mrs. Ellsworth remarked. "Most people don't want their hair to turn gray."

"Why did you want to know what he looked like?" Sarah asked Maeve.

"No reason," she said, although Sarah was sure she had a good one. "Are you and Mrs. Decker going to visit those people tomorrow?"

"We're going to see Mrs. Burke first thing, but not Mr. Sharpe and Mr. Cunningham. After we thought about it, we couldn't figure out any way it was proper for us to visit a widower and a bachelor."

"Oh, my, that certainly *wouldn't* be proper," Mrs. Ellsworth agreed.

"How are you going to question them, then?" Maeve asked.

"Mr. Malloy is going to see them."

"But I thought he couldn't question them without risking his job," Mrs. Ellsworth said.

"He's going to pretend that he's just trying to get more information to use against Nicola."

"But what if they refuse to speak with him?" Mrs. Ellsworth asked.

Sarah sighed. "Then I guess we'll have to figure out something else."

"You could have another séance," Maeve said, surprising them again.

"Another séance?" Sarah echoed.

"Yes," Maeve said, leaning forward eagerly. "From what you said, they'll both want to see Serafina again as soon as they can. They probably are both still very interested in their own plans for her. One of them might have killed Mrs. Gittings just so he could do that very thing! So why not give them the chance?"

"I could invite them for a private reading," Serafina offered.

"I thought you didn't want to go back to the house," Sarah reminded her.

"Not for another séance, but I could do the reading in a different room," the girl said bravely. "I want to help Mr. Malloy."

"And Mother and I could be there to engage them in conversation," Sarah said.

"We're getting ahead of ourselves," Mrs. Ellsworth said. "Perhaps Mr. Malloy will find out all he needs to know without our help."

"Let's hope so," Sarah said fervently.

FRANK DECIDED TO CALL ON JOHN SHARPE FIRST. CUNningham didn't strike him as the type to rise early. Sharpe lived in a tastefully large town house on a quiet, tree-lined street just off Park Avenue. A maid answered the door, a plump Irish girl with a plain face and a fancy starched apron who knew exactly what he was, and she didn't want to let him inside. She acted like she was afraid he'd try to steal the silver or something.

"Just tell Mr. Sharpe that Detective Sergeant Frank Malloy is here. I need to give him some information about Madame Serafina."

"I'm sure Mr. Sharpe don't know no *Madame* anybody," she sniffed.

"Just tell him what I said. I'll wait," he added, shouldering his way inside before she could slam the door in his face.

She gasped in outrage, but short of screaming for help, she had no option but to leave him standing in the entry hall while she went to announce his arrival.

Frank looked around while he waited. Somebody with good taste had chosen the furnishings. A lush carpet covered the floor and ran up the stairs. The wallpaper had fancy swirls in shades of brown, and several chairs that looked like they'd come from a castle sat against the wall, in case visitors got tired while they waited. Frank was admiring one of the large paintings of country scenes when he heard the maid hurrying back down the stairs.

"This way, if you please," she said, her chin high and her nose higher. She wasn't going to apologize for doubting him, and she wasn't going to be one ounce more polite than she needed to be.

He followed her up the stairs to a parlor where Sharpe was waiting for him, and she closed the door behind him.

Sharpe stood with his back to the cold fireplace, legs apart, hands clasped behind him, his expression defensive. He wasn't going to be one ounce more polite than he had to be either. "You have news about Madame Serafina?" he said the instant the door closed. "How is she?"

"She's very well," Frank said, looking around with interest. This was a formal parlor, a room seldom used. The velvet-upholstered furniture looked like nobody had ever sat on it, and the bric-a-brac cluttering every flat surface seemed well dusted but seldom admired.

"Where have you taken her?" Sharpe demanded.

"I haven't taken her anywhere," Frank said.

"The Professor said you did. She isn't at the house, and he claimed he didn't know where she'd gone."

"When were you there?" Frank asked curiously.

"Yesterday. I . . ." He seemed a little embarrassed. "I went to see if she needed anything.

"She doesn't," Frank said. "When she's ready to see clients again, I'm sure she'll let you know. Do you mind?" he added and took a seat on the nearest sofa before Sharpe could say if he minded or not.

Plainly, he did. He hadn't intended for Frank to stay longer than it took to find out where Serafina was hiding. He wasn't going to object, though, not until he had the information he wanted. "When is she coming home?"

"As soon as I find Mrs. Gittings's killer," Frank said.

"I thought you'd already found him."

"How did you know that?" Frank asked. Sharpe had left the house before they'd even known DiLoreto was in it.

"The Professor told me yesterday. He also told me you let him escape," he added with more than a trace of disapproval.

Frank felt a flash of irritation, but he knew better than to let Sharpe see it. "We'll find him," he said with more confidence than he had any right to feel.

"He could be anywhere by now," Sharpe snapped. "You'll never find him."

"We'll find him," he repeated belligerently. "He won't leave town without the girl."

Sharpe's eyes widened. "What do you mean?"

"He's in love with Madame Serafina," Frank said. "Didn't you know?"

"So what if he is?" Sharpe challenged. "The Professor said

he was nothing more than a servant. Madame Serafina would never waste herself on a man like that." He didn't sound very certain, though.

Frank didn't press the issue. "Mr. Sharpe, would you mind answering a few more questions while I'm here? I need to make sure we have all the information we need so that when we do find this DiLoreto, we'll be able to make a case against him."

"I already told you everything I know," he protested.

"I've found out some more information since then, and I need to check the facts with you, to make sure you saw the same things everybody else did. It will only take a minute," he added apologetically.

Sharpe muttered something under his breath, but he chose one of the stiff-looking chairs near Frank and perched on it. "What do you want to know?"

Frank reached into his coat and pulled out his notebook and pencil and made a little show out of finding the right page. He could hear Sharpe making impatient noises, but he didn't allow himself to be hurried.

"When you went into the séance room, did you see anybody except the people sitting around the table?"

"Of course not." This was a stupid question, and now he was annoyed.

"Did you see the Professor before the séance started?"

"Of course. He answered the door when I arrived and showed me into the parlor, just as he always does."

"Did you see him after that?"

Sharpe frowned. "I saw him after the séance, when we realized Mrs. Gittings was dead."

"But not before that?" Frank prodded. "Didn't he escort you into the séance room?"

"I'm sure he did," Sharpe said, fuming. "That was his usual practice."

"But are you sure he did that day?"

Sharpe frowned, disturbed that Frank was making him think about all of this again. "I couldn't swear to it, no," he finally admitted.

"And later, when did he come into the room?"

"I don't know. I wasn't paying any attention to him."

"You said he was standing in the doorway when everyone started leaving the room."

"Then that must have been when I saw him." He was growing exasperated now.

"So you didn't see him until after Madame Serafina opened the door and called for him?"

"No, I didn't. I don't see what any of this has to do with—"

"Do you remember hearing a violin playing during the séance?"

"A what?"

"A violin. Some of the other people in the room remember hearing a strange noise during the séance, like a violin."

Sharpe frowned again, trying to remember. "I think there was something. The spirits often make odd sounds. I was listening to what Yellow Feather was saying, so I wasn't paying attention to anything else."

"Do you remember if you heard the noise through the whole séance?"

"No, I don't, and I can't see that any of this will help you find that boy who killed Mrs. Gittings."

"Madame Serafina said you'd been to lots of spiritualists before you came to her."

Sharpe stiffened in surprise. "What business is that of yours?"

"None," Frank admitted obligingly. "I was just wondering if you'd figured out some of the tricks they use. A lot of them are fakes, you know."

"I certainly do know," Sharpe said indignantly. "You wouldn't believe the balderdash some of them told me."

"Did they try to pull tricks on you, too?"

"Oh, yes. Knocking and table rocking and floating spirits. Parlor tricks, all of it."

"But not Madame Serafina," Frank said.

"No, she didn't stoop to using any of those things."

Frank wasn't going to argue with the man. "And I guess she couldn't do any tricks with people holding her hands like that during the séance."

"Oh, she could have if she'd wanted to," Sharpe said knowingly. "They all make their clients hold each other's wrists, but it's easy enough to get a hand free in the dark."

So Sharpe did know that trick. "But you don't think Madame Serafina did that?"

"I can't think why she would have to," Sharpe said confidently.

"Madame Serafina told me you wanted her to leave Mrs. Gittings so you could keep her," Frank said, catching him off guard.

He'd deliberately made it sound disreputable, and Sharpe instantly took offense. His face flooded with color. "Watch your tongue," he ordered Frank. "Madame Serafina is a respectable young woman, and I had no intention of 'keeping' her, as you so crudely put it. I wanted to provide an establishment for her so she could use her talents without having to worry about supporting herself."

"What's wrong with supporting herself?" Frank asked innocently.

Plainly, Sharpe thought it was very wrong. "She was . . .

That woman was taking advantage of her, turning her talent into a carnival sideshow."

Frank supposed that Sharpe had no idea Serafina used to tell fortunes on street corners, which was probably a step or two below carnival sideshows. "What did Mrs. Gittings say when you told her you wanted to take Madame Serafina away?"

Sharpe's eyes narrowed in remembered fury. "She wouldn't believe that I was only interested in Madame Serafina's spiritual talents. She thought . . . Well, she thought I wanted her for immoral purposes, and she said some very rude things."

"Was she willing to let the girl go for a price?" Frank asked, remembering what the Gittings woman had offered Cunningham.

"Absolutely not. She was getting rich from the business, and she wasn't going to let Madame Serafina go."

Frank nodded. Sharpe could probably easily afford to meet the price she'd quoted Cunningham, and he wouldn't have fallen for some phony investment scheme. No, he would be far more dangerous, so she'd have to refuse him outright. "Didn't you try to convince Madame Serafina to leave her anyway?"

"Of course I did, but she wouldn't hear of it. She said she owed everything to Mrs. Gittings, and she couldn't leave her."

"That's touching," Frank observed, earning a glare from Sharpe.

"Touching or not, she refused my offer, and nothing I said could convince her."

"You were sitting right next to Mrs. Gittings at the séance, weren't you?"

Instantly, Sharpe was back on guard again. "I already told you that."

"Did you notice anything strange during the séance?"

"Do you mean did I know someone stabbed her to death?" he replied sarcastically. "No, I did not."

"She didn't cry out or jerk or squeeze your arm or—"

"No, I told you. I didn't notice anything until she let go of my wrist and fell to the floor."

"And you're sure nobody else was in the room besides the people at the table?"

"No," Sharpe said, annoyed again. "I told you, no one else was there."

"Then how do you think the boy killed her, if he wasn't in the room?" Frank asked with a puzzled frown.

Sharpe gaped at him in surprise. "I . . . The Professor said . . . I suppose he must have gotten in somehow," he tried.

"How?" Frank asked, genuinely curious. "Was it a parlor trick, do you think?"

"No, of course not," Sharpe said impatiently.

"Then how did he do it? Everybody said no one was in the room when they got there, and no one could come in by the door without everyone seeing him. So how did he get in to kill her? You see, that's the first thing they'll ask at his trial, and I have to have an answer."

Sharpe rubbed his forehead as if it ached. "I don't . . . He must have been hiding somewhere."

"Where?" Frank asked with interest.

"I . . . In the cabinet," he finally remembered. "He could have been hiding in there."

"Didn't you check it when you came into the room?" Frank asked.

"No, why should I?" Sharpe asked, defensive now. "I told you, Madame Serafina never used cheap parlor tricks."

"Is that what the cabinet is for, parlor tricks?"

"I have no idea," he insisted.

"Why was it there, then?"

Sharpe sighed in exasperation. "Some spiritualists use them. They climb inside and ask someone to tie them up. Then when the so-called spirits appear, everyone thinks they must be real because the spiritualist is tied up inside the cabinet."

"Are you saying this is some kind of trick?"

"Naturally it's a trick. The spiritualist knows how to hold her hands in such a way that even the tightest knots will fall off when she relaxes them. Then she is free to move around the room in the dark during the séance and pretend to be a spirit. Sometimes they even pretend to materialize and let everyone see them. And when the séance is over, they find the spiritualist still securely tied up in the cabinet because she's slipped the ropes back on."

Frank nodded, impressed. "But Madame Serafina never did that," he guessed.

"No, I told you, she didn't have to use tricks."

"What if I told you the police checked the cabinet after the séance, and it was empty?"

"I'd say the boy had sneaked out while we were all in the parlor."

Frank nodded sagely. "Do you think any of the other people at the séance could have killed Mrs. Gittings?"

He found this suggestion absurd. "What on earth for?"

"Some people didn't like her," Frank confided. "Even you didn't like her."

"I detested her, but that's not reason enough to kill her."

"She was keeping Madame Serafina a prisoner," Frank reminded him. "She was using her like a pimp."

Sharp stiffened in outrage. "How dare you!"

"But it's true, isn't it? She was selling the girl's talents and keeping the money. You just wanted to get her away from all that."

"Any honorable man would have done the same thing!"

"Of course he would," Frank agreed. "But the girl wouldn't leave, would she? That must have made you angry."

"I was furious, but there was nothing I could do short of kidnapping her!"

"You could have killed Mrs. Gittings," Franks suggested.

For a moment, Sharpe just stared at him in stunned silence, until the fact that Frank had just accused him of murder finally sank in. Then he lunged to his feet, his face nearly purple with rage. "Get out of here!" he bellowed. "Get out of here right now!"

Frank rose, betraying not the slightest hint of anxiety. He tucked his notebook and pencil back into his coat pocket and started for the door. He stopped when he reached it and turned back. "Should I tell Madame Serafina that you asked about her?"

He watched the emotions play across the other man's face. His concern for the girl finally won out, and he reined in his outrage with difficulty. "When will she be returning to Waverly Place?"

"I don't know," Frank said quite truthfully. "But I can ask her to send you word when she does."

Sharpe looked as if he were swallowing broken glass, but he said, "Thank you."

Frank managed not to smile. At least Sharpe wouldn't be storming down to Police Headquarters and demanding his head. Not yet, anyway.

SARAH DIDN'T LIKE LEAVING SERAFINA ALONE WITH JUST Maeve and Catherine to watch her. She might very well decide to sneak off and find Nicola and disappear forever. But as Maeve had pointed out to her when they'd discussed it in

treat, decorated with delicately carved furniture in the French style with pink and white wallpaper and draperies. The draperies were still closed, casting the room in shadow. Mrs. Burke reclined on a chaise longue, her legs covered with a light throw. She wore a frilly pink robe with rows of ruffles at the wrist and throat.

"Elizabeth," she greeted Mrs. Decker, holding out a limp hand. "How good of you to come." Then she noticed Sarah and stiffened in surprise. "Who's that with you?"

"My daughter, Sarah," Mrs. Decker said, taking Mrs. Burke's outstretched hand in both of hers. "She was just as anxious as I to see how you were doing after that horrible shock."

Mrs. Burke glanced over to make sure the maid was gone and the door securely shut. "I told Harry that I fell on the sidewalk while I was shopping," she confessed. "I had to tell him something when he saw how upset I was."

"You did absolutely the right thing," Mrs. Decker assured her.

Sarah had pulled up a slipper chair for her mother so she could sit right beside Mrs. Burke and continue to hold her hand. When she had Mrs. Decker settled, she claimed the dressing table stool for herself and positioned it at a discreet distance, so she could participate in the conversation if she needed to but not be intrusive.

"How are you holding up?" Mrs. Decker was asking her friend.

"I haven't slept more than two hours together since it happened," Mrs. Burke assured her. "Every time I close my eyes, I'm back in that room again, holding that woman's hand." She gave a dramatic little shiver of revulsion.

"I know, I know," Mrs. Decker soothed. "I'm sure I'll have nightmares for the rest of my life."

"Has that policeman figured out what happened yet?" Mrs. Burke asked.

"Not yet," Mrs. Decker said sadly. "Everything was so confusing. I haven't been able to make sense of it myself. What do you remember, Kathy?"

"Oh, dear," she said with another shudder. "I haven't even allowed myself to think about it."

"Perhaps we should, though," Mrs. Decker said. "If we could figure out what happened, perhaps we could help the police find the killer and put an end to all of this."

"The killer," Mrs. Burke echoed tremulously. "Oh, dear, oh, dear."

"What is it?" Mrs. Decker asked.

"I just . . . It's all so dreadful. I just can't think about it."

"There, there, you're just overwrought and allowing your imagination to run away with you. You can't continue to sit all alone in this dark room. You'll make yourself truly sick. Sometimes the best thing to do in situations like this is to talk it all out in the light of day."

"I can't," Mrs. Burke insisted faintly.

"Of course you can. I'll help you," Mrs. Decker said bracingly. "Tell me everything you remember from that day."

Mrs. Burke closed her eyes. She really did look ill. "I can't . . ."

"Start with when you arrived at the house," Mrs. Decker suggested. "I was already there. You looked a bit distressed, if I recall."

Mrs. Burke looked a bit distressed now, too, but she was helpless to resist her old friend's iron will. "I was afraid I was late."

"But Mr. Cunningham was even later, as usual."

"That young man has no manners," Mrs. Burke declared.

"No, he doesn't. Mr. Sharpe greeted you, I believe. Mrs.

Gittings was sitting in the corner, as usual, not saying much. She was there when I arrived, but of course she lived there, so naturally she would be the first to arrive. I didn't know that then, though. Did you?"

"Oh, yes," Mrs. Burke said, then caught herself. "I mean . . ."

"You knew that Mrs. Gittings was Madame Serafina's manager, didn't you?" Mrs. Decker said, keeping any disapproval from her voice. "But then you'd been visiting her much longer than I had. However did you keep Harry from finding out you were visiting a spiritualist? I've been terrified Felix would find out. I'm sure he would forbid me to go, if he knew."

"Harry did find out," Mrs. Burke confessed in dismay. "He was so angry. That's why I couldn't tell him what really happened. If he knew I was still visiting Madame Serafina . . ." She closed her eyes again, this time to ward off tears.

"You poor thing. But you were very brave to keep going to see her in spite of Harry's disapproval. I'm not sure I would have your courage."

"It wasn't courage," Mrs. Burke assured her. "I simply had to keep going. I can't tell you how wonderful it was to know that no matter what I asked, the spirits would know the answer. I had no choice."

Mrs. Decker nodded as if she understood perfectly.

"You were talking about when you first arrived for the séance," Sarah reminded them gently.

"Oh, yes," Mrs. Decker said. "And what were we chatting about while we waited for Mr. Cunningham to arrive?"

"I don't recall . . ." Mrs. Burke hedged.

Mrs. Decker frowned, trying to remember. "You were very quiet, now that I think of it. Apprehensive, almost. Were you worried about something, my dear?"

"Oh, no, not at all," Mrs. Burke lied. She lied badly.

"Perhaps you were worried about what your mother would say to you in the séance," Sarah suggested.

"No, no," Mrs. Burke insisted.

"Or perhaps you were worrying about Harry finding out you were still seeing Madame Serafina," Mrs. Decker guessed. "I'm sure that was a concern. And it must have been difficult to hide the expense of it in your household expenditures week after week."

Mrs. Burke's eyes were enormous and the blood had drained from her face. "Oh, Elizabeth, it was horrible! When he found out, he forbade me to see her again, and then he . . . he cut off my allowance!"

"How awful!" Mrs. Decker cried. "You poor dear. But how did you continue if you couldn't pay for the sittings?"

"I . . . I sold some of my jewelry," she confessed. "Not the good pieces," she hastened to explain. "I couldn't, in case Harry noticed, but I had some old pieces that belonged to my family that I never wore."

"How did you sell them without Harry knowing?" Mrs. Decker asked.

"I . . . I couldn't, of course. I wouldn't have any idea how to do it! So I gave them to Mrs. Gittings, and she . . . But she said they didn't bring much. I thought she was cheating me. In fact, I'm sure of it, but I couldn't accuse her, could I? She would have forbidden me to come back!"

Sarah was remembering the séance she'd attended, when the spirit told her it was all right to do something with a gift her mother had given her. Perhaps that was a piece of jewelry she'd been reluctant to sell, and Madame was under orders from Mrs. Gittings to encourage her to turn it over.

Mrs. Decker was making soothing noises, calming her friend and sympathizing.

"You don't know what I suffered, Elizabeth," Mrs. Burke said tearfully. "That woman was horrible, just horrible. The things she said to me, to torture me, you wouldn't believe. She deserved to die!"

12

Frank was right about Cunningham not being an early riser. When he called at his house, the maid told him he would have to come back later in the day. He had to tell her it was official police business and frighten her a bit before she would let him inside to wait. When she returned to fetch him from where he stood cooling his heels in the entryway, she even looked a little pale.

"This way, please," she said. She didn't call him "sir." Servants knew instinctively that he wasn't any better than they were and didn't deserve to be called "sir."

But when he was shown into a comfortable room at the back of the house that was obviously the room the family used for private times together, he found not Cunningham but a small, older lady, who was eyeing him with suspicion.

"And what do you want with my son, young man?" she demanded the moment he entered. She stood in the center of the room, ramrod straight, her hands clasped in front of her, and glaring at him with a disdain that only rich people could master. She was thickening around the waist and her fair hair was beginning to show some silver threads, but her face was as smooth as satin. She'd probably never had a worry or a care to mar it.

"It's a private matter, Mrs. Cunningham," he tried.

"My son has no secrets from me," she insisted. "I demand to know what business the police could possibly have with him."

Frank figured young Cunningham had lots of secrets from his dear mother, and he wasn't about to tell her the truth about this one. He said, "I'm afraid a friend of your son's has gotten himself into trouble, and Mr. Cunningham might be required to give evidence against him."

"He would do no such thing," Mrs. Cunningham informed him. "My son is an honorable man."

"You don't know what his friend did," Frank tried. "Maybe his honor would force him to condemn his friend."

This surprised her, and before she could think of an answer, Mr. Cunningham himself bustled into the room. He'd obviously dressed in a hurry and hadn't had time to shave or even comb his hair. He was still straightening his jacket. He glanced back and forth between Frank and his mother in alarm, trying to judge the mood before speaking.

"Good morning, Mr. Cunningham," Frank said to reassure him. "I'm sorry to bother you, but I need to ask you some more questions about the incident we discussed the other day. I was just telling your mother that—"

"That one of your friends has gotten himself into trouble, and you are going to assist the police in persecuting him," his mother informed him in outrage.

Cunningham gave Frank a look of amazement and hurried to reassure his mother. "I don't know what he told you, but that's not it at all, Mother. It's not that he *caused* trouble but that some rascal is causing trouble *for* him. Calling in the police seemed like the only way to put an end to it."

"I can't imagine anything that would warrant the police at all!" she scolded.

"That's because you are far too gentle to understand the wicked ways of the world, Mother," he said with a charming smile that Frank figured had been getting him out of trouble his entire life.

"If your father were alive, he would never have allowed a policeman in the house," she said, giving Frank a look that could have cut glass.

"Then please leave us alone so we can finish our business and he can be on his way as quickly as possible, Mother," he suggested, turning the full force of his charm on her.

She had probably never refused him anything, and she could not start now. He was already moving her toward the door. "I'll want to know exactly what you talked about," she warned him before sweeping out of the room. Cunningham watched after her to make sure she was well and truly gone and then closed the door securely behind her.

When he turned back to Frank, his charming smile had vanished. "What in God's name are you doing here?" he demanded savagely.

"I need to ask you a few more questions about what happened the other day."

"The Professor told me that some Italian boy had killed that woman," he said. Obviously, he had also paid a visit to Waverly Place in hopes of finding Madame Serafina at home and no longer under the protection of Mrs. Gittings. "Why aren't you out looking for him?"

"We *are* looking for him," Frank said, biting back his own impatience. "In the meantime, I'm trying to get enough information to prove he did it so when we bring him to trial, none of you will have to testify."

Cunningham's eyes grew wide. Plainly, he hadn't considered this possibility. "I can't help you. I didn't see anything at all," he protested.

"Maybe not, but I still have a few questions to ask," Frank said, pulling out his notebook again. "Maybe that will help you remember what happened."

"I remember exactly what happened," Cunningham insisted. "And now I'd like to start forgetting all of it!"

Frank ignored his outburst. "Did you see anyone in the séance room except the people around the table?"

"Of course not. That would have been . . ." He gestured vaguely. "Unacceptable," he finally decided. "Why should anyone else be in there?"

"Did you look in the cabinet?"

"The cabinet? Why should we look in there?"

"To make sure no one was hiding in it," Frank suggested. "Someone who could pretend to be a spirit or something."

He frowned and ran a hand through his rumpled hair. "I didn't look inside it," he said. "I don't know if anyone else did, but I never saw anyone open it in all the time I've been going to Madame's séances."

Frank found that odd, but he didn't comment. "I understand that everyone was holding hands around the table."

"We were holding each other's wrists. I told you that already."

"Which means nobody sitting at the table could have stabbed Mrs. Gittings."

"Nobody sitting at the table would have *wanted* to stab her," he said with frown. "Besides, that Italian boy did it, so why are you asking me all these questions about the people in the room?"

"Because some of the people sitting at the table *did* want to kill her," Frank said baldly.

Cunningham's eyes widened, and then he winced. "I . . . Can we sit down? I have the devil of a hangover, and I'm having trouble following this."

Frank obligingly took a seat on one of the chairs by the fireplace that Cunningham indicated. He sat down on the other and rubbed his temples a moment before looking at Frank again.

"Did you say some of the people at the séance wanted to kill Mrs. Gittings?" he asked.

"Yes, I did," Frank confirmed. "And from what I've been told, you are one of them."

"Me!" he almost squeaked. "I don't know what you're talking about!"

"I'm talking about how you wanted to take Madame Serafina as your mistress."

Cunningham visibly paled. "That's . . . not true," he tried, his voice a croak.

"But she wouldn't leave Mrs. Gittings," Frank continued as if he hadn't heard the denial. "She was loyal because Mrs. Gittings had done so much to help her, but Mrs. Gittings wasn't very loyal in return, was she?' Frank asked. "She offered to sell the girl to you, didn't she?"

"Absolutely not!" Cunningham tried, but not very convincingly.

"How much did she want for her?" Frank asked with interest.

"A gentleman never discusses——" he tried, but Frank interrupted his feeble outrage.

"More than your allowance would cover, I'd guess," Frank

continued relentlessly. "And I already know you won't get your full inheritance until you're twenty-five. Where were you going to get the money, Cunningham?"

While Cunningham sputtered incoherently, Frank pretended to consult his notes.

"Oh, that's right," he recalled. "You were going to make some investments. That's what you were asking your father about at the séances, wasn't it?"

"Who told you that?" Cunningham demanded.

"Just about everybody," Frank lied. "They all heard the questions you asked your father."

"I forbid you to discuss my father," Cunningham tried.

"All right," Frank said obligingly. "Let's talk about those investments. I understand they weren't very successful."

"That's none of your business!"

"But they weren't, were they? And I understand you lost a lot of money. Not what your father would have wanted for you, I'm sure. Do you really think your father would have given you such bad advice?" Frank asked.

The question surprised Cunningham. He stared at Frank in almost comic amazement. "I . . . I never thought of that."

"Well, think about it. What do you know about these men you invested with?"

Cunningham blinked. "I . . . Nothing, really."

"How did you meet them?"

"They . . . they approached me one evening at . . . at a gentlemen's club."

Frank figured the men at this club rarely acted like gentlemen. "Why did you trust them?"

He was rubbing his temples again. "Because my father had told me . . . I mean, his spirit had told me I would meet someone who would offer me an opportunity. Then the next night, I met them. It seemed . . . It seemed like fate!"

Frank nodded sagely. "Let me guess, they told you about this business opportunity, and you offered to invest, but they refused to take your money."

Cunningham was gaping at him again. "Yes, that's exactly what happened! How did you know? I couldn't believe it! I had to practically beg them to let me invest. They said they didn't think it was right to take my money in such a risky venture, but I knew it wasn't a risk at all."

"Except it was."

"What?" he asked stupidly.

"It *was* a risk, because you lost all your money."

Cunningham still seemed confused by this. "But I did exactly what my father had told me to do. It shouldn't have worked out like that."

"Have you ever seen these men again?"

"No, I haven't," he said in renewed surprise. "Not since they told me the venture failed. I suppose they were embarrassed."

Frank let that pass. "So there you were, still wanting the girl—"

"She's not just a *girl*," Cunningham protested. "Stop calling her that!"

"Madame Serafina then," Frank conceded. "You still wanted her, but you'd lost all your money, and your mother wouldn't give you any more, and you couldn't hope to be able to pay Mrs. Gittings what she wanted. What were you going to do?"

"I . . . I don't know."

"Yes, you do," Frank insisted. "What were you going to do?"

Cunningham was starting to look a little sick. "I . . . I needed to speak with my father again, to find out what went wrong. I needed his advice."

"Did he give you advice when he was alive?" Frank asked with interest.

This time, Cunningham's face grew brick red. "He never had time," he admitted reluctantly.

Frank nodded. The boy had been ignored by his father and indulged by his mother. No wonder he was worthless. Six months after he came into his inheritance, the money would be gone.

Frank pretended to consider what he had been told. "So you had lost the money you invested, and you couldn't pay Mrs. Gittings to let Madame Serafina go. What were you going to do?"

"I *told* you, I was going to ask my father!" he cried.

"But if Mrs. Gittings was dead, you wouldn't need any money at all," Frank pointed out.

"That's ridiculous!"

"But it's true, isn't it? She wasn't a very nice woman," Frank reminded him. "Everyone said so."

"I'm sure *I* never heard anyone say so," Cunningham said righteously.

"But it was true. Did you know those men you invested with were working for her?"

He stiffened, and for an instant Frank wasn't sure if he was surprised or just surprised Frank knew. "Why do you say that?" he asked.

"Because it's true. She was operating a fake séance, so why wouldn't she try to cheat people out of money in other ways?"

"Madame Serafina isn't a fake!" he insisted.

"You're sure of that?"

"Of course I am! You don't know what you're talking about."

"Do you have a lot of experience with spiritualism?"

"Well, yes, a bit," he admitted.

"You've visited other spiritualists?"

"A few."

"But they couldn't help you?"

"They . . . Madame Serafina was different," he decided. "She knows what's inside of you. She knows what you're thinking."

"Did she know you were thinking of taking her as your mistress?"

Cunningham jumped to his feet. "How dare you!"

"I'm just trying to figure out what happened," Frank said in apology. "Maybe she was insulted that you thought she would sell herself. Maybe she told you what Mrs. Gittings wanted you to hear so you'd lose all your money."

"She'd never do that!"

"Are you sure?" Frank asked. "I've seen women do some pretty nasty things to men who insulted them."

"I didn't insult her! I would have married her if I could!"

"But your mother would never let you marry a girl like that, would she?"

Cunningham sank back down into his chair in defeat. "No, she wouldn't."

Frank let him consider his miserable situation for a few moments, and then he said, "Professor Rogers thinks that this Italian boy who worked at the house killed Mrs. Gittings."

Cunningham scowled at him. "Then why are you here, bothering me?"

"Because I can't prove it. Everybody says he wasn't in the room and couldn't have gotten in without somebody seeing him."

"He couldn't have gotten in without *everybody* seeing him," Cunningham corrected him. "But what about that cabinet?

Couldn't he have been hiding in there and come out when the lights were out?"

Frank didn't answer. "Everyone was holding hands around the table, weren't they?"

Cunningham needed a few seconds to comprehend the sudden change of topic. "Yes, I already told you that," he replied, suddenly wary.

"And if everybody was holding somebody's hands, then none of them could have stabbed Mrs. Gittings."

Cunningham waited, still not sure what Frank was getting at.

"But isn't there a way that somebody could get one of his hands free?"

"What do you mean?" The color had faded from his face again.

"I mean there's a trick that some spiritualists use. They get up to turn out the lights, for instance, and when they sit back down, they keep one hand free."

"I don't know anything about that," he lied.

"Yes, you do," Frank said. "Madame Serafina told me you do."

His eyes widened again. "Why would she tell you that?"

"Because she wants me to think you killed Mrs. Gittings."

"No, she doesn't!" he cried. "I don't believe it!"

"You don't?" Frank asked with interest. "Then why did she also tell me that you could have managed to keep *both* your hands free that day so you could get up out of your chair and walk around to where Mrs. Gittings was sitting and stick a knife into her."

"That's impossible!" he nearly shouted, lunging to his feet. Instantly, he grabbed his head and sank back down into the chair, clutching it. Frank truly enjoyed questioning someone with a hangover. He hardly had to exert himself at all.

"What's impossible? That you did it or that she told me about it?"

"All of it," he mumbled, wincing with pain. "Why would she say a thing like that?"

"I don't know," Frank said, pretending to try to figure it out. "Maybe she's mad at you for something."

"Why would she be mad at me?" he asked, looking up.

"I'm going to guess it has something to do with the mistress business."

"But she wouldn't do that," he protested. "She's . . . she's . . ."

"What?" Frank asked, truly interested in the answer.

"She's not like other women! She doesn't care about money. She doesn't even know how beautiful she is!"

Frank doubted that, but he didn't say so. "Tell me everything that happened that day at the séance. Start at the beginning."

"Why?" he asked, looking totally miserable.

"Because I need to know if this Italian boy could have done it. When did you arrive?"

He looked as if he could have cheerfully strangled Frank, but he said, "I don't know what time it was. Everyone was already there when I arrived."

"Who opened the door for you?"

"The Professor. He always does."

"Then what happened?"

Cunningham glared at him for a long moment, and Frank couldn't tell if he was just annoyed or if he couldn't remember. Finally, he said. "I went into the parlor, where everyone was waiting."

"Did you talk to anybody?"

"Yes . . . I think so. I'm sure I said hello to everyone, at least."

"Who came to take all of you into the séance room?"

"Madame came. She always does."

"Was she alone?"

"What do you mean? Of course she was alone."

"Didn't the Professor usually come with her?"

"I don't know. I never paid any attention."

Frank nodded, making a note of that. "Then what happened?"

"We went into the séance room and sat down."

"How do you decide where to sit at the table?"

"Madame tells us."

This was something new. Frank managed not to let his interest show. "So you never knew where you'd be sitting?"

"No, we sat in different places, depending on what Madame was sensing about us on that day."

Which meant that the killer couldn't have known he or she would be sitting in a convenient place to stab Mrs. Gittings.

But Madame Serafina could place a killer next to her if she wanted to.

"What happened after you all sat down?"

"Madame talked to us. She said she sensed great unease, lots of anger."

"Does she usually talk to you like that before she starts?"

"Yes."

"Then what did she do?"

"She told us to hold hands, then she got up and turned out the light and closed the door."

"What were you doing while she did this?"

He looked startled by the question. "Nothing. I was just sitting there."

"That's not what Mrs. Decker said."

Cunningham looked confused. "What did she say?"

"She said you started coughing and then you let go of her hand. She said you didn't take hold of it again until the room was dark and Madame Serafina had returned to the table."

"I don't remember," he lied. "But if she said so, I guess it must be true."

"Why were you coughing?" Frank asked.

"What do you mean?" he asked indignantly. "How should I know why I was coughing?"

"Do you cough a lot? I haven't heard you cough since I've been here."

"No, I don't cough a lot. What does it matter if I coughed or not?"

"It matters because you let go of Mrs. Decker's hand, or rather, you made her let go of your wrist until the lights were out and she couldn't see whose wrist she was holding."

"What are you trying to say?" Cunningham demanded.

"I'm trying to say that you could have put your hands in your lap after the room was dark and let Mrs. Decker take Madame Serafina's wrist, thinking it was yours. Then you could have waited until everyone was busy trying to talk to the spirits and gotten out of your chair and stabbed Mrs. Gittings with no one the wiser."

"That's ridiculous!" he cried, outraged. "Why would I want to kill her?"

"Because if she was dead, you wouldn't have to pay her any money to get Madame Serafina to become your mistress."

He exploded out of his chair again, but that was a mistake. He sank back down, clutching it with both hands again. "Damn you!" he whispered savagely. "I didn't kill that bitch!"

Frank let that pass. "When did you first realize something was wrong with Mrs. Gittings?"

He glared at Frank through narrowed eyes, suspicious again. "When Mrs. Burke started screaming."

"You were the first one to notice she'd been stabbed, weren't you?"

"I don't know. Everything happened so fast. I just remember seeing the knife handle sticking out of her back."

"Did you notice anyone else in the room except the people sitting around the table?"

"Anyone else? You mean another person?"

"Yes, another person."

"No, of course not," he snapped.

"What about the Professor? Didn't he come in when Madame Serafina called him?"

He frowned, trying to remember. "I guess so. He was by the door when we all started out."

"And you never saw the Italian boy?"

"I've never seen an Italian boy at the house at all," he said crossly. "Where did he come from?"

"He's a friend of Madame Serafina's," Frank said with just a slight emphasis on *friend*.

"What does that mean?"

"That means that they've known each other for a long time."

"Then he must be the one who killed Mrs. Gittings." He seemed relieved by the thought.

"That's what the Professor thinks."

"He should know, then. All *I* know is that no one at the séance could have done it."

The door opened suddenly, and Mrs. Cunningham bustled in. "What is going on in here? I can't imagine what could be taking so long."

"Nothing, Mother. Mr. Malloy is finished," he added with a note of triumph. Frank wouldn't dare browbeat him anymore in front of his mother.

Frank rose to his feet. "Thank you for your help, Mr. Cunningham," he said politely and gave Mrs. Cunningham a slight nod.

"What will happen now?" Cunningham asked quickly, then glanced apprehensively at his mother. Plainly, he didn't want Frank to say anything about Serafina in front of her.

"I'll keep looking for this Italian boy," Frank said. "If I need your help again, I'll let you know."

"What about . . . ?" He glanced at his mother again. "About that young lady you mentioned? Will she be all right?"

"I'm sure she will be," Frank said, taking perverse pleasure in torturing Cunningham.

"If she needs anything, you'll let me know, won't you?" This time he didn't look at his mother.

"Of course," Frank said.

"The girl will see you out," Mrs. Cunningham said, putting an end to their cryptic conversation.

The maid was waiting for him at the door, and she ushered him to the front door. As he left the room, he could hear Mrs. Cunningham saying, "I hope this young lady you spoke of isn't taking advantage of you."

Frank smiled to himself as the maid escorted him out onto the front stoop, closing the door behind him with an air of finality.

Alone again, Frank shook his head. The more he found out, the more it looked like Nicola was the only one who really could have killed Mrs. Gittings. He hoped Sarah was having better luck today than he was.

S ARAH AND HER MOTHER STARED AT MRS. BURKE IN stunned silence for a moment before Mrs. Burke recalled herself. "Oh, I didn't mean that, not really," she stammered. "I mean . . . no one really deserves to die. Well, perhaps some people do, but surely not Mrs. Gittings."

"I know you didn't mean that, dear," Mrs. Decker said, after a glance to see if Sarah was as shocked as she. "But I never would have dreamed she was such a terrible person. She seemed . . . I don't know, nondescript at best."

"You didn't know her as I did," Mrs. Burke said, pursing her lips in distaste.

"Obviously not. But now I understand why you seemed so anxious that day."

"Mrs. Burke, had Mrs. Gittings threatened you?" Sarah asked.

She looked up in surprise. She'd probably forgotten Sarah was there. "Threatened me? What do you mean?"

"Had she threatened to tell Mr. Burke about your visits to Madame Serafina? Or maybe she threatened that if you didn't give her more money, she wouldn't let you come back to see Madame Serafina again."

"She did both of those things," Mrs. Burke said in despair. "I was at my wit's end!"

"And then Madame Serafina told you to sell the diamond brooch your mother had given you," Sarah tried.

Mrs. Burke's eyes widened. "No, no, she did no such thing!"

"But I heard her, at the séance I attended," Sarah insisted.

"Not Madame Serafina," Mrs. Burke protested. "She didn't

tell me to do anything. It was the spirits! They told me to sell it, but I couldn't! It was all I had left to remember my mother."

"But wasn't it your mother's spirit who told you to sell it?" Mrs. Decker recalled.

"I know, but I still couldn't bear to do it, and there was nothing left that Harry wouldn't have noticed was missing. I didn't know what to do." She began to weep softly into her handkerchief.

"Mrs. Burke," Sarah said sharply.

Mrs. Burke's head snapped up, her moist eyes wide again and full of apprehension. "Yes?"

"That day when Mrs. Gittings died, when did you notice something was wrong with her?"

"Oh, dear," she said with a delicate shudder. "I shall never forget feeling her falling against me. I dream about it and wake up screaming—"

"Did you notice anything unusual *before* that?" Sarah said, jerking her attention back. "Did she make any sound? Or maybe she squeezed your hand or something."

"I was holding her wrist, so she couldn't have squeezed my hand," she reminded them both. "I think I felt her arm jerk a bit at one point, but I can't be sure. People do move around during the séances, you know, even when nothing terrible is happening to them."

"Yes, of course," Mrs. Decker agreed, nodding encouragingly. "But she didn't make any noises?"

"None that I noticed. I was listening to what Yellow Feather was saying, though, so I might not have heard." She seemed to have recovered from her fit of weeping.

"Did you sense anyone moving around in the room?" Sarah asked. "Maybe you thought it was a spirit."

"I don't know," she said with a worried frown. "Everyone

was talking at once, and with that horrible screeching noise, I couldn't understand anything."

Ah, yes, Nicola's violin. "Mother, did you sense anyone moving around in the room?" Sarah suddenly thought to ask.

Mrs. Decker thought for a moment. "I'm really not sure. If someone was very quiet, I don't think anyone would have noticed them, with all that was going on."

"But who could have been moving around?" Mrs. Burke asked plaintively.

"The person who killed Mrs. Gittings," Mrs. Decker said.

Mrs. Burke's eyes widened again, and the little color left in her face drained away. "Oh, dear."

"Of course, we don't *know* that anyone was walking around," Mrs. Decker hastened to explain. "But the Professor seems to think the killer was a boy who worked at the house."

"He does?" Mrs. Burke asked, perking up a bit. "Why does he think that?"

"Because they had an argument the night before, and Mrs. Gittings tried to fire him."

"She was a terrible woman," Mrs. Burke reminded them. "But if they had an argument, why didn't she fire him?"

"Madame Serafina threatened to leave with him," Sarah said.

"Why would she do that?"

"They were childhood friends," Mrs. Decker quickly explained, giving Sarah a warning glance. It wouldn't do to create doubts about Madame Serafina's character.

"She'd had an argument with the Professor, too," Mrs. Burke said.

Sarah and her mother looked at her in surprise. "Madame Serafina had a fight with the Professor?" Sarah asked.

"Oh, no," Mrs. Burke hastened to explain. "At least, not that I know of. I meant Mrs. Gittings had an argument with him."

"How do you know that?" Mrs. Decker asked.

"Couldn't you tell?" Mrs. Burke asked. "From the way they acted that day? Well, perhaps it wasn't an argument, but they were both very angry. The look she gave him when he escorted me into the parlor that day could have burned a hole through him, and he returned it in kind."

"Oh, dear, I'm afraid I didn't notice a thing," Mrs. Decker said in dismay.

"There's no reason you should have," Mrs. Burke assured her. "But I was the first to arrive that day, and of course I was anxious about seeing Mrs. Gittings. I didn't know what terrible thing she might say to me about the money."

"I wonder if Madame Serafina knows what they argued about?" Sarah asked her mother.

"She did say they had disagreed about something," Mrs. Decker recalled.

"When did you speak to Madame Serafina?" Mrs. Burke asked with interest.

Mrs. Decker smiled. "She's staying with Sarah until the killer is caught."

"How wonderful!" Mrs. Burke exclaimed. "Perhaps she could do a sitting for me. I've been afraid to go back to the house on Waverly and—"

"Of course, if everyone was holding hands around the table," Sarah said quickly, diverting her from this disturbing plan, "then no one could have gotten up without someone else knowing it."

"Which proves that the killer had to be someone else," Mrs. Decker added.

"Unless . . ." Sarah mused.

"Unless what?" Mrs. Burke asked apprehensively, clutching her handkerchief to her breast.

"Unless the killer was sitting right beside her."

Mrs. Burke stared at her for a long moment before giving a small cry and fainting dead away.

13

"Do you think she really fainted?" Sarah asked her mother when they were alone in the carriage and heading back to Sarah's house. After calling for Mrs. Burke's maid to attend her, they'd felt obligated to leave rather than upset their reluctant hostess further.

"It's so difficult to really tell," Mrs. Decker said with a sigh. "Properly bred young ladies cultivate the art of fainting from childhood just in case the need ever arises. One can never be certain of actually being able to faint at the precise moment it would be most advantageous, so learning how to pretend is essential."

"I wouldn't know," Sarah said with disapproval. "I've never fainted in my life."

"Exactly," her mother said. "Most people never do, not really. But when you want to escape a difficult situation, nothing drives tormentors away more quickly than a well-timed swoon."

"As we just proved," Sarah sighed. "Would a cold-blooded killer swoon, do you think?"

"I have no idea," Mrs. Decker said. "But she might very well pretend to, if someone was questioning her about it."

"So we're back where we started. I hope Malloy has had more luck than we have today. So far, all we've learned is that Mrs. Burke is very upset by Mrs. Gittings's murder and that talking about it makes her faint, or at least pretend to."

"We also learned that Mrs. Gittings and the Professor were angry with each other the day she died," Mrs. Decker reminded her.

"That's very interesting but hardly helpful. He's the one person we know couldn't have been in that room."

"But if Nicola could have come in through the cabinet, why couldn't the Professor have done the same thing?"

"Because Nicola would have encountered him, either in the cabinet or in the space behind it. Besides, the Professor is a large man. I can't imagine him getting through the false door in the back of the cabinet at all, and certainly not without Nicola knowing about it."

"I suppose you're right," Mrs. Decker allowed. "So the argument between him and Mrs. Gittings is meaningless."

"Probably," Sarah agreed. "But I don't think we can rule out the possibility that Mrs. Burke is the killer. She did act strangely today."

"Yes, she did. I don't suppose I can blame her for detesting Mrs. Gittings. In her place, I'm sure I would have felt the same."

"I hope you wouldn't have murdered her, though," Sarah said with a small smile.

"I hope so, too," Mrs. Decker said, completely serious. "Of course, I've never been in such a desperate situation."

"What would you have done if Serafina had started giving you messages from Maggie?" Sarah asked, matching her mother's somber mood.

Her mother looked sharply at Sarah, trying to judge if there was any underlying meaning to the question. "Do you mean would I have been willing to sell my jewelry in order to keep coming back to see her?"

"Yes, since you put it that way. I can't imagine Father cutting off your funds, but he might very well forbid you to go to another séance. That would force you at least to lie in order to conceal your actions from him. Would you do that?"

Mrs. Decker gave her daughter a pitying glance. "I've often told your father what he wanted to hear instead of the truth, which he would not have found so pleasant."

"I'm sure you have, but have you actually lied to him? Outright lied by telling him you would be in one place when you were, in fact, in another?"

Her mother had to give this some thought. "I don't think so, not outright lied. But if I were desperate . . ."

"Then you think you could do it?"

"If I thought it was important enough," Mrs. Decker admitted.

"Would hearing messages from Maggie have been important enough?"

Her mother considered the question for a long moment. "If I truly believed they were from her, then yes, I would have lied without a trace of guilt."

"Would you have killed?" Sarah pressed her.

Her mother shook her head in disapproval. "Be serious, Sarah."

"I am being serious. Someone cared enough about something to kill Mrs. Gittings. If we can figure out what it was, we'll know who did it."

"Then if you insist, I would have to say no. I don't think I could kill anyone, no matter the provocation."

"Then I suppose you're not the person I should be asking." Sarah said with another small smile.

"But the others at the table are just like me, aren't they? They're all people of privilege whose only real worry in life is whether or not to carry an umbrella when they leave the house or whether they were invited to the most desirable parties."

"But they were much more . . . I'm not sure what to call it," Sarah confessed.

"Obsessed?" Mrs. Decker supplied.

"Yes, that's it. They were obsessed with speaking to the spirits of their loved ones."

"They were convinced Serafina could contact them."

Sarah considered this. "Do you think Serafina is really able to contact spirits?"

This time Mrs. Decker smiled ruefully. "When I was sitting in that dark room, holding hands with strangers, it seemed very possible that she could. Certainly, the others believed it with all their hearts, and perhaps that was part of it. But now . . ."

"Now?" Sarah prodded when she hesitated.

"Now that I've seen Serafina sitting in your kitchen and looking for all the world like an ordinary girl, I'm no longer as sure."

Sarah felt an odd sense of relief.

At Sarah's house, Serafina greeted them at the door, her hope that they had found out something helpful from Mrs. Burke shining heartbreakingly bright on her young face.

Sarah quickly shook her head and, in the moment before Catherine descended upon them, managed to say, "She didn't tell us anything important."

Serafina lifted her chin and put on a brave face as Catherine greeted Sarah and Mrs. Decker with hugs and kisses.

Mrs. Decker agreed to stay for lunch, and Maeve and Catherine were delighted at the opportunity to show off what they had been learning from Mrs. Ellsworth. They had just finished eating the meal of egg sandwiches, cheese and crackers, and pickled peaches the girls had put out when the doorbell rang.

Maeve and Catherine went to answer it, and Sarah couldn't help the small thrill she felt when she heard the rumble of Malloy's deep voice. She was already smiling when Maeve came back to the kitchen, but Maeve was alone and the expression on her face sobered Sarah instantly.

"Mrs. Brandt, Mr. Malloy is here, and he said he needs to see Serafina."

Serafina rose quickly to her feet, but the blood had drained from her face, and her lovely eyes were enormous.

"Does he want to see her alone?" Sarah asked with an anxious glance at Serafina.

"He asked would you come with her," Maeve reported.

Serafina turned to Sarah, and her eyes were terrified.

"Mother, would you make sure Catherine stays in the kitchen?" Sarah asked, taking Serafina's arm. "Perhaps he has some news about who killed Mrs. Gittings," she said encouragingly as she led the girl out of the kitchen and toward the front of the house.

"Of course," her mother said. "Come here, Catherine, and help me finish my peaches."

Sarah could feel Serafina trembling as they made their way into the front room that served as Sarah's office. Malloy was standing at the window, looking out into the street, but he turned when he heard them enter. His expression was too serious to mean he had brought good news.

"Malloy," she said in greeting.

"Mrs. Brandt," he replied. "Serafina, maybe you should sit down."

The girl made a small sound, but she stiffened her spine. "Just tell me," she begged him.

Malloy glanced at Sarah, who shrugged. She didn't know what his news was, so she couldn't judge what Serafina's reaction might be.

"We've found the body of a young man," he said as gently as he could, although the words themselves were so harsh, no amount of kindness could soften them. "We think it might be DiLoreto."

"No," she protested desperately. "That is impossible!"

"What do you mean, you *think* it might be him?" Sarah asked. "Couldn't you identify him?"

"He was beaten pretty badly," Malloy said.

Serafina cried out, and her knees buckled. Sarah grabbed hold of her, but she would have fallen if Malloy hadn't caught her and half carried her to one of the chairs that sat by the front window. "I told her to sit down," he grumbled as he set her in the chair.

"But you do not *know* it is Nicola," Serafina said, clinging desperately to his sleeve. "You said this yourself."

"That's right, I don't, but Donatelli is the one who found him, and he saw him in person. He's the right size and hair color, and Donatelli found him not too far from Waverly Place."

Serafina was shaking her head in silent denial.

"Why are you telling her this if you aren't sure?" Sarah asked, not bothering to hide her annoyance at him.

He gave her an apologetic look. "We need to see if she can identify him."

Serafina made a moaning sound.

Sarah glared at him. "But you said his face . . ."

"The body," he quickly explained. "See if she can recognize the body. They were lovers," he added. "She should be able to tell if it's him."

Tears were streaming down the girl's face now, and her expression was painful to behold. "He killed him! He killed my Nicola!"

"Who did?" Malloy asked in surprise. "Who killed him?"

"The Professor. I know he did it."

"Why would he kill Nicola?"

"For stealing the money."

"And maybe to avenge Mrs. Gittings," Sarah suggested. "He was the one who thought Nicola had killed her."

"He would have had to find him first," Malloy pointed out.

"Maybe he came back to the house looking for Serafina," Sarah said.

"Maybe," Malloy allowed. "Serafina, will you come with me to see if this is him?"

Serafina looked beseechingly at Sarah.

"It might not be him," Sarah said reasonably. "You'd want to know if it isn't him, wouldn't you?"

"And if it is him?" she asked in a small voice.

Sarah patted her shoulder. "You'll want to know that, too."

The girl covered her face and wept for a few minutes before pulling herself together. When she looked back up at Sarah, her eyes were red-rimmed but determined. "I will go." She pushed herself to her feet.

"And I will go with you," Sarah said.

Sarah had to explain to Maeve and her mother what had happened. They both expressed their sympathy to Serafina, who somehow managed to hold herself together.

"Take my carriage," Mrs. Decker offered, and she went out and instructed the driver.

Sarah was grateful that they didn't have to find a cab or, even worse, take the Elevated Train, where they would be an object of curiosity, especially if the body really was Nicola and Serafina was grieving when they returned.

When they were securely inside the carriage and on their way to the morgue, Sarah knew they couldn't just sit there in silence during the whole trip, letting Serafina's imagination conjure visions of her beaten lover. She caught Malloy's eye, sent him a silent message, and asked, "Did you find out anything useful today?"

He understood her instantly and played along. "Not much, except that everything Serafina told us about Sharpe and Cunningham was true."

"I would not lie to you, Mr. Malloy," the girl said, surprising them both. Plainly, she was willing to be distracted.

"Do you think either of them could have killed Mrs. Gittings?" Sarah asked him.

"I'm sure either one of them could have, but I'm not sure either of them did. They didn't like her much, but from what I gathered, Cunningham didn't know she was the one behind the phony investment scheme where he got cheated. He didn't even know he'd gotten cheated."

Serafina smiled grimly. "Mrs. Gittings would be happy to know that. She thought he could be cheated at least three times before he realized it."

Sarah gasped in outrage, but Malloy chuckled his appreciation.

"She might've gotten him even more times than that. He's not very bright."

"But if he didn't know he'd been cheated, why would he have wanted to kill Mrs. Gittings?" Sarah asked.

"Because she wouldn't give him Serafina," Malloy said baldly. "He wanted her, and he was angry because Mrs. Gittings wanted him to give her money. After he lost what money he had on the phony investment, he was starting to feel desperate."

"Did you ask him about freeing his hands during the séance?" Sarah asked.

"Yes. He pretended he didn't know the trick, but he's not a very good liar. That still doesn't prove he did it, though."

"What about Mr. Sharpe?" Sarah asked with a glance at Serafina. She was staring blankly out the window now. Sarah wasn't sure she was even listening to them anymore.

"He was just as angry at Mrs. Gittings. She wasn't going to let him take Serafina either. She wasn't going to lose her meal ticket."

"Was he angry enough to kill Mrs. Gittings?"

"If he was, he didn't let on. He's too smart for that. So what about you? Did you find out anything from Mrs. Burke?"

"Just that she hated Mrs. Gittings, too. And she was terrified that her husband was going to find out she'd been selling her jewelry to pay for the séances."

"We already knew that," Malloy reminded her.

"Yes, but we didn't know she was actually giving the jewelry to Mrs. Gittings to sell for her. She said she thought Mrs. Gittings was cheating her."

"She probably was," Malloy said. "Did she say anything else?"

"Not much before she fainted," Sarah said dryly.

"She fainted?" Malloy and Serafina echoed in unison. At least Serafina was listening again.

"Yes, she did. Apparently, talking about Mrs. Gittings's murder upsets her, although Mother thinks she might have been pretending. According to her, ladies often use a fainting spell to end an unpleasant scene."

"Really?" Serafina asked with credible disbelief, but when Sarah looked at her, she saw a knowing gleam in her eye. That's when she remembered how Serafina had fainted at the séance she'd attended.

"Yes, really," Sarah confirmed with a grim smile of her own.

"Didn't she tell you *anything* you didn't know before?" Malloy prodded.

"Just that Mrs. Gittings and the Professor seemed angry with each other that day. She thought they must have had an argument."

"Did they?" Malloy asked Serafina.

"Yes, I told you, they argued every day. He wanted to use the money from the séances to do something else, but she wanted to keep doing the séances. It was so easy, she said, and so safe."

"Did she think what the Professor wanted to do wasn't safe?" Sarah asked curiously.

"It was dangerous, she said. She said it many times, but he would not listen. He kept saying how much money they would have."

"What does it matter?" Malloy asked impatiently. "The Professor wasn't even in the room when she was killed, remember?"

"Are you absolutely sure he wasn't?" Sarah asked, including both of them in the question.

"I did not see him," Serafina said with a shrug.

"And neither did anybody else," Malloy added. "I asked all of them when they saw him after the murder, and he was in the doorway, so he must have just come in."

"When did they see him come into the room?" Serafina asked with a frown, surprising both of them with her interest.

"Nobody was really sure," Malloy said. "They didn't notice him until they started to leave the room. I guess he came when you called for him and was just standing there, trying to figure out what had happened while everybody else was looking at Mrs. Gittings."

Serafina frowned, as if this information displeased her somehow.

Sarah sighed. "That's really too bad. It would so nice if he was the killer."

"Yes, it would," Malloy agreed. Sarah knew he was thinking of the difficulties he would face if one of Serafina's wealthy clients was guilty.

"Yes, it would," Serafina echoed, and Sarah knew she was thinking of Nicola.

But if Nicola was dead, none of this would matter, because protecting Nicola was the only reason they had for finding the real killer.

WHEN THE CARRIAGE STOPPED IN FRONT OF THE MORGUE, Serafina looked out the carriage window with dread. "What will I have to do?" she asked Malloy.

"I'll take you down to where the . . . where the boy is. He'll be covered with a sheet. You won't have to look at his face if you don't want to."

"I don't," she assured him apprehensively.

"Did he have any birthmarks?"

"I do not know what that is," Serafina said, looking to Sarah for help.

"Any marks on his body that you would recognize," Sarah explained.

"I would know his hands," Serafina said. "And his feet."

"Then Mr. Malloy will show you the hands and the feet," Sarah promised.

Malloy frowned, but he got out of the carriage and helped them down. Sarah put her arm around the girl as they entered the building and found she was trembling again. This must be terrifying for her, Sarah thought. When they were inside, Malloy spoke to someone sitting at a desk in a voice too low for them to hear. Then a young man in a cheap suit that was stained with things Sarah didn't want to identify came out and led them down a flight of stairs to a large room furnished with several metal tables and lots of strange-looking equipment. She had seen autopsies at the hospital during her training, but she'd never been to a morgue. The smell brought the gorge up in her throat, and she swallowed it down hard, refusing to be sick.

Something shaped like a human body lay on one of the tables, covered by a sheet.

"I don't want to see the face," Serafina reminded him anxiously, her eyes wild with fright.

"You don't have to," Malloy said. He spoke to the young man again, and he carefully lifted the sheet on the side of the table nearest them. They could see a bare arm.

Serafina moved closer and looked down at the hand. The knuckles were badly skinned and the nails broken. He had fought for his life. She stared at the hand for a long moment. "Can I see his feet?" she asked. She sounded amazingly calm. She was probably in shock.

The young man covered the arm again and moved to the

end of the table and lifted the sheet to reveal the bare feet. The toenails were long and unkempt. The body had been washed, but dirt was still embedded in the nails. Blisters reddened the small toes of both feet.

"Could you . . . Could I see his back," she asked so softly they could hardly hear her.

The young man looked annoyed, but a glance at Malloy convinced him not to object. "Can you give me a hand, Mr. Malloy?" he asked instead.

Sarah and Serafina turned away while the two men struggled to lift the body. She thought she heard the young man say, "He's stiff."

"All right," Malloy said after another moment, and when they looked, they saw the dead man's bare back. The sheet had been draped to cover the buttocks. Malloy and the young man were holding the body balanced on its side. Rigor mortis was still present, and the body seemed carved of stone. Sarah could clearly see a large, brown birthmark on the left shoulder blade.

The girl made a whimpering sound.

"Serafina?" Sarah asked anxiously.

Serafina sounded for a moment as if she couldn't breathe, and then the awful choking noises collapsed upon themselves into wracking sobs that convulsed her young body.

"Is it Nicola?" Malloy asked, shouting to be heard.

"Yes, yes!" she cried, and ran from the room.

Sarah hurried after her and found her slumped on the stairs, sobbing.

"Come upstairs," Sarah coaxed her. "We'll find someplace quiet and—"

"No, no, take me out of this place!" she begged, lurching to her feet. "Please, I cannot stay here."

"Of course," Sarah said and helped her up the stairs and

out into the street, where the Decker carriage waited in silent splendor. The driver jumped down and helped them inside. Although he'd been trained not to show emotion, even he seemed moved by the girl's anguished grief.

"I'm so sorry," Sarah said, wrapping her arms around the girl's slender body and pulling her close. She held her while she wept out her pain, and by the time Malloy had finished his business inside and rejoined them, she was exhausted and drained and lay limp in Sarah's arms.

Malloy instructed the driver to return them to Sarah's house. The trip back was conducted in near silence, but when they were almost there, Serafina pulled away from Sarah and sat upright, her spine suddenly rigid.

"Nicola did not kill Mrs. Gittings," she told them both.

"We know he didn't," Sarah assured her, earning a black look from Malloy.

When Malloy didn't confirm her sentiments, Serafina turned her marvelous eyes on him. "But you will stop looking for the killer now, will you not?"

"I told you before, I can only question those people once. Cunningham and Sharpe didn't confess, and Mrs. Burke fainted. The Professor is the only other person there, and he wasn't in the room. There isn't much more I can do."

"Nicola is not a killer. I will not let people think he is."

Sarah knew that few people would think about Nicola DiLoreto at all, but she didn't want to upset Serafina again by saying so. She would broach the subject later, when the girl was calmer. "We know he was innocent," she tried. "That's what's important."

"No, finding the real killer is important," Serafina said.

"Do you know who it is?" Malloy asked with great interest.

"I will find out," Serafina said with perfect confidence. "The spirits will tell me."

Malloy ran a hand over his face to hide his exasperation. "When they do," he said when he'd recovered his composure, "let me know."

And just as if he'd made a perfectly logical request, she said, "I will."

BACK AT SARAH'S HOUSE, MRS. DECKER AND MAEVE WERE saddened to learn that the dead man really was Nicola. Even Catherine offered her sympathies by climbing into Serafina's lap and wrapping her small arms around the girl's neck.

Maeve made tea for everyone and set out cookies that she and Catherine had made while they were gone, but Malloy declined the offer and took his leave. Sarah saw him to the door, and when they were alone, he said, "I'm sorry you had to go to that place."

"I didn't mind. I couldn't let her face that alone."

"I was hoping it wasn't him," he confessed. "At least part of me was. The other part hoped it was, because I'm still convinced he was the one who killed Mrs. Gittings."

"So this is the end of the investigation, I suppose."

"Unless something turns up to change my mind," he told her with an apologetic shrug.

"At least Serafina won't have to see Nicola tried for murder."

"Or executed," Malloy added grimly.

Someone knocked on Sarah's front door. "Oh, dear, I hope it isn't a delivery," she muttered. "After the day I've had, I'm not in any condition to do one right now."

Malloy stood back so she could open the door, and they were both surprised to see John Sharpe standing on her doorstep.

"Mrs. Brandt, please forgive me for intruding," Sharpe

said while he was pushing his way into the house, belying his
apology even as he was making it. "I was told . . . What are
you doing here?" he demanded when he saw Malloy.

"I could ask you the same question," Malloy said mildly.

"I have some business with Madame Serafina," he informed
them both. "I was told she is here."

"Who told you that?" Malloy asked with interest.

"Professor Rogers was kind enough to give me the information. He's been quite worried about her, and he asked if I
could locate Mrs. Brandt and make sure Madame Serafina is
all right."

"She's just fine," Malloy told him, "so you can be on your
way."

Sharpe gave him a look that had probably intimidated
many underlings and a multitude of servants, but it didn't
phase Malloy, who gave it right back. "I told you," Sharpe
tried indignantly, "I have business with Madame Serafina."

"What kind of business?" Malloy insisted.

"Mr. Sharpe," Serafina said, surprising them all. While they
had been arguing, she had come out and stood just inside the
office doorway. She still wore the clothes she had worn to the
morgue, the ones that made her look like an ordinary young
woman, but something about her had changed ever so subtly
now that Sharpe was here, Sarah noticed. She carried herself
differently, and her voice was lower, more sensual. "How kind
of you to come."

"Madame Serafina," he said, brushing past Sarah and Frank
to meet her as she crossed Sarah's office, coming toward them.
"How are you? You look like you've been crying," he added
with a glance of accusation at Sarah and Malloy.

"I am still mourning poor Mrs. Gittings," she said without a trace of irony. "She was like a mother to me. I do not

know how I can go on without her." She held out her hand, and he grasped it eagerly with both of his.

"But you must!" Sharpe said. "Your work is too important. That's why I've come, to make sure you can continue."

"You are very good to me." The look she gave him would have melted a much stronger man than John Sharpe.

Sarah suddenly realized that with Mrs. Gittings and Nicola both dead, Serafina was now free to take any of the offers that Mrs. Gittings had refused on her behalf. Sharpe's offer to set her up in a house of her own had certainly been the most attractive and by far the most honorable.

"Mr. Sharpe," Mrs. Decker greeted him as she came into the room as well.

Sharpe looked up in surprise and instantly dropped Serafina's hand, as if he had been caught doing something unseemly. "Mrs. Decker, what are you doing here?"

"I'm visiting my daughter, Mr. Sharpe, and I must admit I'm amazed to see you here. However did you find us?"

"Mrs. Brandt is listed in the City Directory," Sharpe said a bit defensively. "It was merely a matter of giving my driver the address."

"But how did you know Madame Serafina was here?" Mrs. Decker asked with interest.

"The Professor told him," Malloy reported before Sharpe could reply.

Sarah saw Catherine and Maeve lurking in the shadows just beyond the door. They would be watching the scene with avid interest. The only thing missing was Mrs. Ellsworth, and she was bound to show up any minute with a cake in hand to find out who Sarah's latest visitor was.

"The Professor was worried about Madame Serafina," Sharpe quickly explained.

"Then why didn't he come himself?" Mrs. Decker said, asking the question Sarah and Malloy should have thought to ask. "If Mrs. Brandt is in the City Directory, he could have found her as easily as you did."

"He . . . Well, he . . . That is . . ." Sharpe stammered. He really was a terrible liar, Sarah observed.

"What business was it you needed to discuss with Madame Serafina?" Sarah asked to save him from further embarrassment.

Sharpe frowned. "It's private."

Then Serafina made a small sound, closed her eyes, and held out her hand until her palm rested lightly on Sharpe's chest. "You have come to make me an offer. It was very difficult for you to forget your pride and ask again when I had refused you before, but you must follow your heart, as your wife told you to do."

"Yes, yes," Sharpe said in happy amazement.

"But you did something you did not want to do, something you are ashamed to tell me," she continued as if he hadn't spoken.

"No, I wouldn't . . ." he tried, but she ignored his protest.

"The Professor, he wanted money," she said. Then she gasped, as if surprised by her own revelation and her eyes flew open. "Did you give him money?" she asked in alarm.

Sharpe looked around again, as if trying to judge if he needed to be concerned about the opinion of anyone present. Apparently, he decided he didn't. "Only a little," he finally admitted.

"That is not true," Serafina informed him imperiously.

Sharpe actually quailed under her rebuke. "I only gave him a small amount, just what I was carrying with me."

"He would not betray me for a small amount." Her certainty was absolute, and Sarah wondered how she could be so sure of the Professor's loyalty.

Sharpe proved to be no match for her will. "I had to promise him more before he would tell me where you were."

"I would have told you for nothing," Frank informed him.

Sharpe glared at him and would have responded, but Serafina cut him off. "You must not give him any more money. He will run away, and we cannot let him run away."

"Why not?" Sarah asked, stepping forward, intrigued by Serafina's performance and wanting to see how far she would go with it.

"He knows who killed Mrs. Gittings."

"How do you know?" Malloy demanded.

"I feel it."

"Then why didn't he tell me when I questioned him?" Malloy asked with a trace of irritation.

"He may not realize that he knows," Serafina said.

"You should go see him," Maeve said, surprising everyone, who turned to where she stood with Catherine in the doorway. "Maybe you can help him remember."

Serafina dropped the hand she'd been holding to Sharpe's chest and turned to Sarah. "She is right. We must go back to that house. The answer is there."

14

DEAD SILENCE GREETED SERAFINA'S SUGGESTION. AS THE technical hostess to this motley group, however unwilling she may have been in the role, Sarah felt obligated to break the awkward silence.

"What do you think will happen if you go back to the house?"

Serafina turned her remarkable eyes on Sarah, and once again Sarah marveled at the charismatic power the girl possessed and her seeming ability to turn it off and on at will. "We will find out who killed Mrs. Gittings."

"How will you do that?" Sarah asked.

Serafina raised her chin. "The spirits will tell me." She turned the force of her gaze back to Sharpe. "You will return with me, will you not?"

He didn't look as if the idea appealed to him very much.

"Is that really necessary?" he tried. "I thought the Italian boy killed her."

The girl's eyes blazed with fury. "No, he did not." She turned to Malloy. "I will prove he did not, but I must return to the place where it happened, so the spirits can speak to me."

"Couldn't you speak to them here, dear?" Mrs. Decker asked, obviously trying to be helpful. No one wanted to go back to that house on Waverly Place.

"They will not be able to find me here," Serafina declared.

"I don't know why not," Malloy murmured for Sarah's ears only. "You're in the City Directory."

Startled into a laugh, Sarah had to cough to cover it.

Serafina gave her a disapproving glance, then turned her attention back to Sharpe. "We must reenact the séance," she was saying. "Everyone must be in their exact places."

"I can't imagine the others will want to do that," Mrs. Decker protested in alarm. "Mrs. Burke has taken to her bed from the shock. She couldn't possibly go out."

"I could take her place," Maeve offered.

Serafina shook her head. "Mrs. Burke will come," she said confidently. "Mrs. Decker will come, will you not?" She didn't wait for an answer. "And Mr. Cunningham will also come, if I ask him. Only the real killer would refuse. Am I not right, Mr. Sharpe?"

Sharpe had to swallow before replying. "Yes, of course, my dear," he agreed, but he still looked as if he'd bitten into something unpleasant.

"We must send them word," Serafina said. "We will arrange it for tomorrow morning." She turned back to Maeve and said, "You will sit in for Mrs. Gittings."

Sarah opened her mouth to protest, but Malloy grabbed her arm, startling her into silence and giving Maeve the opportunity to reply.

"I'd be happy to," she said with obvious satisfaction.

"It is settled. You will be there at ten o'clock?" she asked Sharpe.

"If you're sure this is the right thing to do," he hedged.

"It is. You will be there, and when it is over, I will give you my answer to your offer." She graced him with a dazzling smile that promised he would not be disappointed.

Sharpe could not possibly resist. "Yes, I'll be there."

"What about the Professor?" Mrs. Decker asked suddenly. "Shouldn't you tell him we're coming?"

"I will send him a message that we are coming and to be ready," Serafina said. "He will expect Mr. Sharpe to bring him money, so he will be there. But you will not give him money," she added to Sharpe. "If you do, he will leave, and he must be there during the séance."

"Yes, yes, whatever you wish," Sharpe assured her.

Serafina nodded, satisfied she had his support. "I am sorry, but I must be alone now to prepare for tomorrow. Until then," she said and gave Sharpe her hand again. He took it in both of his and for an instant Sarah thought he might kiss it, but he simply bowed over it, and stepped back when she withdrew her hand again.

She turned and moved past Sarah and Frank and silently ascended the stairs, moving so gracefully that her feet might not have even been touching the floor.

When she was gone, Mrs. Decker said, "Well," breaking the second awkward silence. "This should be very interesting."

"Do you really think Mrs. Burke is too ill to attend?" Sharpe asked with a frown.

"I don't know," she said with a meaningful glance at Sarah, who recalled her mother's theory that Mrs. Burke was simply pretending to be sick. "I'll take her the message personally, though, so she'll understand the urgency. Perhaps that will persuade her to make the effort."

"I can go see Cunningham," Sharpe said. "He'll do anything Madame Serafina asks of him, I'm sure," he added with obvious disdain.

"Try to get to him before he goes out for the evening," Malloy suggested. "Otherwise, he'll be too hung over to be much use to us."

Sharpe scowled, but he nodded his understanding, then made his apologies to Mrs. Decker and to Sarah and took his leave.

"Oh, my," Mrs. Decker said when he was gone, "what have we gotten ourselves into?"

Sarah looked up the stairs where Serafina had disappeared and wondered if she should go after the girl. She'd had a terrible shock today at the morgue, seeing Nicola's body, and now she had made plans to relive Mrs. Gittings's murder. She really shouldn't be alone, but before she could decide what to do, Maeve came up beside her and called, "He's gone! You can come back down!"

She'd brought Catherine with her, holding the child's hand, and Catherine instantly moved to Sarah's side. Sarah instinctively reached down and picked her up, settling the child on her hip.

Serafina appeared at the top of the stairs and hurried down. "Did he say he would visit Mr. Cunningham?" she asked before she even reached the bottom of the steps.

"Yes, and Mrs. Decker is going to visit Mrs. Burke," Maeve told her. "Do you think you should write her a note?"

"Yes, I must," Serafina said. "She is afraid to come, so I must make her more afraid not to come."

"But that's cruel," Mrs. Decker protested.

"Not if she is the killer," Serafina said coldly.

Maeve bit back a grin. "There's writing paper here in the desk," she said, leading the other girl over to the desk that had been Sarah's husband's. She started opening drawers and pulling out the items Serafina needed.

"Sarah, you'll go with us, won't you?" Mrs. Decker asked. Sarah had rarely seen her mother so unsure of herself. "If that's all right," she added to Serafina.

"Oh, yes," the girl said absently as she selected a sheet of writing paper. "She must be there to see who the killer is."

"So you'll go?" Mrs. Decker asked Sarah to confirm.

"Of course, Mother. I wouldn't miss this for anything."

"I don't want to go," Catherine informed everyone.

"You can stay with Mrs. Ellsworth, sweetheart," Sarah assured her, then she turned to Malloy. "I'll tell you everything that happens."

"You won't need to," Malloy replied smugly. "I wouldn't miss this for anything either. Besides, if the spirits are going to tell her who the killer is, I need to be there to arrest him. Or *her*." He glanced meaningfully at Mrs. Decker, who gasped in outrage.

"I hardly even knew that woman!" she reminded him.

"He's only teasing you, Mother," Sarah said. "Just ignore him."

"It isn't nice to tease people, Mr. Malloy," Catherine told him sternly.

"I'm sorry," Malloy said, feigning meekness. "I won't tease Mrs. Decker anymore."

"Mr. Malloy," Serafina asked from where she was sitting at the desk. "Will you take a message to the Professor? I want to be sure he is there when we come and that everything is ready."

"I would be happy to," Malloy said graciously, surprising Sarah. "I should probably tell him about Nicola, too."

Serafina's head jerked up, and her eyes blazed. "No, please do not tell him. I will do that when I see him. And also do not tell him we are trying to find the killer. It will be better if he thinks I am just going to start doing the sittings again. I will tell him we must begin again since all the money is gone."

"What money is that?" Mrs. Decker asked.

"Nicola took all the money that Mrs. Gittings was holding for us when he ran away," Serafina said before anyone else could speak.

Maeve hastened to confirm her story. "Someone must have robbed him before . . . Well, he didn't have the money anymore when they found him."

Sarah exchanged a glance with Malloy, who shrugged. If that was the story Serafina wanted to tell, it was of no concern to him.

"Please, I must write this note for Mr. Malloy to take to the Professor," Serafina said.

"Let's go in the kitchen," Sarah suggested.

Mrs. Decker led the way. Sarah followed, still carrying Catherine, and Malloy came behind. Maeve stayed in the office with Serafina while she composed her notes.

"What do you make of all this?" Mrs. Decker asked in a whisper.

"She just wants to prove Nicola was innocent," Sarah said, setting Catherine down on one of the chairs. "Would you like another cookie, sweetheart?"

"Yes, please," she said and accepted one.

"I'm starting to think Serafina knows more than she's told us," Malloy said with a frown.

"You mean you think she knows who killed Mrs. Gittings?" Mrs. Decker asked in surprise.

"If she does, why didn't she say so in the first place?" Sarah asked.

"Maybe she couldn't prove it, and she didn't think I'd believe her," Malloy said.

"So she was hoping Mr. Malloy would figure it out for himself," Mrs. Decker suggested.

"But now that Nicola is dead, she knows I'm going to stop investigating," Malloy concluded.

"We could just ask her," Sarah said.

"She'd lie," Malloy said. "She wants to have her séance."

"And what if she has it, and we still don't figure out who killed Mrs. Gittings?" Mrs. Decker asked.

"Then there's nothing else I can do, and I'll be finished with this whole thing," Malloy said with more than a trace of happy anticipation.

"You'd just give up?" Mrs. Decker asked in amazement.

"Mother, Malloy can't badger people like Mr. Sharpe and Mrs. Burke, especially when he doesn't have any reason to think they're guilty. He'd lose his job," Sarah said.

Mrs. Decker sighed. "I just wish there was something else I could do. Serafina is all alone in the world now, except for that Professor fellow, and I don't trust him one bit."

Malloy turned to Sarah. "Have you had a chance to ask Maeve what she thinks of Serafina?"

"No," Sarah said, remembering that Malloy had suggested this the day he'd given her custody of the girl. "She seems awfully anxious to help her, though."

"Or maybe she just wants to go to a séance," Malloy countered.

"I don't like the idea of her playing Mrs. Gittings's part," Sarah said with a frown.

"You can't think someone would try to harm her," Mrs. Decker said. "No one there even knows her."

"I know, but still . . . I just feel uneasy about it."

"Maeve can take care of herself," Malloy reminded her.

Sarah remembered exactly how Maeve had taken care of herself just a few short weeks ago and shivered involuntarily. "I just wish we could be in the room during the séance, in case something happens."

"We can be on the other side of the cabinet," Malloy said reasonably. "We'll hear everything that happens, and we can be in the room in a minute if we're needed."

"But what if the killer decides to . . ." Sarah stopped, trying to think of possible scenarios.

"What if he decides to do what?" Malloy prodded her. "Kill Madame Serafina? I think the killer was trying to help her by killing Mrs. Gittings, so why would he want to kill Serafina now? Nobody even knows Maeve, so she's safe, and what reason does anybody have to kill any of the others? Also, nobody knows who the killer is, so nobody else is in danger of betraying him."

"I know you're right," Sarah admitted.

"Of course I am," he said without a trace of humility.

She glared at him. "I just hate the thought of her sitting there in the dark, helpless."

Malloy considered this a moment. "I think I have something to make her a little less helpless."

"Not a weapon," Sarah protested.

"No, something better."

Before she could question him, Maeve and Serafina returned to the kitchen. Maeve handed an envelope to Malloy. "This is for the Professor."

"Is it going to make him run?" Malloy asked with a doubtful glance at the envelope.

"No, it should make him want to stay," Serafina said. "I

tell him I am going to keep doing the séances because I have no other way to support myself, and he is the only one who can help me."

Malloy nodded his approval and tucked the envelope into his coat pocket.

Maeve handed Mrs. Decker a second envelope. "This is for Mrs. Burke."

"I hope you haven't frightened her too much," Mrs. Decker said, accepting the envelope cautiously, with just two fingers, as if afraid it might explode.

"No, only a little," Serafina assured her. "Just enough so she will come. I also told her I would not charge her for the sitting."

"She'd be a fool to miss that opportunity," Mrs. Decker said.

"Serafina, we were just discussing what Mr. Malloy and I should do during the séance," Sarah said.

"You must do nothing. The others should also not know you are there. They will suspect something."

"We thought we could go into that room behind the cabinet and listen to what's happening."

"No, no," Serafina said. "If you open the false door during the séance, they might hear you. There is a better place to listen, in the kitchen. I will show you tomorrow."

"What do you want me to do?" Maeve asked.

"Just be sure you are holding Mrs. Burke and Mr. Sharpe by the hand and do not let go. Mrs. Decker and I will be holding their other hands. Mrs. Decker and I will also be holding Mr. Cunningham's hands."

"You also must make sure no one lets go or keeps one hand free," Sarah warned them.

"And what are you going to do?" Malloy asked Serafina.

She turned her amazing eyes on him for a long moment, then let her gaze drift until she'd touched everyone at the table with her silent power. "I am going to contact the spirits and ask them who the killer is."

They could not get her to say more or to make any more plans. Serafina insisted she would not know what to do until she heard what the spirits told her.

Frustrated and weary with all of it, Malloy finally took his leave. "I need to go see the Professor before it gets too late. Maeve, will you see me to the door?" he asked.

The girl eagerly complied, leaving Sarah feeling unreasonably slighted. Maeve returned a few minutes later, looking oddly pleased, and Sarah wondered what he had needed to see her alone about. She would have to wait until much later to ask her.

THE PROFESSOR MUST HAVE BEEN WATCHING FOR VISITORS because he opened the door almost the instant Frank knocked.

"Have you found him?" the Professor demanded.

"Aren't you even going to invite me in?"

The Professor stood back and waved him inside with ill-concealed impatience. "Have you found him?" he asked again as soon as he'd closed the front door behind them.

"Are you talking about DiLoreto?"

"Of course I am."

"Not yet," Frank lied. He saw no reason to go against Serafina's wishes.

"Then why are you here?"

With a sigh of annoyance, Frank pulled Serafina's note out of his pocket and handed it to him.

"What's this?" he demanded, accepting it with suspicion.

"Read it and find out." Frank turned away and wandered into the parlor in spite of not having been invited to make himself welcome. This time he paid closer attention to the furnishings, and this time he could see that everything looked slightly shabby and thrown together, as if the items had come from an auction of mixed lots, bought cheap and with an eye to filling space rather than comfort or style.

"She's coming back tomorrow?" the Professor asked from the parlor doorway. He still held the note in his hand.

"That's right. She's invited everybody who was at the séance where Mrs. Gittings was killed to come back for another one. She wants you to have everything ready."

"Does this mean she's free?"

"She's always been free."

"I thought you were . . . holding her," he said with a frown.

"I told you before, she wasn't arrested. She was just staying with Mrs. Brandt for a while, but now she wants to start doing the séances again. She probably needs the money."

"The boy didn't contact her then," he said with some satisfaction. "I didn't think he would. Once he got the money, he didn't need her anymore. He didn't need any of us anymore."

"But you still need Serafina, don't you?" Frank asked.

"What do you mean?" he asked, suddenly wary.

"I mean the boy stole all the money you had. Without Serafina, how else can you make a living?"

"I would manage," the Professor said, drawing himself up to his full height and gathering his dignity around him.

"Like you managed before you found her?"

Now he looked insulted. "What are you insinuating?"

"Nothing at all. I was just wondering how you made your living before you met up with Mrs. Gittings and Serafina."

"I am a professor of philosophy," he lied. He'd told Frank before that it was a courtesy title. "I have taught at some of the great institutions of learning in our country."

"Name one," Frank challenged.

"Harvard," he replied without hesitation, knowing that Boston was far away and such things could not be quickly or easily verified.

"Why aren't you teaching now?"

The man's lips thinned, but he didn't lose his composure. "I am retired."

"You retired from being a professor so you could answer the door and collect money from people going to a séance?" Frank let a faint note of contempt color his words.

"Madame Serafina is doing important work. You couldn't possibly understand, but I felt compelled to assist her in any way I could."

"Does that mean you gave up your plan to bankroll a Green Goods Game?"

Surprise flickered across his face, but he quickly concealed it. "I don't know what you're talking about, Mr. Malloy, but I've never enjoyed games of chance, if that's what this Green Game is."

"That's funny," Frank said, not at all amused. "I thought you looked like the kind of man who liked taking a risk every now and then."

"Not at all. Now I must ask you to leave. I have a lot to do before tomorrow. When will Madame Serafina arrive?"

"She told everybody to come at ten," Frank said. "She'll probably be here before that."

"I'm sure she will. You may assure her that everything will be in readiness." He moved to the front door and opened it, standing expectantly while Frank made his way more slowly, pretending to take an interest in the artwork hanging in the hallway.

"I'll do that," Frank said.

MUCH LATER, AFTER MRS. DECKER HAD GONE OFF TO deliver Serafina's note to Mrs. Burke and supper was over and Mrs. Ellsworth had paid a visit so she could find out what had been going on all day with Sarah's steady stream of visitors, Sarah finally found a moment alone with Maeve. Serafina had gone to bed early, claiming she needed to be rested for the next morning.

"Catherine is asleep," Maeve reported when she found Sarah still sitting in the kitchen. "She just couldn't settle down tonight. I think she's as excited about the séance tomorrow as we are."

"I'm not exactly excited," Sarah confessed.

"You're not worried, are you?" the girl asked in surprise, taking a seat at the table across from Sarah.

"Not worried exactly, but I don't like the idea of you sitting in for a woman who got murdered."

"No one wants to kill me," Maeve said with compelling logic. "Besides, Mr. Malloy is going to give me something tomorrow that I can use if things get out of hand."

"What?"

Maeve frowned. "I'm not exactly sure. He tried to explain it to me, but it sounded more like one of Serafina's séance tricks than something the police would use."

"Is it a weapon?"

"No, it's a light of some kind, but it has a battery, so you don't need a match to light it."

Sarah wasn't sure how a light could help if something

went wrong, but she supposed it wouldn't hurt. "What do the police use it for?"

"I think they use it at night. Some fellow invented it, but nobody wanted to buy it, so he gave some to the police. Mr. Malloy said the beat cops who work at night like it."

"I guess they would appreciate having a light now and then," Sarah allowed. She waited a moment, to see if Maeve had anything to add. Then she asked, "What do you think of Serafina?"

Maeve's expression turned wary. "What do you mean?"

"I'm not sure what I mean, but Mr. Malloy asked me to find out what you thought of her. Do you think she can really contact the spirits?"

"I don't believe in spirits, but I think *she* does. Or maybe she's just a very good actor."

"So she hasn't said anything to you to make you think she's a fake?"

"Oh, no," Maeve assured her. "She's real proud of her powers, and she wants everyone to believe they're real. But there's one thing . . ."

"What?" Sarah prodded when she hesitated.

"Have you noticed, she doesn't seem real sad about that Nicola dying. It's almost like she forgot about it as soon as she got back here."

Sarah considered. "I hadn't thought about it, but you're right. She was nearly hysterical at the morgue this morning, but I guess that's understandable. It's a horrible place. It's true, she hasn't seemed to be grieving, but people sometimes behave strangely when someone dies. Maybe she's still in shock."

"Or maybe she didn't like him all that much," Maeve said.

"I hadn't thought of that. Still, they were lovers. She must have cared about him a little."

"Or *only* a little. I asked her what was going to happen to him now, and she seemed surprised, like she hadn't even thought about it. When my grandfather died, that's the first thing I wanted to know, where was he going to be buried."

"You've never talked about your family before," Sarah said in surprise. She hadn't wanted to press her for fear of bringing up unpleasant memories, but now that Maeve herself had opened the subject, Sarah found she was curious to learn as much as she could about this girl who had become her friend.

Maeve's gaze shifted away and darted around the room, as if she couldn't quite bring herself to look Sarah in the eye. "I didn't want you to think less of me."

"Oh, Maeve, nothing about your family could ever make me think less of you. I told you before, you're part of *my* family now, and nothing will ever change that."

Maeve looked down at where her hands rested on the tabletop. "Even if they were crooks?"

"Even if you were a crook yourself," Sarah assured her.

She looked up in surprise at that. "I can pick pockets," she confessed suddenly. "But I don't do that anymore. Not unless I have to, that is."

Sarah couldn't help smiling at the strange confession. "Of course not."

Maeve rolled her eyes. "I didn't mean it like that. I mean, if I needed to help Mr. Malloy or something."

"I understand. How long ago did your grandfather die?" Sarah asked to change the subject.

Maeve's expression grew wary again. "Almost two years ago."

Sarah heard something in her voice, something that begged her to continue, even though good manners forbade her to pry. "How did he die?"

"He was . . . murdered."

"Oh, Maeve," Sarah cried, reaching out to cover the girl's hands with her own. "I'm so sorry!"

But Maeve just stared back at her, dry-eyed. "Remember when you were telling us about the Green Goods Game?"

"Yes," she said cautiously.

"That was his game. He played the Old Gentleman."

Sarah didn't know what to say to that.

"Mrs. Gittings was right about it, too. It can be dangerous," Maeve continued. "And not just when a mark gets suspicious."

"A mark?"

"A sucker, the ones who come to buy the green goods. Sometimes the operators argue among themselves. That's what happened. One of them thought Grandpap was cheating him. He wasn't, Mrs. Brandt. I swear he wasn't!"

"Of course he wasn't," Sarah said. "I'm so sorry you lost him. Was he your only family?"

"He was all I had left. My father . . . I never knew him at all. He ran off before I was born, and my mother died when I was twelve. Grandpap, he always took care of both of us."

"I'm sure he did. Was that when you came to the Mission, after he died?" Sarah had first met Maeve when she was living at the Prodigal Son Mission, a refuge for young girls with no place to go.

"Yes, and I was so grateful. Grandpap had some money put away, but it wouldn't have lasted forever, and a girl alone . . . Well, people will do terrible things if you don't have somebody to look out for you."

Sarah nodded, understanding only too well the terrible things that could have happened to her. "You did the right thing, going to the Mission, even though that wasn't such a safe place after all."

"It was always safe for me," she reminded Sarah. "And I met you there, and Catherine."

"I'm very glad you did. And I'm also glad you trusted me enough to tell me about your family."

"You really don't mind?" Maeve asked, still uncertain.

"Not at all. I only care about the person you are today, and you are a good person, Maeve."

"I am, aren't I?" she asked in surprise.

"Yes, you are. And I want you to be very careful tomorrow. Catherine needs you and I need you."

Maeve's eyes misted a bit. "Don't worry about me. Nothing's going to happen. And maybe I'll get to talk to Grandpap," she added with a grin.

Sarah grinned back. "I'm sure if you mention it to Serafina, she'll manage to contact him."

"Oh, I'm not going to make it easy for her. She's already been asking me about my family and if there's someone I want to ask a question."

"What did you tell her?" Sarah asked in surprise.

"Nothing true," Maeve replied with another grin. "She'll just have to find out from the spirits."

15

THE NEXT MORNING, AS SOON AS BREAKFAST WAS OVER, Mrs. Ellsworth came to take Catherine. The two of them were going to the market and then were going to bake something very special at Mrs. Ellsworth's house while everyone else attended the séance on Waverly Place.

Mrs. Decker's carriage arrived soon after Mrs. Ellsworth and Catherine had left, and Sarah followed Maeve and Serafina out and climbed in behind them. Serafina was once again dressed in her flowing black gown, but her expression was more determined than Sarah had ever seen it.

"Maeve," Mrs. Decker said when they were settling themselves. "You look lovely."

Maeve blushed prettily at the compliment. Sarah had searched her closet to make sure Maeve's outfit marked her as someone Mrs. Felix Decker would know. They had decided she would be Mrs. Decker's niece, and she looked every bit the part in a suit Sarah hadn't worn in a while and a hat her mother had given her but which Sarah had judged too fancy for her life as a midwife. Maeve touched the hat self-consciously and Mrs. Decker nodded her approval.

Serafina distracted them from their approval of Maeve's clothes. "What did Mrs. Burke say when she read my note?"

Mrs. Decker smiled. "She got very flustered and kept saying she couldn't, she just couldn't, but then I mentioned that you said you wouldn't charge her anything, and she finally decided she would try."

"Good. I have been thinking what we should do," she told them as the carriage lurched away from the curb. "Mrs. Brandt, I think you should not come inside with us. I do not want everyone else to know you are there."

"I'm not going to wait in the carriage until the séance is over," Sarah declared.

"Oh, no, that is not what you will do," Serafina assured her. "I will unlock the back door, and you will come inside that way when we are all in the séance room."

"How will I know when that happens?"

Serafina thought for a moment. "I will go to the front window and move the curtain just before I take everyone into the room."

"I could do that for you," Mrs. Decker said. "No one would think it peculiar if I looked out to check on my driver."

"Yes, thank you," Serafina said. "That would be better."

"What about Mr. Malloy?" Maeve asked. "He'll probably be there when we arrive."

"I will speak with him and ask him to pretend to leave," Serafina said. "I do not want the killer to be frightened by the police. But Mr. Malloy can return with you, Mrs. Brandt."

Sarah nodded her approval. "You said you'd show me where

I could listen to what's happening in the séance," Sarah reminded her.

"I won't be able to show you, but it is easy to find. A picture is hanging on the wall in the kitchen. An ugly picture of a cow. If you lift it down, you will see two small holes stuffed with cotton wool. You can look through them into the séance room, but you will see nothing once the room is dark. They are really for listening. And you must stand in front of them, closely, so no light comes into the séance room once the light is out."

"Why are they there?" Maeve asked.

"For the Professor. He usually listens in case something happens. I call for him and he comes."

"Or when you fainted at that séance I attended, the others called him," Sarah recalled.

Serafina smiled. "Yes, that is right. The Professor will be in the kitchen when you come in, so Mr. Malloy will tell him he must stand aside so you can listen. He will be angry, but do not let him interrupt us."

"I'm sure Mr. Malloy can handle the Professor," Mrs. Decker said with a small smile.

Sarah was sure of it, too.

"Whose spirit will you call for today?" Maeve asked.

"I will call for Mrs. Gittings," Serafina said grimly.

"What if she doesn't know who killed her, though?" Maeve pressed. "What about Nicola?"

Serafina's eyes grew bleak. "I will not call for him. It is too soon. But Yellow Feather will know if she does not. He was there when it happened."

The other three had no answer for that, although Sarah couldn't help wishing she believed in Yellow Feather. If he really existed, he could be very helpful.

They spent the rest of the trip answering Maeve's questions about what would happen at the séance. When the carriage rattled to a stop, Serafina sat up straighter, as if bracing herself.

"I know this must be difficult for you, my dear," Mrs. Decker said.

"I will not be afraid," Serafina told her, although she sounded as if she were trying to convince herself. "I am doing this for Nicola."

The driver opened the door, and the three of them climbed out.

"Mrs. Brandt is going to wait here for a while," Mrs. Decker said to the driver. "Please do whatever she tells you."

He nodded his understanding and closed the carriage door. When the others had gone inside, he climbed back up to the seat and moved the carriage about halfway down the block. Sarah positioned herself so she had a good view of the front window and settled back to wait.

MALLOY HADN'T BEEN THERE LONG WHEN HE HEARD someone coming in the front door. He and the Professor had been staring at each other across the kitchen table for far too long, and the Professor jumped to his feet at the first sound. "She's here," he said and hurried out of the kitchen.

Malloy followed him into the hallway and saw Serafina coming through the front door. Mrs. Decker and Maeve were behind her. Where was Sarah?

"Madame Serafina," the Professor said, obviously pleased to see her. "How are you?"

"I am very well," she assured him. "I am happy to be home again."

"I'm happy to welcome you here," he assured her. "Mrs.

Decker, how nice to see you back again. And you've brought a friend." He eyed Maeve critically, as if trying to judge her potential as a paying customer.

"Miss Decker," Serafina said, "may I present my assistant, Professor Rogers. Professor, Miss Decker is Mrs. Decker's niece. She has always been curious about the spirit world, so she is going to learn more about it today."

"We're very happy to have you here," the Professor assured her, although Frank thought his enthusiasm sounded forced. He gave her a small bow, and then he caught her studying him with more than casual interest. He straightened, probably wondering why this young lady would be so interested in him, and then he said. "Have we met before, Miss Decker?"

"I don't think so, Professor," she said. "What makes you ask?"

"It's just . . . You reminded me of someone there for a moment."

Frank had been watching from the end of the hallway, unnoticed. The Professor's back was to him, so he couldn't see his expression, but Maeve gave the other man an innocent smile designed to disarm him.

Frank didn't wait to see if it worked. He stepped forward. "Good morning, Madame," he said to Serafina.

All the women looked up in surprise, and he was glad to see none of them looked more pleased to see him than was appropriate.

"Mr. Malloy, why have you come?" Serafina asked, as if she really didn't know.

"I thought you might like me to be close by, in case something happened today."

Serafina gave him one of her disapproving frowns. "May I speak with you privately, Mr. Malloy?" She turned back to the Professor. "Will you serve tea to Mrs. Decker and her niece?"

The Professor looked as if he would refuse, eyeing Frank the way he'd look at a rattlesnake from whom he expected the worst. He couldn't think of any reason not to do her bidding, however, so he said, "Yes, Madame." He took charge of the visitors and ushered them into the parlor while Frank and Serafina went across the hall to the office.

Once inside, Frank closed the door with a click and said, "Where's Mrs. Brandt?"

"She's waiting in the carriage. I thought it would be better if the others didn't know the two of you were in the house during the séance. We don't want the killer to be on guard, so I will ask you to leave when everyone has arrived, and then you and she will come to the back door, which I will unlock. I told Mrs. Brandt how to find the holes in the kitchen wall where you can listen to what is happening in the room."

"What about the Professor? Isn't that where he usually waits during the séance?"

"Mrs. Decker said you could handle him," she said with a small smile.

"I probably can," Frank allowed, wondering what he had done to earn Mrs. Decker's confidence.

"Did you tell the Professor about Nicola?" she asked.

"No, you said you wanted to do it," he reminded her.

"Good, I—"

She stopped when someone knocked on the door. It opened before either of them could react, and the Professor stepped in and closed the door behind him. "You can't allow him to stay here for the séance."

Serafina gave him a withering look. "I am the one who decides who is present for the séance," she reminded him.

"Don't get high and mighty with me, missy," he told her. "I knew you when you were telling fortunes on the street."

"And now you live off the money that I earn," she reminded him right back.

He looked as if he wanted to say something else, but he glanced at Frank and changed his mind. He straightened himself again. "Well, perhaps it's good he's here after all. He can protect us in case Nicola comes back."

"Nicola is dead," Serafina said savagely before Frank could reply.

"Dead?" He seemed genuinely surprised. "How could he be dead?"

"Because someone killed him," she told him.

The Professor looked at Frank. "Is this true?"

"Yes, someone beat him to death. We found his body not far from here."

The Professor's face flooded with color. "The little fool, he probably started flashing the money around and somebody killed him for it. Lucille tried to tell you he was no good, but you wouldn't listen."

An excellent theory, Frank thought, but the Professor didn't know Nicola had no money to flash around. "Who's Lucille?"

"Mrs. Gittings," the Professor snapped. "So now he's gone and the money with him."

"Don't worry, you still have me to make money for you," Serafina told him acidly.

"Mrs. Decker didn't give me anything when she came in just now," he informed her just as acidly.

"I told them I would not charge them today."

"What?" the Professor asked, outraged.

"After what happened, they would not come back unless I begged them. You should be glad they are here at all."

"And the others? Are they coming, too?"

"Yes, they are. All of them will be here, just like before."

"Just like before except for that girl. Why is she here?"

"I told you, she is Mrs. Decker's niece."

"No, she isn't. She's somebody's maid, and she's up to something. I don't like it."

"You do not have to like it. She is here because I want her here. Now go answer the door. Someone else has come."

They could hear the bell, and the Professor gave her another glare before going to answer it.

When he'd closed the door behind him, Frank said, "How did he know about Maeve?"

"What does it matter?" She dismissed the Professor with a wave of her hand. "Do you know what you must do?"

"Do you want me to stay until everybody gets here?"

"Yes, and then I will tell you, in front of everyone, that you are to leave, so they all know you are gone. I do not want the killer to think you are here to find him."

"Or her," Frank added.

But she was already on her way out of the room. "I must unlock the back door for you," she said as she disappeared.

Frank sighed. He had a bad feeling about all of this. Why had he let Sarah talk him into it in the first place? If Nicola was dead, nobody cared who had killed Mrs. Gittings. Nobody but Serafina and Sarah. He sighed again and stepped out into the hall. He could hear voices in the parlor, and he crossed the hall to see who had arrived.

John Sharpe was there, and Mrs. Decker was introducing him to Maeve. From the look on his face, he thought she was somebody's maid, too, but Mrs. Decker didn't care a fig what he thought and neither did Maeve. Frank could hear clocks around the city striking the hour. Cunningham would be late, of course, if he showed up at all.

The Professor was opening the door to someone, and Mrs.

Burke came in. She looked pale and drawn and slightly terrified, especially when she saw Frank. He nodded politely.

"What is he doing here?" she fairly squeaked to the Professor.

"Madame asked him to come," he said with obvious
disapproval.

"Mrs. Decker is in the parlor," Frank said, hoping to distract her. He succeeded.

She scurried away, not even waiting for the Professor to
escort her, and Frank could hear Mrs. Decker's welcome.

"Where is Madame Serafina?" the Professor asked.

"I don't know. She had some things to do."

"The boy, is he really dead?" the Professor asked.

"She identified his body."

The Professor looked as if he wanted to swear but remembered just in time where he was. "If he's dead, then why are
you here?"

"Madame asked me to come," he said, repeating the Professor's own words without a trace of irony.

They could hear Mrs. Burke's voice, shrill and too loud
from nervous tension, "I didn't know Mr. Decker had a
niece."

The Professor frowned. "That girl . . ." he said, then shook
his head.

The doorbell rang again. The Professor muttered something under his breath and went to answer it.

Frank waited as he admitted Cunningham. The young
man was only a few minutes late, which meant he must be
eager to see Serafina again. He'd have realized she no longer
had to answer to Mrs. Gittings, and he probably wanted to
make his case to her again about why she should become his
mistress.

The Professor greeted him, but Cunningham wasn't paying attention. "Where's Madame Serafina?" he asked, looking around, and then he saw Frank. "What are you doing here?"

"Madame asked him to come," the Professor said with a touch of irony before Frank could reply.

"Why? Are we in danger?" he asked in alarm.

"Not at all," Serafina said. They all looked up to see her emerging from the kitchen. Her color was high, her cheeks fairly glowing, and her amazing eyes sparkled with some inner light. She carried herself like a queen, and Frank stared admiringly as she moved gracefully down the hallway toward them. "We are all perfectly safe, are we not, Mr. Malloy?"

Frank wasn't so sure about that, but he said, "Yes, you are."

But no one was listening to him. The other two men only saw Serafina. She held out her hand, and Cunningham took it in both of his.

"I'm so glad to see you," he said breathlessly.

"I am glad to see you, too. Please, come inside and greet the others."

She had to tug a bit to reclaim her hand from his eager grip, but then she turned, and he followed her into the parlor. Frank followed, too, but stopped, hovering in the doorway and aware that the Professor was hovering just behind him, listening intently to what she might say.

Everyone greeted Cunningham, and Sharpe made a remark about how he was only five minutes late. Everyone chuckled politely.

"We are all a little nervous today," Serafina said when they were finished greeting the newcomer. "But we have nothing to fear. I asked Mr. Malloy to come, but now that I am here, I know that everything will be fine. I can feel it. The spirits are surrounding us, protecting us."

"I thought he was here to tell us he found whoever killed Mrs. Gittings," Cunningham said with a frown.

"The boy who did it is dead," the Professor said over Frank's shoulder.

The three people to whom this was news gasped, and the others stared at him in surprise.

"Do you mean that Italian boy who worked here?" Sharpe asked.

"That's right," the Professor confirmed. "Mr. Malloy had arrested him, but he managed to escape and now . . . Well, they found his body, didn't they, Mr. Malloy?"

"That's right," Malloy said, loath to agree with the Professor about anything but unable to think of a reason to lie.

"How did he die?" Mr. Sharpe asked with obvious disapproval. "I hope it wasn't at the hands of the police."

Frank could have taken offense, but since many people had died at the hands of the police while in custody, he chose not to argue the point. "No, he was beaten to death before we could find him."

"So there is no longer any danger," Mrs. Burke said with palpable relief. "Nothing to worry about at all."

"Of course not," Mr. Sharpe assured her.

Frank glanced at Serafina and was surprised to catch her eyes burning with anger in the moment before she got control of herself again and smiled sweetly. "We are in no danger here. I told you, the spirits are surrounding us with protection. That is why I will ask Mr. Malloy to leave us. We do not need you here."

Frank looked around to see the reactions. No one protested. No one wanted the police around if they didn't have to be. In fact, they were all looking at him as if he were a skunk at a picnic, except Maeve, who was staring at the Professor with the oddest expression on her face, as if she wanted to knock him over the head with a vase. Maybe he had accused her of being a maid. "If you're sure you won't need me," he said.

"Why should we need you?" Cunningham said with forced bravado.

"If you're *sure*, Madame Serafina," Frank repeated, ignoring Cunningham.

"I am, Mr. Malloy. Thank you for your help." She gave him a gracious nod of her head, and Frank turned to see the Professor had already fetched his hat and was holding it out to him.

In another moment, he found himself on the front stoop with the door closed securely behind him. He saw Mrs. Decker's carriage waiting down the street and headed for it. By the time he reached it, the driver was helping Sarah out.

"Good morning, Mrs. Brandt," he said, unreasonably happy to see her, considering the circumstances. Although, he had to admit, these circumstances were far better than many they'd been in. At least no one was in danger of getting murdered today.

"Good morning, Mr. Malloy. Why are you smiling?"

He hadn't realized he was and quickly stopped. "No reason. Serafina told me the plan." He glanced around and saw they were almost to the corner. They'd have to walk down the side street to the alley and then half a block back to the back door of the house. "Are you ready for a little stroll?"

"I'd be delighted." She took his offered arm, and they started down the street.

"We arranged that Mother would move the front curtain when they started into the séance room, so I would know when it was safe to make my entrance. I saw it move just after you came out. What was going on inside?"

"Did you know Maeve is your cousin?"

"Yes, that was the story we decided on."

"I thought she looked very nice, but the Professor knew her for what she was the instant he saw her."

"He can probably smell an Irish girl a mile away," Sarah sighed. "I don't suppose it matters, though, so long as they let her into the séance."

"They'll do whatever Madame Serafina wants. Serafina told the Professor that Nicola is dead, and he told everyone else that Mrs. Gittings's killer was dead."

"Why would he do that?" Sarah asked in surprise.

"Because they were nervous about being in the house with the killer still running loose, I guess. Or maybe he was just happy Nicola is dead and wanted to let everyone else know, too. Anyway, when they heard the killer was dead, they wanted me to leave, so I did."

"How rude of them," she said sympathetically.

Frank stopped when they reached the alley. "I forgot to count the houses."

"I did while I was waiting," she assured him. "We don't want to go barging into the wrong kitchen."

"No, we don't," he agreed. He had to admit he was enjoying walking along with Sarah's hand tucked into the crook of his arm, as if they belonged together. But if Maeve didn't belong with those people in the house, Frank Malloy certainly didn't belong with Sarah Decker Brandt. Under any other circumstances, he would never even know a woman like her, much less be her friend and . . . well, and whatever else he was to her. He couldn't even think about what she was to him.

"This is it," she said. "Yes, I remember those curtains in the kitchen window."

Frank opened the back gate, and they made their way up the flagstone path that had been overgrown with weeds last summer and was now covered with their withered remains and the first green shoots of this spring's crop. Sarah was the first to the back door, and it opened easily. She gave Frank a conspiratorial grin and then slipped inside. He followed, ready to do very quiet battle with the Professor for possession of the kitchen.

But when they got inside, the room was empty.

"Where is he?" she asked in a whisper.

Frank shrugged. "Maybe he's in there." He pointed to the curtained alcove. He stepped over and pulled back the curtain, but no one was in there either. He shrugged again.

Without a word, she went to the wall opposite the back door and started to remove a picture hanging there. He hurried to take it from her. When he'd set it on the floor, he saw her pulling a plug of cotton wool from one of two holes. She pointed to the other one, and said, "Stand close to it so the light doesn't shine into it."

He pulled the cotton wool out of the other hole and peered through. He had a perfect view of the séance room. Serafina had just put out the gaslight and was closing the door. He could see everyone seated around the table, their hands clasped just the way Serafina had demonstrated. Maeve was looking all around, taking in every detail of the room in the last seconds before the door closed, plunging them into darkness. She'd probably learned that from her short stint as a Pinkerton Detective a few weeks ago.

Then the room was dark, and Frank and Sarah could see nothing, but after a few moments, when Serafina had taken her place again, she spoke, and they could hear her clearly.

"Yellow Feather, are you there? What do the spirits have to tell us today? Yellow Feather, speak to us."

Someone at the table murmured something, and Cunningham called out, "Is my father there? I need to speak with him!"

Serafina kept calling for Yellow Feather, pleading with him to make his presence known, and just when Frank thought maybe the spirit guide wasn't going to cooperate, he heard her make an odd sound, and suddenly a new voice started speaking, one he'd never heard before.

"This is Yellow Feather. I am very confused," the voice said. A man's voice, but not the voice of either of the men in the room. "So many spirits, too many, all shouting, all wanting to be heard."

Frank looked at Sarah, and she gave him a nod, telling him everything was as it should be.

"Is my father there?" Cunningham asked desperately.

"Soon, soon," Yellow Feather soothed. "You must be patient. A new spirit is here. I have never seen him before. He is looking for someone, someone young. Are you there?"

"Is it me?" Cunningham asked. "I'm here, Father!"

"Who is it? Who are you?" Yellow Feather asked, sounding uncertain.

Someone moaned, a plaintive sound that gave Frank gooseflesh, although he never would have admitted it.

"The new spirit is searching. He is old, very old. And rich."

"It's my father!" Cunningham insisted. "It must be!"

"No, no," Yellow Feather moaned. "No, I am seeing money, much money, but it does not belong to him. He only pretends to be rich. He lies. He lies to steal money from people."

Frank glanced at Sarah, but she looked as puzzled as he.

"He is old," Yellow Feather was saying. "No, not old, not very old, but he says he is old. He calls himself the . . . the Old Gentleman."

Sarah's breath caught, and when he looked at her, her eyes were wide with surprise. She put her hand over the hole in the wall and whispered, "Maeve's grandfather played the Old Gentleman in the Green Goods Game."

Now Frank's eyes widened in surprise. When had Sarah come by that interesting piece of information? She had some explaining to do when this stupid séance was over.

"I see money," Yellow Feather was saying. "A lot of money, and blood. There is blood on the money, and the Old Gentleman is dead. Someone killed him."

"Who is he?" Mrs. Burke asked in alarm. "Why is he here?"

"He has a message for someone," Yellow Feather said. "He wants to say . . . Maeve! Maeve, are you here?" Yellow Feather's voice rose with desperation.

"Yes," someone said faintly. Was it Maeve? Was she terrified? Too frightened to speak aloud?

"Maeve, he wants to tell you something. He has a message for you."

"Who killed him?" Maeve asked, not sounding at all frightened. "Tell me that! Who killed you? Say his name!"

Yellow Feather moaned. "I can't hear him. Too many spirits. They are all shouting. They all want to speak through me, but I can't—"

"Is Mrs. Gittings there?"

Sarah started. That was her mother's voice.

Yellow Feather gave a chilling moan. "I do not want to speak to her."

"Let her speak," Mrs. Decker insisted. "Can she tell us who killed her?"

"Oh, Elizabeth, please don't!" Mrs. Burke cried.

"So many spirits," Yellow Feather complained. "I am so tired."

"No, no, you must find my father before you go!" Cunningham cried.

"Someone is here, someone new . . ." Yellow Feather's voice broke, and he made some strangled sounds. "He wants to speak. He's trying so hard to speak."

Suddenly, a piano started to play. The notes were slow and uncertain, as if the player was just learning. Frank looked at Sarah. She covered her peek hole again and whispered, "It must be the Professor playing the gramophone."

Frank knew the Professor hadn't been in the secret room a few minutes ago, but he stepped over again and pulled back the curtain. Sure enough, the gramophone was turning, the needle pressed against one of the wax cylinders, and the bell-shaped speaker was turned toward the door that led to the cabinet. But the room was still empty. Who had started it up?

He hurried back to Sarah and shook his head to tell her no one was there.

Apparently, Yellow Feather was still trying to get the new spirit to speak up and encountering resistance. "He can't . . . He is still too close. The pull of life is still too strong."

Suddenly, everyone gasped, and they all started talking at once.

"What's that?"

"Who's there?"

"Did you feel it, too?"

Mrs. Burke made a sound like a sob.

"He is here," Yellow Feather said. "He needs to speak to you. Spirit, who are you? Why are you here?"

This time the moan was a different voice, higher pitched and keening, and everyone gasped again.

"Speak, Spirit," Yellow Feather called out. "Do not be afraid!"

"I . . . did . . . not . . . kill . . . her!"

"Who is it?" Mr. Sharpe demanded. "Who are you?"

"Nic . . . Nic . . . Nicola," the spirit wailed, as if the word was torn from his throat.

More gasps and sobs. The piano music had grown more confident.

"I'm going to stop this," Frank said, but Sarah grabbed his wrist and shook her head.

"Let her go," Sarah whispered fiercely. "Maybe she really knows who the killer is."

The new spirit was keening and Yellow Feather started shouting to be heard. "Stop it! Listen to me! What else do you have to tell us?"

That was when Frank realized with a start that Serafina couldn't be doing both voices at once. From the way Sarah's eyes had nearly popped out of her head, she had realized the same thing.

"Tell us!" Yellow Feather begged. "Tell us who killed her!"

"I did not kill her," the spirit insisted.

"I know! I know! We believe you!" Yellow Feather said. "Tell us the truth. Tell us who killed her."

"The same . . . The same . . ." the spirit sputtered.

"Who is it?" Yellow Feather cried.

"The same who kills Serafina!"

Someone shouted and suddenly a burst of light illuminated the room, and he could clearly see everything.

Frank peered through the hole, desperate to see what was happening, but he could hardly make sense of what he saw.

Nicola's ghost stood in front of the cabinet, staring in wide-eyed shock at the dark figure holding a stiletto poised to strike, but not at Serafina at all.

He was going to stab Maeve.

16

MALLOY PRACTICALLY KNOCKED SARAH DOWN IN HIS
frantic haste to get to the kitchen door and out into the hall
so he could force open the door to the séance room. She
caught herself and took out after him. He'd just forced the
door open when she reached him.

She could hear screams and shouts and the sound of a
struggle. Malloy lunged for the struggle, which was taking
place on the other side of the table, just where Maeve had
been sitting, but she was gone. Dear heaven, had someone
killed her, too?

But in the next instant, she saw her good hat bobbing
above the edge of the table, and an arm came up holding
something long and cylindrical that had some kind of light
streaming out of it and brought it down with a sickening
thud. As quickly as that, the struggle ceased and the light
went out, and from the other side of the table, people started

to reappear. Malloy first, and then Mr. Sharpe, and finally
Nicola.

Nicola?

Sarah blinked to make sure. He looked furious and
slightly disheveled but very much alive. And he was helping
Maeve to her feet.

"What did you hit him with?" he was asking her.

But Maeve wasn't listening. She didn't even seem to know
she'd been assisted by a ghost. She was too busy glaring down
at the body on the floor. "Is he dead?" she asked, obviously
hoping he was.

"Not likely," Malloy said. "Probably just stunned, but
we'd better truss him up before he comes to." He turned and
realized everyone else was staring at them in horrified silence.

"Who is it?" Sarah asked, hurrying over to see for herself,
and she looked down at the body sprawled unceremoniously
on the floor, a nasty gash across his powdered hairline.

"The *Professor*?" she said in surprise. "But he couldn't be
the killer. He was the only one who wasn't in the room!"

"Just as he was not in the room today," Serafina said. "Did
anyone see him come in?"

"No, I didn't," Cunningham replied. At some point he'd
gone to her aid and now held her arm as if to support her in
case she fainted. Sarah had never seen anyone who looked less
likely to faint.

"Neither did I," Mrs. Decker agreed. She was supporting
Mrs. Burke, who did look like she might faint, although she
was probably too interested in what was happening to risk
missing any of it. "But I didn't see that young man in here
either," she added, nodding toward Nicola.

"He was probably hiding in the cabinet, weren't you, Nicola?" Malloy asked.

"Yes, I was," he admitted a little defensively.

"But the Professor wouldn't fit in there," Malloy pointed out. "And Nicola would have noticed him, so how did he get in?"

"He hid behind the door," Serafina said.

Everyone looked at the door in question, and Malloy walked over to it. When he passed Sarah, he said. "Hold this," and handed her the stiletto that she'd seen the shadowy figure ready to stab Maeve with. She looked at it with horrified fascination.

Malloy was examining the door.

"I did not think of it that day, not until later, but he would always come with me to escort the clients into the séance room," Serafina was explaining. "He did not come that day, and I did not know where he was. Then I remember, I also did not see him come in at the end, when I called him to help when Mrs. Gittings fell over. He was just there, but he did not have the smelling salts. He always brings the smelling salts from the kitchen when he comes. Later, when I think about everything, I knew he must have been hiding behind the door. As the door closes, the room gets dark, and if he was very still, no one would notice him."

Malloy stepped behind the door, and Serafina demonstrated. Sure enough, if he pressed himself back into the corner behind the door, by the time he was really visible, the room was almost totally dark.

"Everyone would be looking at me and not expecting to see anyone there," she added.

"Distraction," Maeve said. "It's an old magician's trick." She looked down at the figure still lying at her feet. "He used to do some magic, too."

"You know him?" Sarah asked in surprise.

"Yes, I know him," she said simply.

"Nicola," Malloy said, having emerged from behind the door, "do you have some rope we can tie him up with?"

Nicola scrambled to do his bidding, and as he passed Mrs. Decker, she said, "I thought he was dead."

He flashed her an impudent grin and was gone. Sarah noticed Serafina's gaze followed him, her feelings for him glowing in her eyes.

"You identified the body," Sarah reminded her.

"I had to protect Nicola," she said simply. "If we could not make you believe the Professor was the killer, then you would think Nicola was dead, and he would be safe."

"But you were so upset when you saw the birthmark on . . . on that poor fellow's back," Sarah said.

"What poor fellow's back?" Cunningham cried. "What is she talking about?"

"Madame Serafina had to look at a dead body," Malloy said. "We thought it might be Nicola, and she told us it was."

"How horrible for you," Cunningham said solicitously. "You should have sent for me."

Serafina ignored him. "I was not sure at first. That is why I asked to see the back. Nicola has a scar from when he fell against the stove as a child. When I saw no scar, I knew it was not him."

"So you were crying from relief," Sarah guessed. Serafina simply smiled.

Nicola returned carrying a length of heavy twine. The Professor was starting to moan, and Malloy made short work of tying his hands and feet. By then he was awake, and he started cursing Malloy.

"Watch your language, man," Sharpe cautioned him as Malloy hauled him to his feet and sat him in Maeve's former chair. "There are ladies present."

"You bitch," he spat at Serafina, who simply glared back at him.

"Mrs. Decker, allow me to take you and Mrs. Burke into the other room," Sharpe offered.

"You'll do nothing of the kind," Mrs. Decker said. "I want to hear what this man has to say for himself." To her credit, Mrs. Burke stood her ground as well.

But the Professor didn't say anything at all. He just looked at each of the people standing around the room, one by one until he got to Maeve. Then his eyes narrowed and he lurched to his feet and made a lunge for her.

Malloy caught him and slammed him back into the chair.

"I knew he would try to kill someone today," Serafina said with more confidence that Sarah could believe she felt.

"But why would he try to kill Maeve?" Sarah asked.

The Professor didn't reply. He just gave Maeve another black look.

"He killed my grandfather," she said, drawing renewed gasps from everyone. "I guess he recognized me the same way I recognized him, and he was afraid I'd tell."

"How astonishing that you should be here practically by accident today!" Mrs. Decker said.

"It wasn't an accident," Maeve said. "He always called himself the Professor, even in the old days. I suspected it was him the first time Serafina mentioned him."

"And you've been trying to get her to hold another séance right from the start," Sarah remembered.

"So I could see him for myself," Maeve said.

"But why would he kill Mrs. Gittings?" Mr. Sharpe asked impatiently.

"They argued right before the last séance," Mrs. Burke said, surprising everyone. "I told you that, didn't I, Elizabeth?"

"Yes, you did," Mrs. Decker confirmed. "You were the only one who'd noticed that."

Mrs. Burke beamed.

"They argued all the time," Sarah said. "Why was this different?"

"Why *was* it different?" Malloy asked, kicking the chair leg to give the Professor a jolt.

He glared at Malloy but refused to speak.

"Let me guess," Malloy said thoughtfully. "She wasn't going to give you the money to set up your Green Goods Game."

The Professor's eyes widened in surprise, but he still refused to speak.

"You couldn't stand being pushed around by a woman," Malloy continued, still thoughtful. "And you weren't man enough to stand up to her."

"Coward!" Cunningham supplied helpfully. "Afraid of a woman!"

"That's right, you were afraid of her," Malloy went on, "so you took the easy way out and stabbed her when she was helpless so you could take all the money Serafina made for yourself—"

"Stealing from a defenseless girl!" Cunningham cried, outraged.

"She's not defenseless!" the Professor snarled. "And I wasn't afraid of Lucille!"

"Then why did you kill her?" Malloy asked curiously.

"Because she was causing too much trouble!" he said, then caught himself, realizing what he had done.

"Too much trouble," Malloy repeated thoughtfully, and glanced around at the people assembled there. "You mean the way she was trying to get extra money from everyone here? By offering to sell Serafina to Cunningham so he'd fall for that phony investment scheme she arranged?"

"What?" Cunningham roared.

"And by frightening Mrs. Burke into paying more and more for the séances, and—"

"She couldn't be satisfied!" the Professor moaned. "We had a perfect setup here, but she always wanted more and more. I told her she was going to ruin everything, but she wouldn't listen! She just wouldn't listen!"

"But why take the chance of killing her like that?" Malloy asked.

The Professor's eyes narrowed, and he looked as if he wanted to slip a knife into Malloy. "Because a normal policeman wouldn't have investigated at all, not with all these important people involved, and if he did, he would have been satisfied to charge Nicola with it and be done."

Sarah realized with a start that he was absolutely right. "But weren't you afraid killing Mrs. Gittings would frighten clients away?" Sarah asked.

He just glared at Sarah, but Maeve said, "You could always move to another city, couldn't you, Professor? Just like you did when you killed the Old Gentleman?"

He glared at her venomously. "My only mistake was coming back."

THAT NIGHT, AFTER CATHERINE WAS SAFELY IN BED, SARAH, Maeve, and Malloy told Mrs. Ellsworth the story of the séance as they sat around Sarah's kitchen table. Sarah's mother had felt she must go home so her husband wouldn't wonder where she had spent her day. Serafina and Nicola were enjoying a reunion at the house on Waverly Place.

Everyone was particularly fascinated by the light that Malloy had given Maeve to use and the way she had turned it on in the dark room just in time to catch the killer.

"I thought I broke it when I hit the Professor with it," Maeve said as Malloy demonstrated the device for them.

"No, it just went out by itself. The power doesn't last too long at a time, so you only get a short flash of light each time you turn it on," he explained. "Then the battery has to rest before it will light again. That's why they call them flash-lights."

"You used it at just the right moment," Sarah said.

"I was afraid it might be too soon, but when Nicola said someone was going to kill Serafina, I couldn't wait."

"I'm glad you didn't," Mrs. Ellsworth said, laying her hand over Maeve's. "If anything had happened to you . . ." She gave a little shudder.

"I didn't think the Professor recognized me, or I wouldn't have taken a chance."

"He kept looking at you," Malloy recalled. "But he said he was sure you were somebody's maid, so I thought he just didn't approve of you being there. If I'd suspected the truth, I never would've let you go in that room."

Maeve smiled sweetly. "I know."

"How did that boy Nicola get in the cabinet?" Mrs. Ellsworth asked. "After he escaped, I thought we'd never see him again."

"That's something Serafina didn't explain," Sarah said, "but I have a feeling he'd been watching the house, and he would have known she was back."

"While we were waiting for everybody to get there, she disappeared for a few minutes, into the kitchen," Malloy said. "She told me she was going to unlock the back door for us."

"She must have contacted Nicola then," Sarah guessed. "And he could have sneaked into the cabinet then, too."

"I noticed she looked a little . . . excited," he said, choosing his word carefully, "when she came back. I thought it was just because of the séance, but if she saw Nicola, that would explain it."

"It would have to, since he wasn't really a ghost," Sarah said with a grin.

"And speaking of ghosts, I'm so sorry about your grandfather, dear," Mrs. Ellsworth said to Maeve. "But how interesting that the spirits knew the Professor had killed him."

"I don't think the spirits did know that," Maeve said.

"But I thought you said—"

"No, I never told anyone that until after the séance was over," Maeve reminded them all. "All that the spirits knew was that my grandfather had played the Old Gentleman in the Green Goods Game and that he'd been murdered."

"Just what you'd told me," Sarah recalled.

"And Serafina," Malloy guessed.

"No, Serafina had already gone to bed that night," Sarah said. "It was just Maeve and me."

"So it really was the spirits," Mrs. Ellsworth said in wonder.

"I don't think so," Maeve said with a grin. "I should have remembered, because I've done it enough times myself." She pointed toward the ceiling, and they all looked up to see the grating that allowed the heat from the kitchen to pass into the bedroom upstairs. And which also allowed conversations to be overheard.

"So she was listening to your conversation," Mrs. Ellsworth said, disappointed. "I was so hoping it was really the spirits."

"Serafina will never admit it, but I think we can explain just about everything that happened," Sarah said with some satisfaction.

"We know the music and the baby crying were records Nicola played on the gramophone," Malloy said, starting to tick them off on his fingers.

"I've been thinking about the way we all smelled roses that first time," Sarah said. "I think Mrs. Gittings may have had some cologne that she sprinkled on the table. She could have done that if she had one hand free."

"But she did know about your sister," Mrs. Ellsworth reminded Sarah.

"I thought so then, but Maeve pointed out that practically every family has had a baby die at one time or another. When the baby cried, my mother was the one who said it must be Maggie's baby."

"But didn't Serafina know the first time she saw Mrs. Decker that she'd lost a daughter?" Mrs. Ellsworth reminded her.

"Mrs. Burke probably told her that," Maeve said. "I'd guess Mrs. Gittings was trying to get her to think of friends who had a loved one they'd want to contact, and she remembered Mrs. Decker had a daughter who died young."

"So you see, we can explain all of Serafina's powers," Sarah said.

Mrs. Ellsworth smiled mysteriously. "Perhaps not all of them, dear. Remember Serafina told me where I would find my late husband's watch?"

"That's right," Maeve remembered. "Didn't she say it would be something with the letter B?"

"Yes, she did," Mrs. Ellsworth reported. "And that's just where I found it, hidden in the fireplace."

"Fireplace doesn't start with a B," Sarah pointed out skeptically.

"No, it doesn't," Mrs. Ellsworth agreed with some satisfaction of her own, "but it was behind a loose *brick*, just where my husband had left it."

Author's Note

I HAD A WONDERFUL TIME RESEARCHING SÉANCES FOR this book. I found lots of interesting information about how to do "cold readings," which means how to make people think you know things about them when you really don't. What I learned is that most people are eager to help a self-professed psychic and will try to find meaning in anything that is said, no matter how vague or meaningless. This is called "subjective validation," which is the process of validating words, initials, statements, or signs as accurate because one is able to find them personally meaningful and significant. If you go back and read Serafina's "readings," you will find that the subjects were the ones who found meaning in them and that she gave them few, if any, real facts. I'm afraid I'm even more of a skeptic since researching the subject than I was before, but I do still enjoy getting my Tarot cards read.

When I got to the end of the story, I realized I needed to

give Maeve a way of lighting up the dark room. I thought immediately of a flashlight, so I looked up when they were invented. Sure enough, the first ones were developed in 1896, the year before this book takes place. The lights performed poorly, so they were not successful, but the inventor gave some to the police department. Even though the flash of light didn't last very long, the police on the night shift found them very useful and gave the new invention favorable testimonials. Inventors improved the batteries that powered the lights so they no longer flash as they did in the early days, but the name seems to have stuck just the same.

Please let me know how you liked this book. If you send me an e-mail, I will put you on my mailing list and send a reminder when the next book in the series comes out! Contact me through my website at www.victoriathompson.com.